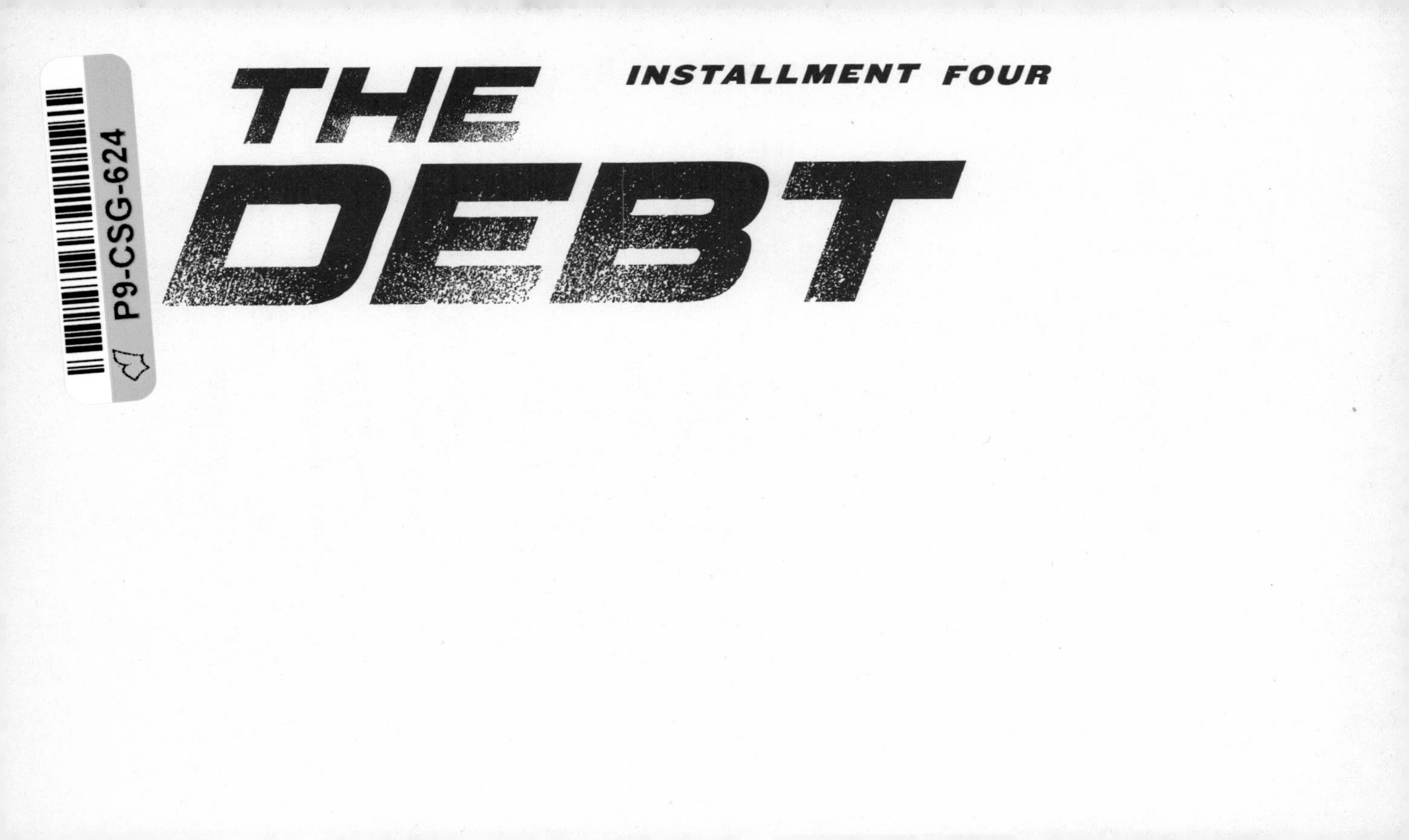
THE DEBT
INSTALLMENT FOUR

THE DEBT

THE DEBT

INSTALLMENT FOUR

FETCH THE TREASURE HUNTER

PHILLIP GWYNNE

First American Edition 2014
Kane Miller, A Division of EDC Publishing

Cover and text design by Natalie Winter
Cover photography: (boy) by Alan Richardson Photography, model: Nicolai Laptev; (Colosseum and scooter) by Getty Images

For information contact:
Kane Miller, A Division of EDC Publishing
PO Box 470663
Tulsa, OK 74147-0663

www.kanemiller.com
www.edcpub.com
www.usbornebooksandmore.com

Library of Congress Control Number: 2013953413

Printed and bound in the United States of America
1 2 3 4 5 6 7 8 9 10
ISBN: 978-1-61067-306-8

For Colleen and Megan, and kids

TOBY, TOBY, TOBY

By the time we got back to Halcyon Grove from the national titles Toby had been missing for hours.

Dad and I rushed into the house, Gus hobbling after us, to find Mom in the kitchen with Roberto, the head gardener. Although if you saw the two of them sitting there at the table I doubt you would have pegged them as employer and employee. More like friends. Maybe even relatives, because I noticed something I'd never really noticed before: my mum and Roberto the gardener actually looked a bit alike. I'm not sure what it was: the same-shaped nose, the color of their eyes, something.

Mom must've noticed that I was scoping them because she snapped, "Roberto's been a great help with you all away in Sydney."

"Thanks, Roberto," said Dad. "We're here now."

Roberto didn't move.

Dad said, "We can look after this now, Roberto."

Still no movement from Roberto and I could see the anger rising in Dad's face.

"Roberto!" he said.

Throwing Mom a sort of half smile, Roberto walked slowly away, disappearing out the door.

Okay, there's always stuff going on between adults that us kids don't know about. But it occurred to me then that the stuff going on between these three was big stuff, important stuff. So I had yet another entry on my Things To Do list: investigate stuff between Roberto and Mom and Dad.

Miranda came hurtling down the stairs and said, "I've totally plastered the net with his photo and everybody's tweeting like crazy."

"The police have looked everywhere," said Mom. "They can't find any trace of him."

Hound's clever, I thought. *Of course, he's not going to leave any clues.*

"Do you think ..." started Mom, her voice trailing off, as if what was in her mind was too horrible to put into words.

Dad moved in for a reassuring hug, but I'm not sure how reassured Mom was because she seemed to squirm out of his grip.

"Did Toby say anything to you?" she said, her eyes searching mine.

"No, Mom," I said as I recalled Hound's words:

I reckon it would be really, really difficult to make ice cream if you had ten broken fingers. You know, with all that whisking they do.

"You sure?" said Mom, studying my face.

"Of course I'm sure," I said.

My little brother and I weren't exactly close, especially not since The Debt had taken over my life. But it was my fault he'd been taken. And I had to get him back, I had to rescue him, not stand around wasting time talking like this.

"I think we should go for a drive," I said to Gus. "Have a look for him."

"And what good is that going to do?" said Mom. "Like I said, the police couldn't find him."

"Really can't do any harm," said Dad. "Miranda and I can go in one car, Gus and Dom in another, and you can stay here and hold the fort in case the police call."

Reluctantly, Mom agreed.

As we hurried towards his truck Gus said, "You've got some idea where he is, don't you?"

"Some idea," I said. "There's this man, Hound, and he –"

Gus didn't let me finish the sentence.

"You know if it's The Debt I really can't help you."

"Relax," I said. "It's not to do with The Debt, not directly. Besides, all I'm asking you to do is drive."

Gus considered this for a second and said,

"Where to?"

"The Block," I said as we got into his truck.

Gus frowned. "No place for a kid."

"That's for sure," I said, thinking that it was especially no place for a kid like Toby.

Despite his no-place-for-a-kid misgivings, Gus drove much quicker than usual, took all the right shortcuts, and we reached the Block in no time at all.

It looked even shabbier, more ominous, than last time I was there and my mind was taking me to places I didn't want to go. We pulled up right outside Cash Converters.

"If I don't come back in half an hour," I said as I got out of the truck, "you better come looking for me."

Gus said something in reply, but I didn't hear it as I was already running towards the entrance. Cash Converters was strangely quiet, none of the usual loiterers loitering. Which suited me fine, because I wasn't sure what would happen if I ran into Red Bandana again, especially after our recent encounter at Electric Bazaar.

Behind the counter the rat-faced man with the ponytail was engrossed in an iPad and he gave me only a cursory glance as I passed. I took the stairs three at a time to find that Hound's office was closed. Really, I don't know why I was so surprised:

if I'd kidnapped somebody, would I take him to my place of work?

Of course not!

I'd take him to an isolated farmhouse or an abandoned warehouse, somewhere I could break a kid's fingers, one by one, without his agonized screams disturbing the neighbors.

Don't Even Think About Breaking In, said a sign on the door.

I'm not sure whether it was for my benefit or it was more a general warning, but it seemed like pretty sound advice – I hurried back down the stairs.

When I got back into the truck Gus said, "No luck?"

"No," I said. "Nobody there."

"Where to now?" said Gus.

It was the obvious question, one that had already occurred to me, but I didn't have an answer for it. Because I didn't have a clue where that isolated farmhouse or abandoned warehouse was.

One step at a time, I thought.

"Hound's house," I said.

"And where would that be?"

"I don't know."

"That makes it a bit difficult."

"Give me a minute," I said, and as soon as I did I realized that a minute was probably all the time it would take to – *snap!* – break a kid's finger.

I did a quick Google search on my iPhone, checked

the online White Pages. Just as I'd expected, there was nothing – what private investigator is going to put his private address up for public consumption?

So then I did a memory trawl, casting the net wide and deep, starting from my first encounter with Hound when I'd visited his office, to our time together on Reverie Island, to the quest for the Cerberus. All that time I'd spent with him and I couldn't remember him ever mentioning where he lived.

I was so angry with myself – why hadn't I found out before?

Gus was humming that song again, the Brazilian one about sick feet and a bad head.

"So where we at?" he said eventually.

"Dead end."

"Hmmm," said Gus. "Dead ends aren't good."

I shook my head – no, dead ends aren't good.

Five more minutes had passed – five more broken fingers.

"Look, for what it's worth, there's a technique I sometimes use," said Gus, scratching at some flaky skin on his scalp. "It's a bit hard to explain, but maybe you're trying too much. Just relax, don't give yourself such a hard time."

It sounded like so much Zen crap, but what did I have to lose?

I did – or tried to do – as Gus suggested. Instead

of trawling the past, I tried just floating through it. Like a scuba diver, like a snorkeler. Again, past my first meeting with Hound. Our time on Reverie. When he got me out of school that time.

"That's it!" I said. "He said once that where he lives he's got the ocean at his front door and the river at his back step."

Gus thought for a while and said, "If he's talking about the Gold Coast, then really that's only two places: Millionaire's Row or the Spit."

"I'm pretty sure he's no millionaire," I said.

"The Spit, then?" said Gus, ramming the gear into first.

"The Spit!"

Once we got to the Spit, I could see that it matched Hound's description perfectly: a single row of houses, facing the ocean, ran along the edge of a canal. *Ocean at my front door, river at my back step.*

Gus parked the truck outside the first house and I got out. Moving quickly from one house to the next I looked around for a parked Hummer, anything that might indicate that this was where Hound de Villiers lived.

I raced from one end of the Spit and back again and there was nothing.

Getting desperate now, I yelled "Hound!" at the very top of my voice. "You there, Hound?"

Unfortunately even the very top of my voice was

no match for high walls and double glazing – not one person came out.

"No luck?" said Gus when I returned to the car.

I shook my head.

"I need something big, something noisy, something to make him come out and take a look."

"Why didn't you say?" said Gus, pressing on the accelerator.

The engine kept revving, higher and higher, until it was screaming and the old truck was shaking like a maraca. And just when it seemed as if the engine was going to combust, Gus dropped the clutch. The tires spun, rubber burned. Already people were appearing from their houses. The tires kept spinning. Rubber kept burning. And the truck snaked up the road. More people appeared. Quite a few of them were on their phones. One man, clad in only his Homer Simpson boxers, was carrying a rifle. But not one of them was Hound.

"Okay, that's enough," I screamed at Gus.

He took his foot off the accelerator and immediately I could hear the wail of a police siren.

"Better get out of here," said Gus.

He hurtled down one side street, then another one, then another. Finally he pulled up in a service station.

Wow, I thought, *the old fellow's got some moves I didn't know about*.

"What now?" I said, because I'd pretty much run

out of ideas.

Gus thought about this for a while before he said, "Maybe you could just call this Hound character."

"Call Hound?"

"Call Hound."

Yeah, right. Call the person who had kidnapped my brother and was currently snapping his fingers like shortbread cookies.

"What have we got to lose?" said my grandfather.

Of course Hound wouldn't pick up, but so what?

I called his number.

Hound picked up.

He said, "Hello!" in a big beery voice.

In the background there was noise, music blaring, people talking.

"Hound, it's Dom," I said.

"Youngblood, my boy!" he said, and he seemed genuinely excited to hear from me.

"Where are you?" I said.

"Vegas!"

"Las Vegas?"

"No, Port Vegas, you idiot. Of course, Las Vegas. Me and the boys go every year for some R and R," he said.

I could hear somebody in the background say, "Show us what you've got, Big Dog!"

"So you didn't kidnap my little brother?"

Hound laughed raucously, and there were all

sorts of other noises, hard to identify, before he said, "I've got to go." The line went dead.

My first thought was: *Hound obviously didn't kidnap Toby.*

But something I'd learned from The Debt was that all thoughts, especially first ones, needed to be interrogated. So had Hound kidnapped Toby and the Las Vegas thing was a big ruse? But that didn't make sense – why go to all that trouble when all he had to do was not answer my call? Hound hadn't kidnapped Toby.

But then who had?

I tormented myself for about five minutes trying to come up with a likely culprit when – total lightbulb moment – I got it. What if nobody had kidnapped Toby?

What if Toby had kidnapped himself?

I remembered that time when Mom had all these people around to watch *Ready! Set! Cook!* and Toby had let his usual mask slip, just for a second, and I'd seen a look of terror on his face.

But if Toby had lost his bottle, if he'd kidnapped himself, where would he be hiding? I called Mom.

"You found him?" she said

"Not yet, Mom," I said. "Do you know how much money Toby had on him when he went into the *Ready! Set! Cook!* house?"

"Not much," she said. "I think I gave him twenty. Because everything was supplied, he didn't need money."

"Did the police say they checked his bank account?"

"No, they didn't mention it," she said.

So much for the exhaustive police search. But kids went missing on the Gold Coast all the time. I didn't really blame them for not taking it seriously for a few days at least.

I opened my CommBank app on my iPhone.

I knew Toby's account number was one more than mine, because Dad had opened the accounts for us at the same time.

As for his password, it always used to be "nigella."

I tried that – no luck.

I tried "jamie."

Again, no luck.

I called Mom again.

"Who's Toby's favorite chef at the moment?" I said.

Mom sighed.

"I'm getting close," I said.

"That mad Spanish fellow," she said. "Ferran Adrià."

"How do you spell that?" I said.

She spelled it out and I entered it into the password field.

Bingo!

"I'll get back to you soon," I said to Mom before I hung up.

At 12:45 today Toby had made a withdrawal of two hundred dollars at an ATM located at the Palazzo Versace hotel.

"Palazzo Versace," I said to Gus. "Let's go."

PALAZZO VERSACE

Palazzo Versace is the glitziest, tackiest, most over-the-top hotel on the whole coast and it is Toby's favorite place in the whole world, maybe even the universe. If he had his way we would go there for every vacation and he would lie by the pool and listen to Lady Gaga on his iPod and read food magazines and order double Swiss chocolate milkshakes.

Gus parked outside and I ran inside and there was Toby, by the pool, on a lounge chair. Despite the fact that it was now nighttime, his face was hidden by an enormous pair of sunglasses. His fingers, unbroken, were flicking through a *Gourmet Traveler*. On the table beside him was what looked like a half-finished double Swiss chocolate milkshake.

Relief, several truckloads of it. I almost felt obliged to get to my knees and thank the god I didn't always believe in.

I immediately texted Mom – *found him and he's okay* – and then made for the pool.

If Toby was surprised to see me, neither he nor his sunglasses showed it.

"You look all sweaty," is all they said.

"Can I have some of that?" I said, indicating the milkshake.

"It's pretty chocolatey," he said.

"That's okay."

Pretty chocolatey? It was chocolate multiplied by chocolate and it tasted amazing.

After I'd finished, slurping every last bit, I said, "Everybody's really worried about you, Tobes."

He said nothing.

"Tobes?"

He pushed the shades up onto his forehead, revealing eyes that were red and puffy.

"Do you think ice cream's easy?" he said, before he launched into a monologue about the precarious world of making ice cream, about how it was both a foam and an emulsion, how …

I let him go on. And on. And on.

When he'd finished he looked down at his fingernails. He looked up at me again and said, "I just didn't want to muck it up. Not in front of all those people. Not in front of Mom."

"Mom wouldn't care if you mucked it up or not," I said.

Toby just gave me this look. *You don't know what you're talking about. You don't know Mom like I know her.*

Okay, it was a look, not an essay, but it took a while to absorb it. Would Mom really care if Toby mucked up some ice cream?

My phone was ringing like mad, jumping around in my pocket, and I knew it wasn't fair to keep Mom and Dad in suspense.

"Hey, what say we go home?" I said to Toby. "Gus is waiting outside."

"I guess so," he said, getting up.

I noticed the tears glistening on his cheeks.

"Look, you want a hug or something?" I said.

"Really?" he said. "You'd really give me a hug?"

"Of course I would," I said. "Hey, you're my little brother, aren't you?"

Toby nodded. *I am your little brother. I do want a hug.*

So I hugged him.

He felt sort of squishy. And he smelled really chocolatey.

"Okay, that's probably enough," said Toby, attempting to de-hug.

But I wasn't letting go of my squishy little brother.

Not yet.

BARBIE TIME

Later that night I sat on the leather couch in Gus's office, the only light coming from a lamp on the battered wooden desk. All the books, all the posters on the wall, all the newspaper clippings, were hidden in darkness. But I knew that Dr. Roger Bannister was still there, breaking the four-minute mile; John Landy was still there, setting the 1500 meters world record in 1954; and Hicham El Guerrouj was still there, setting the current world record of three minutes and twenty-six seconds. And as my father, sitting at the desk, heated up the tip of the branding iron with an ancient Zippo lighter, I felt sort of glad that they were there. Because they were my friends. I know that's pretty ridiculous, because I'd never met any of them and probably never would. But at least I knew who they were. They wouldn't suddenly become somebody else, they wouldn't double cross me, or trick me.

"You ready, son?" said Dad, standing up.

I'm not sure you can ever be ready to have the skin on the inside of your thigh branded, but I gave him a "yes" anyway.

I looked across to where Gus was sitting on the other couch, stump pointing at me like an oversized thumb. He shook his head slowly, mournfully, as if to say, *I'm sorry this has to happen.*

Well, I'm sorry, too, I thought as I undid my shorts and pulled them down so that my thigh was bared and the letters *PA* were visible.

I'd caught the Zolt, I'd turned off the lights, and now I'd brought back the Cerberus.

Dad approached, the brand in his hand, the letter *G* on the tip of the brand glowing white-hot. He had this look on his face that's hard to describe. Like he was sorry he had to do this, but maybe not that sorry.

He sat down on the couch next to me. And already it seemed I could smell that barbecue smell.

Dad clamped my leg with his hand.

"You don't have to do that!" I said, pushing his hand away.

"Just helping," he said, and again I couldn't work out the look on his face.

"Dave, just get it over and done with," said Gus, his voice full of gravel.

"You ready?" said Dad, and I could feel the heat of the brand as he brought it closer to my leg.

"Just get it over and done with," I said, using Gus's words, his gravel.

I was trying to convince myself that it wasn't that bad, that it wouldn't hurt that much, but my body was having none of it. My body was sweating, and had gone from dry to damp in a second. My body wanted out of here.

The familiar sensation of hairs singeing, white-hot metal searing flesh, the nauseating smell, and then the pain – pain upon pain.

I looked over into the shadows for support, towards my friends, Dr. Roger, John, Hicham.

"Done!" said Dad, removing the brand.

I went to zip up my shorts but Gus said, "Don't you want to put something on that?"

"I can deal with it!" I snapped.

Three installments repaid, four brandings, and he thought I didn't know what to do?

ANOTHER PROTEST

To say it was tense in the car as we made for school the next day is a bit like saying that Israel and Palestine don't quite get on.

"Toby, I want you to personally go in and apologize to the police," said Mom, firing the first missile from the driver's seat.

"Why?" said Toby, with a retaliatory strike from the backseat. "They couldn't even find me. Dom did."

"Don't be a bloody brat," said Mom. "And when you're finished apologizing to them, you can apologize to the *Ready! Set! Cook!* people as well."

"Why? It was the highest rated program in their history," said Toby.

I wanted to step in, UN-style, and make them stop.

But it was Mom who fired the next Scud missile. "And when you're finished with them, I wouldn't mind an apology, either."

I looked over at Toby.

He said nothing, but he didn't need to because his eyes said it all: right then, he hated our mother.

It was actually a relief when we pulled up at the school drop-off zone and Mom said, "Looks like there's another protest!"

The way she said it made it sound like protests were a weekly event outside the wrought iron front gates of Coast Boys Grammar, but from memory the last one had been about two years ago when some local residents had gotten upset that our school had acquired an adjoining playground.

"Haven't these people got jobs to go to?" continued Mom.

There were many more demonstrators than last time, maybe fifty or sixty people swarming around the entrance to the school, many of them holding up placards.

Coalition of Islam Youth was written on one.

A Fair Race for All Races! was written on another.

Obviously this wasn't about the acquisition of a playground, but what, exactly, was the Coalition of Islam Youth protesting against?

Refugees Always Run Last, said another placard.

I opened the door and got out of the car.

As I made for the entrance there were shouts of "That's him!" and "There he is!"

That's who? I wondered. *There who is?*

But when I was engulfed by a group of jostling

protestors I realized that who was me, that they were protesting against me being awarded third place in the 1500 meters at the national titles.

I had no doubt that Rashid had beaten me, but somebody – The Debt? – had gotten to the photo and doctored it so that it looked like I had beaten him. So it ended up that I was on the team going to Rome for the World Youth Games and Rashid wasn't.

A man pushed his placard right into my face. Then somebody gave me a shove from behind. Just as it was about to get ugly, five student protection officers pushed their way through the protestors and surrounded me.

Now, with me inside, this carapace of SPOs made towards the entrance. Once we were safely in through the gates I said, "It's okay now."

But the carapace kept going, moving me towards the headmaster's office. It was only when we were inside that they released me.

Mr. Cranbrook, the principal, was there in his suit. Mr. Iharos, the vice principal, was there in his suit. Another man, who I think was head of security, was there in his suit. Mrs. Zipser, the school PR person, was also there in her suit.

Seriously, it looked like a suit-off – and may the best suit win.

"Please take a seat, Dominic," Mr. Cranbrook said.

I took a seat, and there was a knock on the door.

"Come in," said Mr. Iharos.

A man entered; he was very smooth-looking, wearing – you guessed it – a suit.

If the suit-off did happen, I had all my money on his; it looked like one of those Italian jobs my dad wears.

Mr. Cranbrook introduced him as Mr. Theissen; apparently he was going to assist Mrs. Zipser with the PR on this "delicate issue."

Firstly Mr. Cranbrook gave him a "heads up."

Which was pretty fortunate for me, because I learned some things that nobody had bothered to tell me.

The most surprising being that Rashid was no longer attending this school.

"You suspended Rashid?" I said, ready to be outraged.

Mr. Cranbrook did that thing men in suits like to do, where they smooth down their lapels.

"Let me explain," he said.

I let him explain, and explaining was something the principal of Coast Boys Grammar did very, very well.

The school hadn't suspended Rashid at all, he'd suspended himself.

Apparently the school had received an email

from the Coalition of Islam Youth saying that as a protest Rashid would no longer attend the school.

"But that's crazy," I said.

Nobody was arguing with me.

"Rashid loves Grammar more than anybody I know," I said. "He's a girly swot from hades."

Mr. Cranbrook concurred. "Rashid is certainly one of our more diligent students."

Apparently they'd tried to contact him directly to ascertain whether it was he who had made this decision or it had been made for him. But they hadn't been able to get through.

It was, Mr. Cranbrook said, "a very delicate situation and one that needed to be handled astutely."

Mrs. Zipser and Mr. Theissen exchanged knowing nods. Very astutely.

Apparently, there was the school's brand to consider. Not to mention emerging markets in predominately Muslim countries like Indonesia and Malaysia.

Mr. Cranbrook continued. "What we wanted to talk about, Dom, is some strategies we intend to put in place this week in order to circumvent any other unfortunate events like this morning's. Fortunately there's only a week of the school term left, so this makes it much easier for us."

He went to say something further, but I thought I'd save him a whole lot of breath – and enunciation –

by getting in first. "It's totally okay with me if Rashid goes to Rome instead of me."

It actually wasn't totally okay, it wasn't even just plain okay, but this was crazy – Rashid belonged at Grammar!

The principal and the vice principal and the two PR people exchanged looks and Mr. Cranbrook said, "That certainly won't be happening."

"But Rashid did actually beat me," I said, trying to convince myself as much as them.

"Not according to the judges, he didn't," said Mr. Iharos. "Not according to the photo."

So I sat there and listened to the strategies that were going to be put in place. Basically they involved me sneaking in through the back entrance when I came to school tomorrow.

When I walked into the classroom fifteen minutes late, Mr. Travers looked up from his desk and gave me a look.

But that's all it was, a look, and a pretty feeble one at that. Because we both knew that I had something on him.

As I made for my desk I could sense there was something different about the classroom today.

And it didn't take long for me to work it out, because suddenly – *biff!* – I got a playful punch on the shoulder.

Playful for him. Painful for me.

Yes, Tristan was back.

I hadn't seen him since the day I'd given him up to the cops at Electric Bazaar.

The day he'd been Tasered.

"Dom, as you can see, Tristan has joined us for the last week of term."

"Welcome back, buddy," I said.

But I could tell that this wasn't the Tristan who'd woken up from the coma.

That Tristan had been sort of sleepy, but it was like that Taser had given this Tristan his old electric energy back. And when I say electric I mean electric: Tristan was dangerous, he was lethal.

The next lesson, English, was even more of a disaster than usual, because all I could think about was Rashid.

One part of me was absolutely sure that it was only right that I should go to Rome.

But another part of me was absolutely sure that it wasn't.

And these two parts kept brawling, no holds barred, UFC style, in the Octagon of my mind.

"And Dom, what do you think Whitman is saying here?"

Mr. McFarlane's voice managed to find a way through all this conflict.

I looked up.

Mr. McFarlane was standing at the front of the class. His eyes, magnified by his glasses, gave him an owlish look.

"Whitman?" I said.

"Yes, Mr. Walt Whitman. You do remember him, don't you, the poet we've been studying this term?"

This brought forth some tittering from the class – Mr. McFarlane, when he puts his mind to it, has a solid line in sarcasm.

I looked at the board, on which was written in chalk: *Walt Whitman, 1819–1892.*

And under that, *I am large, I contain multitudes,* which I gathered was a quote from Walt Whitman, 1819–1892.

Mr. McFarlane continued, "So what do you think Mr. Whitman is saying here? Bevan, for example, believes he might be referring to obesity and the multitudes is, in fact, a multitude of hamburgers."

Like I said, a solid line in sarcasm.

The two parts of me had stopped brawling, however. It was like they, too, were reading the quote. I looked over at Mr. McFarlane, at his owl eyes, at that haircut that was some sort of relic from the swinging seventies. He had this encouraging look on his face: *Just say it.*

So I just said it. "Is it like he's saying, even though we're the same person we can have different ideas and opinions inside us and that's sort of okay?"

Just then the bell went and Mr. McFarlane wasn't able to say anything over the resulting noise. But he smiled at me, raising his eyebrows, tilting his head.

I left the classroom and hurried straight to Mr. Ryan's office.

Knocked on the door.

"Who is it?" he said.

"Dom," I said. "I need to talk."

"Come in," he said.

He was leaning back in his chair, several mountains of paper on the desk in front of him. But I didn't think he'd been doing much marking because his earbuds were in. He waved at the chair and as I sat down he started playing air guitar. Whether it was for my benefit or not I'm not sure, but it was pretty embarrassing. When he'd finished his solo he removed the earbuds.

"You know what?" he said. "Your father is so right: those early Rolling Stones albums really do stand up well."

"I want to pull out of the team for Rome," I said.

Mr. Ryan's boyish mood instantly changed – he was my teacher again. And a fellow runner.

"Are you sure?" he said emphatically.

"If I pull out and they reinstate Rashid on the team and the demonstrations stop, then I'm sure he'll come back to Grammar."

Mr. Ryan considered what I'd just said in that calm, unhurried way he had when he wasn't playing embarrassing air guitar.

"Possibly," he conceded.

"So how do I officially withdraw from the team?" I said.

Mr. Ryan seemed to choose his words very carefully. "If you withdraw, you might do your career irreparable damage, Dom. And yes, you are withdrawing for noble reasons, but even that will work against you. You see, successful athletes have a certain mindset where they … now, what's the best way to put this …"

"They always look after number one?" I said.

"I guess that's one way of putting it."

I fully understood what Mr. Ryan was saying. And I wanted to say, "Forget it, then." Or "Hey, I was only joking."

But I couldn't.

"I've made my mind up," I said. "Could I send them an email?"

"You could do that," said Mr. Ryan with a resigned shrug. "Let's find the appropriate email address, shall we?"

We found the appropriate email address and Mr. Ryan helped me compose the email.

All I had to do now was hit the send button and it was done: Rashid would go to Rome instead of me and my career would be trashed.

I hesitated.

"It's often a good idea to sit on these things for a day or two," said Mr. Ryan. "Give it some considered thought."

A day or two?

I grabbed the mouse and I clicked on send.

As I left his office and walked along the corridor I was feeling really good about myself – I'd made absolutely the right decision.

Not for long, though. Because Tristan Jazy, all one hundred and ninety-five centimeters of him, all one hundred kilos of him, ran straight into me and kneed me in the knurries.

Before his accident Tristan Jazy was a champion cricketer, a star rugby player, a state-ranked swimmer, but now I knew that these talents were nothing compared to the one he had as a knurrie knee-er. I collapsed onto the floor. I rolled around the floor. And I screamed out in agony.

Tristan Jazy looked down at me, not a trace of pity in his conventionally handsome face, and said, "Payback for the pool, Silvagni."

"What pool?" I managed to say, but this was more for the benefit of the quite large crowd that had quickly gathered to enjoy the spectacle of a fellow student and his shattered knurries.

Tristan knew that I'd set fire to his pool. I knew that I'd set fire to Tristan's pool. I knew that Tristan

knew that I'd set fire to his pool. Tristan knew that I knew ... Put it this way, Tristan and I shared the same body of knowledge about the fire and the pool.

Tristan brought his foot back as if to kick me again. The crowd started clapping, chanting in unison, "Kick him in the knurries, kick him in the knurries!"

By now Mr. Kotzur, the tall, bearded librarian who rode a recumbent bicycle to school and was vice president of the Gold Coast Stars Wars Society, had appeared.

"What's going on here?" he said.

With one last lingering look at my knurries, Tristan uncocked his foot. The crowd dispersed as quickly as it had persed.

"Are you okay, stormtrooper?" said Mr. Kotzur, helping me to my feet.

"I'm fine," I said.

And, despite my throbbing groin, I was fine, because I figured I totally deserved that knee in the knurries.

Setting fire to the Jazys' pool had been a low act, the lowest act of my life. I remembered the terrified look on the face of Tristan's little sister as she stood at the back door, rattan furniture exploding like firecrackers.

"Would you like to make a formal complaint against your assailant?" asked Mr. Kotzur.

"No," I said, because I almost wished that Tristan would come back, keep kneeing me in the knurries over and over until my knurries were nothing but mush and the shame I felt had all gone away.

For the rest of the afternoon my aching knurries and I waited; I'd pulled the pin on going to Rome, surely the explosion must follow.

We expected Coach Sheeds to come storming into the classroom.

We expected to be called before Mr. Cranbrook to explain the email.

But we were disappointed, because the school day just meandered on as usual.

And eventually my knurries stopped aching and I was by myself.

After school, I decided to walk home.

I hadn't gone too far, just a little past the bus stop, when a taxi pulled up in front of me.

Not Luiz Antonio! I wasn't in the mood for him and his bad head and his sick feet.

But when the window wound down it wasn't Luiz Antonio, it was Father of Rashid.

Remembering the violent looks on the faces of the demonstrators, the nasty shove I'd received in the back, I got ready to make a run for it.

But when he said, in an accent twice as thick as Rashid's, "What you did was the honorable thing," I knew I didn't need to.

"So you know?" I said.

"Yes, my son receive a call that say you withdraw from national team."

"Well, he deserves to go to Rome," I said.

"Rome, that does not matter so much," he said. "What matters is school. Those hotheads almost ruin my son's education."

Those hotheads? It took me a second or two to realize that he was talking about the demonstrators, the Coalition of Islam Youth.

"So they will stop now?"

He gave a sort of exasperated look. "Yes, now they must stop."

"That's great," I said.

"Great!" he said, and he held out his hand for me to shake.

ACROSS THE ABYSS

That night, at dinner, things between Mom and Toby hadn't gotten much better; there was a lot of glaring across the lasagna.

Apparently Toby had apologized to the police. Apparently he had sorted it out with the *Ready! Set! Cook!* people.

But he still refused to say sorry to Mom.

With Toby playing the role of Rotten Son, the pressure was off me for a change; it sort of sucked, though. So I told everybody about my decision to withdraw from Rome, hoping it would break the ice, somehow. Mom said that she was proud of me. Miranda said I'd done absolutely the right thing. Toby said that pasta was just as good in Australia anyway. But Dad really didn't say much at all.

After dessert everybody drifted off until it was only Mom and me at the table, drinking tea.

"Can I ask you something?" she said.

"Sure."

"Do you think I put too much pressure on Toby?"

Too much pressure? It was only a cooking show, for Pete's sakes! What was that compared to what I was going through?

I finished my tea.

"Probably," I said.

Mom's eyes were on me now, an expectant look on her face; I wasn't going to get away with just a "probably."

I continued. "Maybe it's because Toby is so, you know, Toby. We all think he's totally got it together. All the time. But maybe it's not as easy as it looks."

Mom took a while to digest what I'd said.

Then she smiled at me. "Okay, I did put too much pressure on him. That's good to know."

She reached across the table and took my hands in her hands.

"Toby's not like you, is he, Dom? He's fragile, and you're as tough as old boots."

I felt both chuffed: she had just hit me with a pretty major compliment; and peeved: why couldn't I, too, be fragile?

We talked some more and then I went upstairs.

As usual the door to Dad's study was closed, but I could hear his voice from the other side. I could tell from the way the volume kept changing that he was walking and talking, something he did all the time. I went to knock but stopped.

"Don't worry, Ronny will ensure there's no enquiry, or if there is, he'll make certain it's got no teeth. We've all invested too much in this home loans thing," I heard him say.

And then he must've moved to another part of his office, because the rest of the conversation wasn't audible.

When I was sure he'd finished, I knocked on the door. "It's me, Dad."

"Come in, Dom," he said.

Dad's office is pretty Spartan: there's a desk and a bookshelf with a few management books and a couple of computer screens, but that's about it. It didn't really say "mega-successful businessman," but I guess it didn't really need to, as nobody went in there except Dad. And it wasn't as if he had to prove it to himself.

"What's up?" he said.

I noticed there was something different about him – he didn't look as relaxed as he usually did. I'm not sure what it was exactly – a certain tightness around his jaw, perhaps – but there was definitely something.

"It's about Rome," I said. "I sort of get the sense that you don't agree with my decision to withdraw from the team."

I was surprised as to how formal I sounded. This was my dad! But it wasn't the same dad I'd had half a year ago, or even a few months ago. That dad didn't speak Calabrian. That dad didn't wield white-hot branding irons.

Dad smiled, but it was a professional smile, one that he'd use over a bargaining table. There was no joy in it, no warmth.

"That's perceptive of you, Dom," he said. "And I'd have to say that you're pretty much spot on."

"Why?" I said, even though I had a fair idea.

Dad gave my question quite a lot of thought before he answered.

"I'm not saying this is the case, but from the outside it might look like you got scared of the mob."

"The mob?" I said, thinking of the Mob, the Mafia, and wondering whether he was making some reference to the 'Ndrangheta.

"That mob of Afghanis, or Iraqis, or whatever they were," he said.

"Oh, that mob," I said.

"And the other thing is, obviously somebody wants you to go to Rome."

Immediately, I knew he was talking about The Debt. It had been circling around in the back of my mind, but now that he'd actually said it, it stopped circling and took up residence smack bang in the middle.

I went to say something, but Dad put his hands up as if to fend off any potential questions fired in his direction. It was The Debt: no discussion allowed!

"Okay, thanks, Dad," I said tersely, and went to walk out.

"Wait!" said Dad, with a force I wasn't used to.

I stopped.

"I've said this before, but I'm going to say it again. It was me who dragged this family out of the gutter. And it's your job to keep it out," he said.

I said nothing, just got out of there.

Why had I even bothered talking to him?

Inside my bedroom, I slammed the door shut and threw myself on my bed. More than anything, I needed to hear Imogen's voice. I needed to hear her say, like Mom and Miranda and Toby (sort of) had said, that I'd done the right thing.

I took out my iPhone and scrolled down the contacts until I came to her. I sat there looking at it, at the photo with the two numbers I had for her – mobile and landline.

I know it was pretty pathetic, like some bad country-and-western song: my baby done left me but I still look at her contact details.

I knew I wouldn't call either of the numbers, and after a while my eyes were drawn away from the iPhone and towards my desk where ClamTop was sitting, its seamless surface gleaming.

Come over here, it seemed to say. *Open me up.*

Again, I knew it was wrong.

Again, I knew it was immoral.

Again, I knew it was unethical.

Again, I couldn't help myself, because I had to see her, even if that "her" was the digital "her." I succumbed to ClamTop, bringing up all the networks in the area.

Opening HAVILLAND, I cloned SYLVIA, Imogen's computer. But she wasn't there; no programs were open, all the icons were lined up in perfect rows and perfect columns.

I noticed that it was the same wallpaper as last time, the newspaper clipping of her father after his election win.

Again my eyes fell on that person – who was he?

I opened her email program. Bang! Bang! Two messages downloaded.

The first was from somebody called Joy Wheeler, who was the secretary of the Gold Coast Branch, Australian Labor Party.

"Dear Ms. Havilland," it read. "Thank you for your enquiry. Though we understand your predicament, and still remember your father fondly as a foot soldier of our organization, I'm afraid it's the Labor Party's policy not to divulge any information regarding its membership, now or in the past."

I scrolled down so I could read Imogen's original request.

Dear Ms. Wheeler,

I have attached a photo taken during my father's election. I wonder if you are able to identify any of the people standing behind him.

Yours sincerely,
Imogen Havilland

I had to give it to Imogen: she didn't give up very easily.

But maybe I wouldn't either if my dad disappeared like that.

During the last installment I'd done a contra deal with Hound de Villiers, PI: find out who the people in the photo were and I'd help him with his tech stuff.

I figured that if I – or Hound – did this, then surely Imogen would start talking to me again. That it would build a bridge over the abyss that separated us.

Unfortunately, Hound had done nothing.

And the abyss was still there.

Maybe even more abysmal than it had been then.

Forget Hound de Villiers, PI. There was only one way to find out who these people were: I had to do it myself.

I turned my attention back to the photo. Looking closer there was a man towards the background.

Most of his face was obscured by the man holding up Graham Havilland's hand in victory, however, there was something familiar about what I could see – his ear and curve of his jaw.

I used Windows "snipping tool" to remove his head, created a JPEG of this, and saved it onto my desktop.

Just as I'd finished doing this there was a knock on my door.

"Who is it?" I said, thinking these crazy, spooky thoughts – like there was some decapitated person on the other side wanting to know why I'd snipped off their head.

It was only Miranda, though, just about the least-decapitated person I know. I mean, she was just about all head, all brain.

"What is it?" I said.

"Well, you know how you asked me about Cerberus, that time?"

"Sure."

"And you know there was that thing about why it was never released? How it wasn't sexy enough, or something?"

Again I answered "sure," but to tell the truth, once I'd managed to obtain Cerberus, I'd hardly given it another thought.

"Well there's another theory floating around the place, now," she said, pausing, the way an actor pauses before they're about to deliver a killer line. "That it was actually too good."

"Too good?" I said. "As in lots of sick apps?"

She gave me a look – *we share DNA so, please, don't be so dumb.*

"No, the architecture was so adaptable – 'plastic' is the word they kept using in this piece I read – that it could be used for a whole range of applications. Not all of them for the benefit of mankind, if you know what I mean. So the US Government stopped them from producing it."

"What sort of applications?" I said.

"Like remote control of weapons," she said. "Imagine if some mad terrorist got their hands on that?"

I did imagine, but that didn't seem like The Debt to me.

"What else do they reckon?" I said, though I was feeling really, really tired now, and just wanted to go to bed.

"It's pretty technical stuff," she said. "I can email you the link if you like?"

"Hey, sis, that'd be great."

Miranda frowned. "Did you just refer to me as 'sis'?"

"Sorry," I said.

"You're forgiven," she said. "Just."

She left then, and a couple of minutes later her email with the link came through. I didn't open it, however. I was too tired and let's face it: Cerberus was so last installment.

LABOR PARTY

"Thank God they got rid of those ludicrous protestors," said Mom as we pulled up at the school drop-off zone.

I was surprised that she hadn't made the connection: me withdrawing from the team and Rashid being reinstated meant that they no longer had anything to protest against.

"I'll be home a bit late," I said, trying to think of an excuse why. In the end I decided to go with the truth. "I'm going to visit the Labor Party offices."

"What in heavens for?" said Mom.

I might as well have said I was going for swim at the sewage farm.

"School project," I said.

"This late in the term?"

"Catch-up," I said.

Mom just rolled her eyes – what was Grammar coming to?

As I walked through the school gates I could see Coach Sheeds standing near the entrance to my classroom, waiting for me. The anger was coming off her, wave after wave of it, like heat off the asphalt on a hot summer day. So I kept my head low and headed in the opposite direction. But she'd already seen me, and she was after me. I increased my pace. She increased hers.

The mature thing to do was to stop and face the music. She had a right to an explanation, after all.

But I just couldn't stop – she was too scary.

I took a sharp right and made for the sports field. Another glance over my shoulder – she was still behind me. Despite the predicament I was in, I couldn't help but admire Coach's turn of speed – she must've been some athlete in her day.

Through the gate and I was on the rugby field. A couple of groundsmen who were moving sprinklers looked up as I flew past them, schoolbag bouncing on my back.

Surely I've lost her by now.

I sneaked another look behind. *Surely not!* If anything, she'd gained on me.

Through another gate and I was on the running track. A couple of galahs flew into the air, screeching.

Down here, there was nobody around, just Coach Sheeds and me.

Just stop and face the music, Dom, I kept telling myself. But my legs and arms continued pumping.

And Coach Sheeds kept coming.

Another lap and she was still gaining on me – she was now only about ten meters behind me.

I increased my pace and it was starting to really hurt.

Just stop!

Another lap and I hit the wall.

I could hear her breathing – she was only a few paces behind.

The finish line was twenty meters away.

She was alongside me.

We lunged for the line together.

And, then, bent over, I sucked in the big ones.

Coach Sheeds was doing the same. Her hands were on her hips. Her face was an alarming shade of heart attack red.

A couple of times she went to say something, but got no further than "Uhh" before her oxygen ran out and she had to suck in some more air.

Eventually we both had enough hemoglobin in our blood for conversation.

But before she said anything, I said, "I know."

"What do you know?" she said.

"I know exactly what you're going to say."

"You do?"

"You know, lions, gazelles, that sort of thing?"

"Go on," said Coach Sheeds.

"How you threw away your chance to compete and there's not a day passes when you don't think about what could've happened?"

"You wouldn't have any water in your bag, would you?"

"I do, actually," I said.

I took off my bag, opened it, took out the bottle and handed it to Coach Sheeds.

She gulped down half the contents and then handed the bottle back to me.

I took a hefty swig.

"You ran a really crap race at the nationals," said Coach.

"Tell me something I don't know."

"And Rashid Wahidi is getting better," she said. "He will never be the runner that you are, but he is improving."

I shrugged.

"But he beat you fair and square. I'm not sure what happened to that photo, but I was right there at the finish and he came in before you."

I took another swig of the water. Handed it back to Coach Sheeds.

"So are you saying I did the right thing withdrawing?"

"That's exactly what I'm saying," she said. "You've done your career absolutely no favors, but you did the right thing."

Coach looked at her watch.

"I've got a class to get to!"

"Me, too," I said.

We walked together back up to the main building.

As we were about to go our separate ways, Coach said, "And thanks for the workout. I don't think I've run that fast in years!"

Ω Ω Ω

The Labor Party office was easy to find.

It was an otherwise ordinary-looking building in an ordinary-looking street except for the two enormous pictures of Ron Gatto, the long-standing local member, that took up both of the windows.

I guess you have to be pretty confident about your looks before you get them blown up to that size.

No volcanic pimples about to erupt, no crazy nose hair, no stray snot.

But Ron Gatto had the look of man who was pretty confident about everything: his looks, his golf game, his electoral majority.

Seeing him like that, larger than life, immediately reminded me of the last time I'd seen him in real life, in Nimbin, walking with my dad and Rocco Taverniti and another man, speaking in Calabrian.

I stepped inside and there were even more large photos of Ron Gatto, long-standing local member. As well as all sorts of political propaganda: the Labor Party is great, the Labor Party is wonderful. Ron Gatto is great. Ron Gatto is wonderful.

"Mate, can I help you?" asked the man at the reception desk.

"Hello," I said, my voice loud and clear. "My name is Dominic Silvagni, I'm from Coast Boys Grammar, and I'm here because I'm currently doing an assignment on the history of the Labor Party in the Gold Coast area."

The man looked at my face, at my school uniform, back at my face, and said, "Really?"

"Absolutely!" I said. "And I'm aiming to get an excellent mark."

I'm not sure what role I was playing, and why exactly I was playing it, but now that I was in character, I had trouble getting out.

"Is there anybody I could speak to?" I said.

"Well, Joy's your woman," he said.

I figured that Joy must be Joy Wheeler, the woman who had sent the less-than-encouraging email to Imogen.

"I'll just see if she's free."

While he went back to see if my woman Joy was free, I took the opportunity to, as we say in the business, case the joint.

Because the way I was seeing it, if I couldn't personally coax Imogen's data from Joy Wheeler, and if ClamTop didn't work, then I'd have to resort to less subtle methods, like break and enter.

I don't want to brag or anything, but Diablo Bay, Fiends of the Earth office, Hound's office; you name it, I'd broken it and I'd entered it.

But straightaway I could see that this place would be a challenge.

It was an electronic fortress, CCTV all over the place, and I could tell that it was all good-quality stuff, not some crappy DIY kit bought off eBay.

I guessed there were two ways of looking at this: either they were really, really cautious or they really, really had something to hide.

If I did have to break and enter, it wouldn't be easy.

Was I willing to take that risk?

The man returned with Joy Wheeler.

It didn't take me long to realize that Joy Wheeler should have been charged with false advertising because there was nothing joyful about her at all.

She had one of those emoticon faces that seemed to be stuck in frown mode.

And when she talked she had a habit of taking what I said, sticking a question mark on the end and then handing it back to me.

"So you're doing some sort of project, are you?"

"So you go to Grammar, do you? So your name's Dom, is it?"

Eventually I decided it was time to go on the attack.

"Are your records all electronically archived?" I said, thinking that if they were I might be able to access them with good old ClamTop.

For a second I thought she was going to say, "So you're asking me if all our records are electronically archived, are you?"

But instead she said, "The Labor Party of Queensland takes its rich history very seriously."

"I'm sure it does," I said.

It was a pretty innocent comment, but I could see that Joyless Joy thought otherwise, that she took it as a challenge, because she said, "Come with me, please!"

I followed her into a windowless room that was obviously some sort of library: there were shelves crammed with books, overflowing filing cabinets.

Another woman, also pretty joyless, was placing a newspaper clipping on a scanner.

She looked up when we entered.

"How we going with the digitization, Helen?" said Joy.

"Almost there," said Helen. "The sooner we get this stuff off-site, the better."

Joy threw me a triumphant look, but I'd already

seen enough to know my next move would include ClamTop.

"Look, I've probably got more than enough information to start with," I said.

And that's exactly when long-standing local member Ron Gatto walked into the room.

Obviously this Ron Gatto wasn't as big as the two Ron Gattos outside – I mean, there was no way his face was two meters wide – but he still had an enormous presence.

It was almost like he was radioactive, because he had these waves coming off him, and like radioactive waves they were dangerous.

"What's going on here?" he said.

After Joyless Joy explained what was going on, Radioactive Ron fixed me with a look.

"What did you say your name was?" he demanded.

"Dom," I said, thinking that it was probably a good idea to keep my surname well out of it.

"Dom," he said, rolling the word around in his mouth. "So let me guess: you're like Prince, or Madonna, or Warnie, you're so famous you only need the single moniker."

As he said this, he threw Joy a look and she responded with a stuttering laugh. Joyless Joy laughed!

Okay, Mr. Gatto, if that's how you want to play.

Now I wished his face was two meters wide, because I wanted to study it, see what his reaction was when I pulled the pin on the grenade and said, "My surname's Silvagni."

But there was no reaction, nothing. The blankest of poker faces.

"Silvagni?" said Joy. "I've seen that name in the archives somewhere."

Ron Gatto's paw grabbed me by the shoulder and he said, "Why don't you come into my office, and I'll show you some stuff. The Labor Party of Queensland has a rich history of which we are immensely proud."

Which is exactly what I did.

Most of the rich history he showed me was about the many and varied accomplishments of the Gold Coast Labor Party under the stewardship (his word!) of Ron Gatto. But I didn't absorb much of what he was saying, because I kept thinking about what Joy had said about the Silvagni name. As far as I knew, we were the only Silvagnis on the whole Coast, but when had my family ever, ever been involved with the Labor Party?

It was time to get out of here. I thanked Ron Gatto and I thanked Joy Wheeler and I thanked the man behind the counter and walked back onto the street. As I did, I noticed a parked fire truck and a small crowd gathered around an open manhole.

"Well back, please, folks," said a man in a yellow fluoro jacket.

He peered into the manhole and said, "Any luck, Mal?"

"There she is," said Mal from somewhere in the drains. "Here, pussy! Here, pussy! Gotcha!"

There was a cheer as a bedraggled cat appeared, handed from Mal to Mal's workmate and then to its owner.

And Mal himself got a round of applause as he appeared, a huge cat-saving smile on his face. The two men pulled the cover back on the manhole and made for the fire truck.

On the bus on the way home I googled *Silvagni* and *ALP*.

All I got was an Italian mountain climber called Claudio Silvagni who had managed to climb all the major peaks in the Alps in one season.

So I put *Gold Coast Labor Party* instead of *ALP*, but I got nothing.

No connection at all between Labor and Silvagni. I recalled what Miranda had said, that Google wasn't the friend I thought it was, that it censored results.

Surely not, I thought.

But what if it had no results to censor? What if the information had been censored before Google even got its electronic hands on it?

Instead of heading straight through the door of our house, I diverted to Gus's house. He wasn't in the kitchen or his office, but I could hear the *doof-doof* sound of techno from the garage and I knew he must be in there. I know what you're thinking: *Gus likes techno?* When he's lifting weights, yes.

The garage door was open.

"Gus," I called through it. "It's me."

"Enter!" he said.

There was nothing sophisticated about Gus's gym: a bare concrete floor, a few benches, bars and free weights. And a boom box belting out techno.

Gus was spread out on the bench, one foot on the ground, hands on a bar lumpy with weights, ready to press. I did some mental arithmetic: seventy kilos, including the bar! What, at seventy-four years of age, was Gus trying to prove?

My grandfather hoisted the bar from the rest and started pumping. The first seven lifts he did easily, a study in style and economy of power. He struggled a bit with the eighth lift. Struggled even more with the ninth. And on the tenth lift his elbows remained bent, the bar hovering only a few centimeters above his chest.

"You okay, Gus?" I said, worried that those seventy kilos were going to crash back onto him. "You need a spot?"

The answer was a grunt so loud it out-technoed

the techno. And slowly Gus lifted, willed the bar upwards, every muscle, every fiber in his arms straining. Until the bar dropped back onto the rests with a seventy-kilo clang.

Gus sat up. "Not bad for an old codger, eh?" he said, his face brick-red from the exertion.

"For an old codger," I said.

I'd thought that Gus had lost his leg because he hadn't been up to it, because he, unlike Dad, hadn't had what it took to repay The Debt. But it occurred to me that maybe I had this wrong: Gus had been totally up to it; he lost his leg because of other reasons.

"Hey, Gus, were us Silvagnis ever involved with the Labor Party?"

Gus laughed and said, "Lucky you didn't ask your father that question."

"I'm asking you," I said, getting some of that seventy kilos of iron in my voice. "Were we?"

Gus sighed and got up from the bench.

Now that we were eye to eye he said, "I've told you before, but now I'm begging you: please stop digging, Dom. Because if you don't, there's going to be serious trouble"

"Okay," I said, but *Okay* I didn't think, because a terrible thought had found its way into my head. *Did we Silvagnis somehow have something to do with the disappearance of Mr. Havilland?*

SCHOOL BREAKUP

It was the last assembly for the term and Mr. Cranbrook was in his element, perched high up there on the podium, microphone in his hand.

"Boys," he said, and lots of other stuff as well, but I was so not tuned in to Radio Principal.

There were too many other frequencies out there competing for my attention. Like Radio What Am I Going to Do over Vacation? And Radio Did I Really Make the Right Decision Not Racing? And Radio How Am I Going to Bust into the Labor Party Office?

I was so tuned in to these that I didn't notice it when it started.

It was only because the other kids around me started reacting that I tuned out of all those stations and tuned in to what was happening inside the Great Hall. Or more specifically, outside. Because there was a clattering sound from above.

"Whoa, what's that?" I said.

"I reckon somebody's throwing rocks," said Charles.

Now I got it: the Great Hall was actually close to the main road. A few times previously some kids – I assumed they were kids – had lobbed rocks onto the roof. And even those few rocks had made an incredible sound. But this was more than a few rocks and the sound was actually pretty scary.

"Calm now, boys," said Mr. Cranbrook.

SPOs were swarming all over the place now. But why were five of them headed in my direction?

"Dominic Silvagni?" said one of them. I nodded. "We're getting you out of here," he said.

Before I could say anything, they'd surrounded me in a carapace again and smuggled me out of there and into the principal's office.

Within a few minutes, a posse of authority arrived: there was the de-podiumed Mr. Cranbrook and Mr. Iharos and Coach Sheeds and Mr. Theissen.

"Who in the blazes were they?" I said.

"Language, please!" said Mr. Iharos.

"Given the circumstances, the language might not be so inappropriate today," said Mr. Cranbrook.

Mr. Iharos didn't say anything, but he looked peeved.

"They're the same people who were here the other day," said Mr. Cranbrook.

"But what are they protesting about now?" I said.

Mr. Cranbrook and Mr. Iharos exchanged looks.

"Dominic, though we fully support your decision, we do wish you had warned us that you intended to retract your withdrawal."

"Retract my withdrawal?"

"Yes, your withdrawal from the team to go to Rome."

"But I didn't retract anything," I said.

More looks were exchanged.

"Have you checked your emails lately?" said Coach Sheeds.

No, actually I haven't, because your school has a policy about checking emails during school hours.

"Do you mind?" I said, taking out my iPhone.

"No, of course not," said Mr. Cranbrook.

Mr. Iharos looked even more peeved.

I clicked on the Mail app.

Checking for mail …

Bang. Bang. Bang. Bang. Bang.

I scanned the emails.

Your decision to retract …

After much discussion …

Reinstate your position …

Our investigation shows that the original withdrawal email was indeed "phished."

Suddenly, the room felt as cold as a freezer.

The Debt had doctored the photo because they

wanted me to go to Rome. Now they'd phished these emails to stop me withdrawing from the team.

I remembered what Zoe Zolton-Bander had once said, that I was "so owned."

Yes, it was a pretty common expression: it seemed like everybody was "owned" nowadays.

A surfer falls off his board; the wave "owned" him.

Some kid got sick; the flu "owned" him.

But I really was owned; not only was The Debt reaching deeper and deeper into my life, they were controlling it, too.

Now I noticed that four sets of eyes were on me, waiting for some sort of explanation.

My first instinct was to deny it.

No, of course I didn't withdraw!

But imagine the hoo-ha that would result from that – a full freaking enquiry.

And what if the school somehow got close to The Debt? That just couldn't happen.

"Oh, that retraction of that withdrawal," I said, not quite believing how utterly lame I sounded. "It was sort of spur of the moment."

"Spur of the moment?" said Mr. Cranbrook.

I don't think he quite believed how utterly lame I was sounding, either.

I nodded.

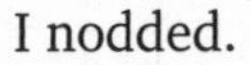

There was silence in the room; nobody knew what to do.

I thought of Father of Rashid, the handshake he'd given me last night because I'd done the "honorable thing."

Mr. Theissen shot his cuffs, adjusted his tie.

"Here's how I think we should handle this," he said.

I could see why he got to wear expensive Italian suits: he knew exactly what to do.

When he'd finished, Mr. Cranbrook looked at me and said, "Okay, then our first priority is to get Dominic out of here safely."

"I need a word first," said Coach Sheeds.

Here we go, I thought. The big speech from Coach. How disappointed she was with me for changing my decision. How she thought I was made of better stuff. But I got nothing of the sort.

Instead she gave me a whole lot of logistical information about the trip to Rome.

"I assume you have a passport," she said.

"Yes, of course," I said.

"Well, as long as your parents agree, you're off to Rome!" she said, slapping me on the back.

And I couldn't help buying into it – I was off to Rome. To run! To compete!

Then the five SPOs took me down to the back of the school where there was a car waiting to drive me all the way home.

A GRATE WAY TO DIE

It didn't seem possible, but the next morning at nine thirty I would be joining the team at Brisbane Airport where we would board a plane bound for Rome, Italy.

As you'd expect, Dad was totally fine with it; he even said that I didn't have to worry about money, he'd keep my card topped up. Mom was less fine with it, but Dad soon brought her around.

"He'll be the first Silvagni to visit the old country," he said.

"You've seriously never been to Italy?" said Toby, obviously shocked that his own parents had not visited the land of the fabled tiramisu.

Mom and Dad exchanged looks.

"Not technically," said Dad. "But we might've sneaked over the border during that last ski trip to the Alps. The way your mother skis, you never know."

Ski humor, like golf humor, is pretty much wasted on me.

Besides, I was still coming to terms with how I felt about going to Rome. *I contain multitudes*. I shouldn't be going, I lost the race. *I contain multitudes.* I should be going, I was a better runner than Rashid. But cutting through all that was one absolute – The Debt had spoken.

And I still hadn't talked to Imogen.

Instead of playing the usual country-and-western song: my baby done left me but I still look at her contact details, I played another one: my baby done left me but I'm gonna try to call her.

Her phone rang and rang, however.

I walked past her house hoping to get even a glimpse of her at her bedroom window, but the curtains remained resolutely closed. And I guess Mr. McFarlane would have said they were some sort of symbol that represented how closed Imogen had become to me. Yeah, well, Mr. Mac didn't know about ClamTop.

I powered up it up. Brought up local networks. Imogen's network was up, her computer connected to it.

But instead of feeling ashamed as I had last time, I felt weirdly justified. I mean, Imogen was behaving stupidly. I hadn't done anything that warranted her cutting me off so completely. Even the detestable knurrie-kneeing Tristan had admitted that I wasn't to blame for his accident.

I cloned her desktop but this time, instead of the icons sitting there, turd-like, they were moving about as though they were in a Beyoncé video.

I read an article once that said in girls this part of the brain called the corpus callosum is bigger than it is in boys. This results in more traffic between the two hemispheres of girls' brains, which means they are much better at multitasking.

Well, Imogen's corpus callosum must've been humungous, because wow! was she multitasking or what?

There were about a thousand websites up. Facebook was open and she had three conversations going with three different people. And Windows Mail was open on a half-written email. uTorrent was downloading an episode of *Modern Family*. And she was listening to music in iTunes.

Where to start?

Emails, I thought.

I scanned the list of senders, expecting to see sixpack, sixpack and more sixpack, but there actually weren't that many from Tristan.

Imogen's dialogue with Joy Wheeler seemed to have continued since last time I'd snooped … I mean, looked.

Dear Imogen,

While I am personally sympathetic to your requests, I hope you understand that I must adhere to Labor Party regulations regarding this matter. I would also like to inform you that, tragically, most of the Gold Coast Labor Party archival material was destroyed in a flood some years ago.

Yours sincerely,
Joy Wheeler

What flood? She hadn't mentioned any flood when I'd gone there. All I'd gotten was that "rich history of which we are immensely proud" crap. And what about all that stuff Helen was digitizing?

Joy Wheeler, emoticon on legs, was telling lies, and big ones at that. But what was she hiding?

When I come back from Rome I'll find out, I promised myself.

But it would be more than a week before I got back from Rome and by then, going by what Helen had said, all archival material might be off-site.

If I was going to do it, it had to be tonight.

I recalled the surveillance inside the Labor Party office. The lack of cover outside the office. How could I get ClamTop anywhere near it? Then it came to me – *of course! That's how.*

But at one in the morning, when my alarm went

off, I managed to convince myself yet again: *Of course you're not going to do it, you idiot. You've got to catch a plane at 9:30 a.m.!* I rolled over, readjusted my pillow, closed my eyes. And changed my mind yet again.

I was going to do it tonight.

Sneaking out of the house wasn't an issue. Because of the care I took each morning not to disturb anybody when I went out for my run, I knew where each loose floorboard, each creaky door was.

But sneaking out of Halcyon Grove: not so easy. I couldn't just leave through the front gates, because there was no way Samsoni, or whoever was on duty, would let a minor like me through. And since I needed to get into the storm water drain anyway, then why not do it from here?

I slunk past Imogen's house, past Tristan's house, but instead of continuing on, I turned left and into the recreation area. *Please Do Not Walk on Grass* said the sign, the sign I disobeyed.

Right at the back of the park, hidden by some gardenia bushes, was the grate. When we were little kids, monsters lived beneath this grate. The biggest, meanest, ugliest monsters the world had ever seen. But later, when we were older, they went somewhere else to live.

One day we even managed to pry the grate up and Nathan Cordeiro climbed down.

"There's a tunnel!" he said, but then he froze.

He just wouldn't move, so we had to get his mum to coax him out. They concreted the grate in after that.

But now I'd come prepared – a raid of the gardener's shed had yielded a hammer and a cold chisel. I used these to chip away the concrete, loosening the grate, until eventually I was able to remove it.

I put on my headlamp, took the waterproof holder with the storm water map I'd found on the Internet out of my backpack and hung it around my neck.

I zipped up the pack and put it on my back, tightening the straps so that it didn't bounce around. If there had been any hint of rain, there's no way I would've lowered myself into that storm water tunnel. But the skies were clear, and had been for weeks, and the tunnel was dry, so I started crawling on hands and knees, my headlamp picking out the concrete cylinder ahead.

According to my map the pipe had a diameter of one and a half meters, but it seemed much, much smaller than that. It also smelled much smaller than that, that dusty, irritate-your-nostrils smell of places that don't get a whole lot of fresh air.

But it didn't smell damp and that was the main thing. Technically I was coimetrophobic, not claustrophobic, but I still wasn't that happy to be in such a confined space.

And if I'd wanted to turn back: bad luck, this was about as one way as a one-way street gets.

After about half an hour of crawling I came to a T-junction, where another pipe joined the one I was in. According to the map, I was below Chevron Heights, and the next major feature, a large sump, was about the same distance as I'd already come.

I kept crawling.

And crawling.

And crawling.

Something's wrong, I told myself as I checked the map again. *I should be there by now.*

I wouldn't say I was panicking, but I could feel my heart rate going up, sweat forming on my palms. So when I heard voices I figured they were some sort of hallucinatory response to the discomfort I was feeling. But as I continued and those voices became louder and more distinct, I knew I wasn't imagining them.

"Pass us the vodka, will ya?" Male voice.

"You've had enough!" Female voice.

The drain became wider, higher, and I could feel the waft of fresh air in my face.

"I said, you've had enough!" Female voice.

"Who cares what you say?" Male voice.

I better say something, I thought, *or I'm going to scare the crap out of them.*

"Hi, honey, I'm home," I said, thinking that the comedic approach was often effective.

Except my voice reverberated outrageously: there were hundreds of honeys in hundreds of homes.

The tunnel opened out and I dropped down into a sort of chamber, like a square room with other tunnels leading off in four directions.

Candles threw a surprisingly strong light over the scene, over the sleeping bags and vodka bottles and empty Pringles containers. And two street kids: a boy and a girl. I knew them; in fact, I'd once employed them. It was Brandon and his sister, PJ. I was aware that they hung around the storm water drains because I'd seen them disappear down one at Preacher's Forest. Brandon looked even gaunter than the last time I'd seen him. Again I thought of that Neil Young song, "The Needle and the Damage Done."

He looked at me with bloodshot eyes.

"Hey, what you want?" he demanded.

I noticed that his sister was holding a spray can, finger on the nozzle – what, she was going to graffiti me? – but then I realized it must be pepper spray.

"Hey, chill," she said, putting the can down. "It's what's-his-name. The dude from Cozzi's that day. The one we got the phone for."

The last time I'd seen her she'd had black hair, now it was blond. It was the same messy style, though. And she still looked like an anime character.

Brandon squinted at me.

"You're right," he said, and he closed his eyes and slumped back.

PJ shrugged.

"He's a bit sick," she said.

"Look, I'm totally out of here," I said, pointing to the entrance to a new tunnel. "Is that the way to the city?"

PJ nodded. "Rich kid like you, thought you could afford something better than these rat runs."

I'm not sure why I thought she deserved an explanation, but I did.

"Everybody at school's into urbex these days," I said.

"Urbex?"

"Urban exploration," I said.

"Oh, is that what you call it at Grammar?" PJ smiled and her whole face seemed to come alive. "Take care."

"I will," I said.

Brandon had toppled right over now, the vodka bottle still clutched in his hand.

"Is he okay?" I said.

"Like I said, he's just a bit sick," said PJ.

I hoisted myself into the drain and started shuffling as quickly as I could away from there. It

didn't take long, about ten minutes, before the drain opened up again into another chamber, this one smaller than the previous one. Overhead there was a grate, street-light filtering in. I didn't even need my headlamp to check the map.

There was a makeshift ladder made from milk crates stacked on top of each other and I figured this was at least one of the places where Brandon and PJ got in and out of the drains.

I was exactly where I'd hoped I'd be.

Now I had to take the tunnel to my left. I did this, and after fifteen more minutes of crawling I was at my destination, another sump. The one the cat had been rescued from. Again an overhead grate provided some street-light. There was enough room for me to sit down, my back against the concrete.

I took ClamTop out of my bag, out of the plastic sleeve I'd put it in, and powered it up. There was only one network available in this area, and that was LABORNET.

Of course it was secure, but ClamTop and its little red devil had no trouble cracking it. And in what seemed like no time I was in there, on the main server.

I had a quick look through the directory – it was very complex, lots of directories, with lots of layers.

How to navigate through this and find what I was looking for when I really didn't know what it was?

But then I had a brain wave: if Helen had been working this week, digitizing files, then all I had to do was run a file search where the date modified was "earlier this week."

I tried that and it worked a treat.

Now I knew where all the documents she'd digitized were stored.

But again, there were so many of them I could sit here all night searching through them and still not find what I was looking for. I needed to make a copy.

But how did I do that on ClamTop?

I racked my brain for a while before it occurred to me: the obvious way, that's how.

I highlighted the directory and dragged it out of its window and into ClamTop's window.

And of course it worked.

If ever they marketed ClamTop, that should be its motto – The Obvious Way.

Satisfied that I now had everything, I put ClamTop back in its plastic sleeve and back into my backpack.

I had planned to return via the storm water drain but now I was having serious second thoughts. It was past three, so I'd been underground for more than two hours. It was time to get some fresh air.

And yes, I'd have to get back into Halcyon Grove via the main gate, but that was something I'd deal with.

I crawled back to the previous sump, the one that looked like it was one of the places where PJ and Brandon got in and out. Taking advantage of the milk-crate ladder, I reached up and pushed the grate aside.

Hoisting myself up through the hole wasn't that difficult. Still squatting, I slid the grate back over the hole. It was only when I stood up that I realized I had company. Of the uniformed variety. I also realized something else. There was a low guttural rumbling and the sky was host to jagged strikes of lightning.

RAIN, RAIN, GO AWAY

"So how many of you?" asked the policeman, the pimply one who looked like he wasn't much older than me.

Plop! A fat raindrop landed right on the tip of my nose.

"They're not actually my friends," I said.

"I don't think you quite understand," said the other copper. "Forecast is for torrential rain and if anybody is caught in there they're goners."

I thought about those two kids who not long ago had been caught in one of these tunnels and swept out to sea.

Their bodies had never been found.

I thought how quiet it had been in the chamber – there was no way they would know about the rain until it came gushing in on them.

"There's a boy and a girl," I said.

"Terrific!" said pimply cop, and he was on his radio, calling in Special Ops.

Another seismic peal of thunder, a violent crack of lightning, and the rain got serious. It didn't fall, it pelted down, and I knew I had no choice.

"I'm going back down there," I said, wrenching the grate away.

"No, you're not," said pimply cop, trying to grab me.

I easily slipped out of his grasp, however, and dropped down into the hole. The milk crates collapsed under me and I tumbled to the bottom of the sump.

Back on my feet, I dived back into the tunnel. If I thought I'd crawled quickly before, I was flying now.

There were no voices this time and when I reached the chamber I could see why: PJ and Brandon were sleeping, the guttering candles throwing weak light over their pale faces.

"Hey, wake up," I yelled, my voice echoing. "Wake up! Wake up! Wake up!"

PJ opened her eyes, but Brandon remained slumbering.

"It's raining!" I said. "There's water coming!"

She blinked a couple of times.

Drunk, half-asleep, I could understand why she was having trouble taking it all in.

"Raining," I repeated. "There's water coming!"

"Crap!" she said, and she started shaking her brother. "Brand, wake up, it's raining."

Brandon remained motionless. But when PJ slapped him hard across the face he opened his eyes.

"Rain!" she said. "We have to get out of here."

"Rain, rain, go away, come back another day," said Brandon in a little kid's singsong voice.

I could hear it now, the distant gurgle of water, and it was coming from the drain I'd just been in. Going back that way wasn't an option, then.

"Where does this go?" I said, pointing to another drain.

"The sea," said PJ.

Also not an option, I told myself, thinking of those two drowned kids.

"This one?"

"Preacher's," said PJ. "It's the fastest way out."

"We head for Preacher's, then," I said.

The gurgling was getting louder and then dirty brown water, carrying with it a flotilla of cigarette butts, ice cream sticks, twigs and leaves, burst into the chamber.

"We have to go now!" I yelled.

Brandon had nodded off again.

PJ slapped him again, so hard that the sound reverberated around the chamber.

She was small, I could see the ladder of her ribs against the thin material of her T-shirt, but she sure packed a wallop.

"What the –" he said, bringing his hand to his reddened cheek.

"We've got to go, Brandon!"

"There's water coming!" I added.

The proof was pretty irrefutable: the water, ankle deep, was rising quickly, and the smell, of all the accumulated muck that had been washed off the street, was almost overpowering.

The second slap seemed to have done the trick because Brandon stumbled to his feet, and we all splashed our way over to the drain entrance.

"You go first, sis," he said.

PJ scurried into the tunnel.

"Okay, you're next," he said to me.

"You sure?" I said.

If Tristan had – or used to have – the Smirk, then Brandon had the Snarl, a permanent look of disdain on his face.

"We live down here, kid. You're just a tourist."

I got a glimpse of the resourceful kid Brandon must've been before the needle or whatever it was got to him.

I dived into the drain.

Crawling, I figured, was just the precursor to running, so I did all the stuff I did when I ran:

I concentrated on form and rhythm and I tried to ignore the pain.

Mostly the pain was coming from my hands, because all that friction against the wet concrete floor was rubbing them raw, and my knees, too, were starting to react to the battering they'd had.

It wasn't long before my headlamp picked out the bottom of PJ's shoes.

"Keep it moving," I said, splashing through water.

"Is Brandon behind you?"

"Yes," I said, though I didn't know if he was or not.

PJ slowed.

"Keep it moving!" I said, my voice echoing back down the drain.

We picked up speed again.

But then slowed again.

"Keep it moving!"

And despite the predicament I was in, the pain I was feeling, I had this sense of – I'm not sure how to describe it – teamwork, togetherness, like me and these street kids were in this together, and together we were finding a way to get out of it.

"Here!" echoed PJ's voice from ahead.

The tunnel opened out into another chamber, on the side of which was an iron ladder that led to another level, high above the water. Up there I could see sleeping bags.

"Where's Brandon?" said PJ.

I maneuvered my head so the headlamp illuminated the drain.

A river of water, gushing, gurgling, but no sign of Brandon.

He's dead, I thought.

Drowned.

"Let's go!" I said.

But PJ didn't move.

"I'm going back," she said, trying to push past me.

Again I was surprised at how strong she was.

"It's no use," I said. "He's gone."

"Out of my way!" she screamed.

"He's gone," I repeated, but with much less conviction – I didn't know that.

I went back into the drain, into the water.

"Brandon!" I yelled as I crawled, even though I knew there was very little chance he could hear me above the insane gurgling noise.

"Brandon!"

One more minute, I kept telling myself, looking at my watch. *One more minute.*

But that minute elapsed and I kept going.

Until there he was.

Improbably, he was on his back, sort of wedged sideways, the water cascading over him: how had he managed that?

Eyes closed, body still. I'd been right: he was gone.

Better make sure, I told myself, and I dug my fingers into his neck as we'd been taught in the first aid course Coach Sheeds had made us all do.

Nothing: he was dead.

My first dead person, and I felt like I should be having these momentous feelings, but, to tell the truth, I wasn't feeling much at all.

But suddenly: a pulse.

At first I thought it must be something to do with the gushing water.

But no, it was a pulse, weak but regular.

I grabbed Brandon by the scruff of the neck and yanked as hard as I could.

His T-shirt tore and he remained where he was.

Great!

So I grabbed a handful of his hair instead, squeezing my fingers tight, and again I yanked.

This time he moved.

I shuffled back.

I repeated the process, yanking him towards me.

Now the water was pouring into me, there was no avoiding it, no escaping the water and I copped mouthful after mouthful of it.

It tasted putrid, and I fought to keep it out, but it was no use, water poured down my throat.

I yanked Brandon forward.

Shuffled back.

We were moving, but too slowly, and my energy was rapidly diminishing.

A hand grabbed each of my ankles, sending a bolt of terror through me. I screamed – the biggest ugliest scariest monsters in the world lived in these drains.

"It's me," said PJ. "He's alive?"

"Just," I said.

"Okay, how we going to do this?"

It wasn't something to be explained, we just did it, somehow found a technique, a rhythm: PJ pulling me, me pulling Brandon, like some sort of dislocated caterpillar.

And weirdly enough, the water, the same water that so wanted to drown us, was our biggest ally, because Brandon was almost floating now.

"I'm here," said PJ.

Thank God!

But now we had to get him up the ladder.

There wasn't much to Brandon, and I was able to push him from behind while PJ pulled him from above.

Eventually we managed to drag him onto the higher level, out of the reach of the rising water.

It was like a room here, with a ceiling high enough to stand up. There was a round entrance at one end, through which I could make out the shapes of bushes.

There was more than just sleeping bags here, I could see foam mattresses as well. And open suitcases with clothes inside. And, surprisingly, a lot of paperbacks.

We put Brandon into the recovery position and I checked his pulse again.

It seemed stronger now, more regular.

"We still need to get him to the hospital," I said.

"It's okay, he's better here," said PJ, stripping off his wet clothes. "Hospitals freak him out too much."

I checked my watch.

It was past four.

"I need to get home," I said. "I have to catch a plane to Italy at nine thirty this morning."

"Skiing, are we?" said PJ.

"No, actually I'm running for ..."

But I didn't have the energy for any more words, any more justification.

I had to go.

But when I tried to go, when I tried to get out of there, I just didn't have the energy for that either.

I collapsed back onto one of the mattresses.

"Hey, you," said PJ, sounding just a bit like my mother, "don't lie on there in those wet things!"

"But this is all I've got," I said.

PJ threw me a T-shirt and some jeans that I assumed were Brandon's.

"Here, put these on," she said.

I hesitated – she was staring right at me.

"I'm not looking," she said, turning to face the other direction.

I stripped off my wet clothes and put on the dry ones.

Punk may have ended about a thousand years ago, but nobody had told Brandon that. So I squeezed into a torn black T-shirt and torn black jeans that were at least one size too small for me. It didn't matter, though, because they felt so good, so warm.

I opened my backpack, checked ClamTop, my iPhone.

Thank goodness, both of them were dry.

Again I checked my watch: four twenty. I had to get going. But I couldn't. I had no energy whatsoever. My eyelids were getting heavier and heavier. I could hear PJ somewhere near me. And I could hear Brandon's breathing. And I could hear the splash of the water below.

And I had this incredible feeling of well-being, of happiness.

I wasn't going to Rome. So what?

The Debt would come after me. So what?

Tonight I'd helped save another person's life. And there was nothing at all "so what" about that.

"Good night," I said to PJ.

She didn't answer, but her hand found mine, and she squeezed it.

The very last thought I had before I went to sleep was that there was no way I was going to let go of it.

TO THE AIRPORT

Somewhere, out there, beyond this sleep that held me in its soft arms, my phone was ringing.

There was nothing I could do about it, though. Not now.

Again my phone was ringing.

This time I managed to open my eyes. Brandon was right next to me. For a split second, as I took in his face, so thin and white, I thought he was dead. But I realized that the sound I was hearing, that regular wheeze, was his breathing. No, Brandon was alive. And that lump on my other side must be PJ, I reasoned. I closed my eyes.

The third time I woke it wasn't to the sound of my phone ringing.

There was a terrible smell.

And I was being shaken.

And somebody was saying, "Awake, thou that

sleepest, and arise from the dead, and Christ shall give thee light!"

"Go away," I said.

"Awake, thou that sleepest, and arise from the dead, and Christ shall give thee light!"

I opened my eyes, and it was the most horrible thing, outside of a nightmare, I had ever seen.

Actually, it was the most horrible thing, inside of a nightmare, I had ever seen.

The Preacher, his face centimeters from mine, his toxic breath scorching my face, his hands clawing at my shirt.

I screamed, shuffling back.

"Go away!"

"So must thou bear witness also at Rome!" said the Preacher.

"What did you say?" I said, and by this time PJ's tousled head had appeared from under a sleeping bag.

"So must thou bear witness also at Rome!"

Was the Preacher telling me I had to catch that plane?

"So must thou bear witness also at Rome!" he said for the third time.

"Okay, already! I heard you," I said.

"What does he want?" said PJ.

"He wants me to catch that plane to Rome," I said. "But how does he know anything about it?"

"You better do what he says," said PJ. "He's a pretty spooky old dude."

Spooky?

He was terrifying.

I checked my watch.

"It's almost six," I said. "And I have to check in by seven-thirty. There's no way I can get there on time."

"So must thou bear witness also at Rome!" said the Preacher, one hand digging into the rags he was wearing.

It came out jangling a set of car keys.

"He wants me to drive there?" I said. "What is he, mad or something?"

Of course he was mad or something.

PJ held out her hand, and for the first time I noticed that her fingernails were painted alternate colors, pink and purple, pink and purple. The Preacher tossed her the keys.

"Let's go, then," she said.

"You're going to drive his car?" I said.

"It's not exactly a car," she said. "He lets us use it sometimes."

Like Alice, I'd fallen into a topsy-turvy world where normal rules no longer applied.

"So must thou bear witness also at Rome!" said

the Preacher, taking a step towards me.

I got quickly to my feet.

"Okay, let's go, then. Let's go bear freaking witness in freaking Rome."

I realized that I wasn't wearing shoes, however.

Brandon didn't seem to have any spare ones, black and torn or otherwise, so I had no choice but to use my old runners.

It was like putting some sort of disgusting bottom-feeding marine creature on each foot.

"Will he be okay?" I asked, pointing at Brandon.

"Sleep's good," she said.

We left the sleeping Brandon and the now-silent Preacher and quickly made our way out of the sump, down that last little piece of drain, and through the park, my feet squelching with every step. It was a really nice morning: the sun was shining, birds were singing, and the rain had made everything look and smell clean and fresh. And despite the night I'd just had, I could feel my spirits lifting. I wondered if this wasn't more than just meteorological, if it might also have something to do with being around PJ, the anime.

When we came to the turnoff to the path that led out of Preacher's, PJ kept walking.

"Isn't this the way out?" I said.

"You trust me or not?" she said.

She was a street kid, a scam artist, a thief – not the type you usually trusted – but for some reason

I did trust her.

We continued along this path before we turned onto an even smaller path.

I looked around for a landmark – who knew, one day I might have to use this route.

There was a gum tree with a split trunk.

That'll do, I told myself, making a mental note. *Turn left at the tree with the split trunk.*

This path wended through scrub until it eventually came out at the back of Preacher's.

I hadn't been here before and I was sort of glad of that, because it had the look – a couple of burned-out car shells; the smell – like squashed insects; the feel – totally creepy – of a major badlands.

"Lovely place," I said.

"Remember that murder case last year?" she said. "The husband who killed his wife?"

I nodded, though I only had a vague recollection.

"That's where they found her," she said, pointing to a crop of bushes we were walking past. "Or what was left of her."

"And the Preacher's wheels?"

But my question was redundant, because they'd already come into view. The Preacher's wheels was big and it was black.

"Wait a minute," I said. "Isn't that a hearse?"

PJ nodded.

"Hop in."

"You're really going to drive?" I said.

"Look, do you want to get to Italy or not? No skin off my nose either way."

It was a pretty good question: did I want to get to Italy or not? And it didn't take me very long, about a nanosecond, to decide that there were a number of reasons, some of them Debt-related, others not, why my answer had to be yes.

"Okay, let's go," I said, getting into the front passenger seat.

The hearse had a very strong, very unpleasant smell. And I wondered if maybe there was still a client in the back. A quick inspection revealed nothing coffin-like, however, just a whole lot of garbage; old newspapers mostly.

PJ pumped the accelerator, twisted the key.

"Come on, Hearsey," she said, in a way that suggested she was quite familiar with driving it.

Hearsey responded with a couple of barks and then the throaty roar of an internal combustion engine. I was about to say something like, "So you're okay to drive this beast?" but I managed to bite my tongue before the words were out. Of course she was okay to drive this beast, otherwise she wouldn't be driving this beast, would she?

We rumbled through the badlands and then onto a main road. I guess if I was a minor illegally driving

a car I would probably choose something a little less conspicuous than a hearse. A Barina maybe. Or a Ford Festiva. But weirdly enough, nobody gave us a second look. Admittedly there weren't many people around, but those that were didn't seem that intrigued or interested as we passed.

I needed to call a few people, but my phone had run out of juice.

"Does your phone have any charge?" I asked PJ.

"A bit," she said.

"Can I borrow it?"

"Sure," she said, extracting a Nokia from her front pocket.

Mom?

Or Dad?

Neither.

I called Gus instead.

He was concerned but surprisingly calm.

"You're okay?" he said.

"I'm fine," I said. "I'm on my way to the airport."

"You are?" he said.

"Yes, can you bring my stuff? It's all in my room."

"Your passport?"

"It's in the messenger bag. The orange one."

"Okay, I'll meet you at check-in."

"And Gus?"

"Yes."

"Can you tell Mom and Dad that I'm okay?"

"Will do," he said.

Well, that was surprisingly straightforward, I thought.

We'd turned onto the freeway and were heading north to Brisbane.

"How long from here, do you reckon?" I said.

"About an hour," said PJ.

I checked my watch: we were on track. Just.

The hearse was barreling along, PJ was driving well, and again I had that crazy feeling of well-being, that the world wasn't such a evil, rotten place after all. And again I wondered if it had something to do with her, with this street kid.

"So how did you end up on the streets anyway?" I asked.

"That's a highly original question," she snapped.

"I was just trying to make conversation," I said, trying to keep the hurt from my voice.

"I get that," she said. "But what if I asked you how you ended up as rich kid?"

"Then I'd probably attempt to give you a civil answer. Maybe something like 'because I got born to rich parents.'"

"Yeah, well we didn't," she said. "And that's how we ended up on the streets."

As far as explanations went, it wasn't much of one, but I got the idea that it was all I was going to get.

"Has anything, like, really bad happened to you?" I said.

"Crap!" said PJ.

At first I thought it was an answer to my question, as in "crap" had happened to her, but then I realized it had more to do with what was up ahead. There were flashing lights and barricades, a couple of ambulances, two smashed-up cars and a tow truck. And there were police, police cars and police officers. Crap, indeed. A baguette full of it.

"We're done," I said, and I could see Italy fading from view.

"You didn't give up that easily last night," said PJ as we pulled up at the back of the line of cars.

"That was different," I said. "Brandon could've died."

"And this Rome thing isn't important?"

"Of course it's important!" I said. "It's the most important thing that's ever happened to me."

"Okay," she said. "That's all I needed to know."

The cars moved slowly forward.

"Do you think they're checking registrations?" I said, wondering if the hearse was up to date.

"No, they're just making sure everybody takes it nice and slow while they clean up the mess."

If that was the case, then we did have some chance of getting through.

We rolled slowly forward. I checked my watch: we had twenty-five minutes to get there. I could see two uniformed cops directing the traffic. The car in front of us, a gray Toyota Kluger, passed through, and it was our turn.

The cop was looking straight at us. Surely he must see us. Surely. But then something occurred to me: the sun that was rising in front of us must be glinting off the windshield, obscuring his view.

As long as we kept going the way we were we'd be okay.

Keep coming, beckoned the copper. PJ took her foot off the clutch and the hearse stalled. She turned the key, the engine sputtered, but that's all it did. I checked the fuel gauge: the needle was on empty.

"There's no fuel," I said.

"The gauge doesn't work," said PJ, pumping the accelerator.

The car behind us beeped. The policeman was still making the beckoning motion, but he was walking towards us now as well. The engine sputtered, there was another beep from the moron behind, the policeman still beckoned, still walked, and the sun went behind a cloud.

I could see the expression on the policeman's face change from one of slight annoyance to one of surprise and then shock. *There's a bloody kid driving the hearse!* The beckoning gesture became a stop gesture as he yelled something to his colleagues.

The hearse's engine kicked into life.

"It's up to you," said PJ, revving the engine.

I had no time to think; there seemed to be police converging on us from all directions.

"Rome," I said.

PJ dropped the clutch, rubber gripped road, and the hearse seemed to rear up like a wild horse before we shunted forward.

A couple of the cops had to jump out of the way, a barricade went flying, but we were away.

A very loud "Whoa!" was all I could come up with.

PJ slalomed through the traffic.

Behind us, the sound of sirens.

Airport turnoff 2 km ahead said the sign.

The sirens were getting louder.

"We've got no chance," I said.

PJ laughed.

"You're a bit of a wuss, aren't you?"

A wuss?

I could show her the brands on the inside of my thigh – how wussy were they? Tell her how I caught the Zolt. Turned off the lights. Got a Cerberus. How wussy was that?

She knew nothing about me, my supposed wussiness or otherwise.

I gave her a "Whatever."

Probably not the wittiest of replies, but right then I didn't have much else in the arsenal.

One kilometer to the turnoff.

The sirens didn't seem to be getting much louder.

I checked my watch.

Eight minutes.

The hearse was rattling so much that a piece fell off the dashboard.

"The Preacher won't be happy," I said.

"The Preacher is never happy," said PJ.

I'd been so engrossed with our trip that I hadn't had any time to think about PJ's relationship to the Preacher.

"So how do you know him?" I said.

"Us outcasts, we watch each other's backs," said PJ.

"You know much about his history?" I said.

"Nah, he doesn't talk about that much," she said. "Mostly it's just stuff from the Bible."

The sirens had suddenly gotten louder and my hopes, ballooning just a second ago, deflated again.

PJ wrenched the wheel and we were on the exit.

"Maybe they won't notice that we went this way," I said.

"I'd say they'd have a fair idea," said PJ, pointing skyward, where a helicopter was buzzing. "The old eye in the sky."

"Whoa!"

"You say that a lot, don't you?" she said.

"Not usually."

We turned onto the airport road.

"Here's the deal," said PJ. "I pull up and you get inside."

"What about the cops?" I said.

"Cops?" she said dismissively. "I've been dealing with cops since I was ten. Just leave them suckers to me."

We did exactly as she said, pulling up in the drop-off area.

I opened the door.

"Thanks so much," I said.

I went to get out, but PJ said, "Hey, rich boy?"

"What?" I said.

"My mum, she used to have this little model on her dressing table, you know, that tower that's leaning right over."

"The Leaning Tower of Pisa?"

"Yeah, that's it," she said. "Can you bring me back one?"

"Sure," I said.

"You promise?"

"I promise."

It was the first time she'd mentioned her parents and I wondered what had happened to them.

But not for long, because it was time to get out of there.

"Better get on your bike," said PJ.

I slid out of the hearse and managed to tack onto the back of a family group headed into the terminal building.

I glanced behind as the hearse took off with a beep of its horn, so loud it would wake the dead.

"Thanks, PJ," I mouthed.

Two minutes to go.

With each footstep, vile-smelling liquid oozed out of my shoes.

I don't think my newfound family was that happy with their latest member, because they quickened their pace.

But I quickened mine, ensuring that I was surrounded by family members as we passed the two security guards standing at the entrance.

Gus was exactly where he said he'd be, standing off to the side of the line at the check-in counter.

My bags hanging off him.

His face, when he saw me, was a like a two-minute soap opera.

First there was relief: I'd made it; and then concern: I'd made it but what state was I in?; and then revulsion: what was that smell?

"I need to get changed first," I said.

Gus held out his hand so that I could see the face of his watch.

"Time isn't exactly our friend," he said.

I saw what he meant: the minute hand was already past half-past seven and there'd be no coaxing it back.

The check-in line was enormous, snaking this way and that way. I went to join the end, but Gus had other ideas.

"Bugger that," he said, dragging me by the arm, past the line and straight to one of the attendants, a pale man with an expensive haircut.

"My grandson needs to get to Italy," he said. "He's representing his country."

The attendant leaned over the counter, gave me the once-over.

He obviously wasn't happy with what he saw – and I can't say I blamed him – because he said, "Unfortunately the flight's closed, sir."

But Gus wasn't moving.

"He's representing his country," he said. "Do you know what that means?"

The man stood there, arms folded, a look on his face that said: *I've got the power here.*

"Fifty years ago I was in the same situation," said Gus. "I was picked to run for my country, for Australia."

The man still wasn't impressed.

"Come on," I said to Gus.

But Gus wasn't going anywhere.

He leaned down and next thing I knew the prosthetic leg was in his hand and he was placing it on the counter.

"But I didn't make it," said Gus. "A shark took my leg."

The man looked at the prosthetic, then at Gus,

then at me, the expression on his face unchanged.

"It's no use," I said to Gus.

But as I said this the man turned to the computer screen.

"You'll only be able to take cabin baggage," he said.

"That's fine," I said, figuring I could punk it for a while longer.

"Passport," he said.

I handed him my passport and he entered my details into the computer.

"The plane is boarding soon," he said. "You better get yourself through customs."

"Thanks," Gus said to the attendant.

The attendant picked up Gus's prosthetic in both hands and held it out.

"I believe this is yours, sir," he said.

I quickly sorted out what luggage I had.

"Can you take this?" I said, handing him ClamTop. "Stick it in my room."

Then it was a quick hug, a stamp in my passport, and I was through customs.

As I sprinted past all the shops and all the other gates, my shoes still leaked and when I looked behind I could see smears of liquid tracking my progress across the tile floor.

I approached Gate 24 and I could see the group of athletes and officials, all of them wearing the green and gold of Australia.

Among them I caught a glimpse of the distinctive chinos and blue shirt of Mr. Ryan.

Our school had decided that since there were five Coast Grammar students representing Australia, they would – at the school's expense, of course – send two chaperones, Mr. Ryan and Mrs. Taylor.

Coach Sheeds was also going as part of the national coaching team.

She hurried over when she saw me.

"Where in the blazes were you?" she said. "I thought you weren't going to make it."

"Neither did I," I said.

"And what in the blazes are you wearing?" she said, taking a step back so that she could fully take in my clothes.

"It's a long story," I said.

"Well, you're on the flight and I guess that's the main thing," said Coach Sheeds.

I nodded: *yes, that's the main thing.*

But then it finally sunk in, what she was saying: I was on the flight, I was going to Rome, I was competing in the World Youth Games!

And then I saw him.

Standing next to an ancient-looking suitcase, wearing an ancient-looking suit, an ancient-looking teacher.

Dr. Chakrabarty!

What is he doing here? I wondered, but not for long.

Because when he saw me he ambled over.

"Pheidippides!" he said. "Like Alaric the Goth we descend on Roma, eh?"

Okay, there were two questions that needed answers here.

I went with the least important one first.

"Alaric the Goth?" I said, imagining a skinny person clad in clothes not dissimilar to those I was wearing.

"Yes, Alaric, King of the Visigoths. Sacked Rome in 410 BC, which many see as the start of the decline of the Roman Empire."

Okay, first question answered in typical Chakrabartian style. Now for the second one: "Are you going to Rome, Dr. Chakrabarty?"

"Indeed I am," he said.

"I thought Mrs. Taylor was coming."

"Mrs. Taylor had an accident," he said, and there was something ominous in his voice. "So the school asked if I would take her place."

I couldn't imagine why the school would ask him to take her place. Somebody who had no interest in athletics. Somebody who was so old that he was probably there when that Goth dude sacked Rome.

"Loose as a goose on the juice," came a voice from behind me.

Seb!

In the excitement I'd forgotten all about Seb. Because he wasn't affiliated with any school, he'd had to make his own way to the airport. He was wearing the official tracksuit, though.

An announcement came over the loudspeaker: it was time to board.

But as I showed my boarding pass to the attendant with the stuck-on smile, I was still expecting somebody to stop me, to say, "Young man, you're not allowed on this plane!"

Because it seemed like I'd gotten one past the universe; there was no way I should be going to Rome.

As I trudged down the aisle towards my seat, I knew the universe wouldn't forget; there would be payback, serious payback.

FASTEN SEAT BELTS

My seat, 34C, was a window seat.

Good, I thought as I squeezed past the corporate-looking man in 34A, *I can look at all the fluffy clouds passing by.*

But as soon as I sat down my guts gurgled.

And gurgled some more.

The gurgling started to move from my guts in both directions, upwards towards my mouth, downwards towards my bowels.

No, forget the fluffy clouds, a window seat wasn't good at all.

Obviously I'd picked up some horrible gastrointestinal organism during my time in the drains, and it was now blitzkrieging through my bowels.

I needed an aisle seat, to be as close as possible to the lavatory.

Actually, I probably needed to be in the lavatory. But that wasn't going to happen.

Well, at least the seat next to me is vacant, I thought.

I concentrated on watching the remaining passengers walking down the aisle, willing them not to take seat 34B.

My telekinesis worked, the aisle was empty, all the passengers were seated, and seat 34B was still empty.

I even lifted up the armrest to give my intestinal tract some more room to squirm.

And that's when I saw her: Mrs. Jenkins, an amazing number of laminated passes dangling around her neck.

I'm not sure what her official title was – head of the Queensland delegation, something like that – but she was pretty much the boss of everybody and everything.

I reckon it's true of any junior sports team that at least one of the officials is, well, not very sporty. Mrs. Jenkins was one of those.

No, it can't be, I told myself as she rolled down the aisle.

There have to be other empty seats.

There weren't.

Mrs. Jenkin's seat was 34B.

She looked over at me and said, "If I'd had my way, you wouldn't be on this team, young man."

What a lovely way to start a relationship, I thought.

The flight attendant hustled over to help Mrs. Jenkins put her bag in the overhead bin, but she practically pushed him out of the way.

"I can manage it very well by myself," she said.

See what I mean: boss of everybody and everything.

I wouldn't have been surprised if some time during the flight she introduced herself to the pilot and gave him a few flying tips.

The man in 34A had to get out of his seat to let her in. And then Mrs. Jenkins squeezed into her seat. As she did, I belched. But belch is probably too polite a word for what my bug-infested guts produced. For a start there was the sound: a sort of volcanic rumble. And then there was the smell: sulfuric, also like something that would emanate from a volcano.

Mrs. Jenkins gave me a look, but said nothing.

As the plane taxied down the runaway I clenched my buttocks tight.

"Our flight time today until our stopover is fifteen hours," said the captain over the intercom.

Fifteen hours – no, that wasn't possible! I couldn't be on this plane, with this intestinal tract, for fifteen whole hours.

I had to stop myself from yelling, "Let me off!"

As the attendants went through their routine I belched again. This one was even more volcanic than the previous one. The stench even more sulfuric.

Another glare from Mrs. Jenkins.

As the plane took off, I could feel the gas gathering in my bowels. I clenched my buttocks tighter. My guts were writhing. And I was sweating.

What if I unclenched just a little bit, let some of the gas escape, released the pressure?

But what if that wasn't the only thing that escaped?

That couldn't happen.

The plane started to level out.

I looked at the illuminated fasten seat belts sign, willing it to switch off so I could get up and go to the bathroom.

It was like my whole body had tied itself into one great writhing knot.

And the sweat was rolling off me.

Mrs. Jenkins and her jiggling flesh seemed to be encroaching on my space, forcing me to press against the side of the plane.

The seat belt light was still illuminated. I was sure the pilot was some sort of sadist.

I could see him giving his co-pilot a friendly nudge in the ribs. "Hey, check out the monitor – the kid in 34C is doing it tough! Let's make him suffer, shall we?"

The sweat was coming off me in torrents now. And I'm not talking about downloading protocols.

I couldn't stand it any longer – I had to get to a toilet.

Ignoring the still-illuminated light, I stood up.

"I have to go," I said.

"Don't be ridiculous," said Mrs. Jenkins. "What has gotten into you, young man?"

What has gotten into me?

A bug, that's what's gotten into me, a bug that has turned my guts to slush.

I practically crawled over her.

"I have to go," I said to the man in the aisle seat.

He gave me an alarmed look.

By which time the flight attendant had arrived.

"Excuse me," she said. "The captain hasn't turned off the fasten seat belts light yet."

Well the captain is a sadist.

"If I don't get to the bathroom right now," I said, regressing to a two year old, "I'm going to do a number two in my pants!"

The attendant didn't hesitate. She took me by the hand and pulled me into the aisle.

"This way, sweetie," she said, hurrying me towards the back.

Every pair of eyes, and I mean every pair of eyes, was on me as I made my way to the rear of the plane. Dr. Chakrabarty's. Seb's. Mr. Ryan's. And a whole lot of people I didn't know.

But I was there, and I opened the door, and I undid Brandon's punk belt and I lowered Brandon's punk jeans and I sat down and I let it all come out.

A symphony of wind and poo. They were all there: the flute, the oboe, the horn, and the bassoon. All amplified by the small boxy lavatory.

But now I knew the real meaning of the word "relief."

Finally my twisting guts stopped twisting.

I cleaned myself up.

Opened the door and went back outside.

And as I made my way up the aisle I could tell from the looks on the people's faces – some shocked, some amused – that my private moment hadn't been private at all. And now I knew the real meaning of another word: "embarrassment."

The flight attendant took me gently by the elbow.

"Young man?" she said.

"Yes."

"You having some tummy issues?"

I nodded.

"We might have something to help you with that," she said, handing me a strip of pills. "Imodium. Take two."

"Thanks so much," I said.

Head down, I found my way back to my seat.

The man in 34A gave me a wry smile. Mrs. Jenkins gave me another of those looks.

"Well, that was quite the performance, wasn't it?"

Quite the performance?

Mrs. Jenkins was the boss of everybody, and everybody knew that if you got on the wrong side of her, you were gone. There were even stories of athletes whose careers she'd sabotaged.

I bit my tongue.

And ate two Imodium.

And I closed my eyes.

And slept.

NOTHING TO DECLARE

Niente da dichiarare.

Nothing to declare.

Well, that's me, I thought as I walked in that direction. *All I've got is this orange messenger bag.* But a uniformed customs officer stood in my way and pointed towards the counter.

"I've got nothing to declare," I said.

"Over there, please," he said.

I did as he asked.

By this time Mr. Ryan had appeared by my side. Despite the fifteen-hour flight, stopover and last leg of the trip, his chinos and blue shirt seemed as clean and crisp as ever.

"How's the tummy?" he said. "Everything settled down in that department?"

"It's fine now," I said.

"What's the problem here?" he said, waving his hand at the counter.

"Not sure," I said.

He turned to the customs official and said something in what sounded vaguely like Italian. Obviously he'd been practicing.

"It's just a routine check, sir," replied the customs officer in perfect English. "Could you place your bag here, please," he said to me.

I did as he asked.

"Open it for me, please."

Again, I did as he asked.

He pushed up his sleeves and his practiced hands explored inside my bag.

Why had he chosen me? Why me?

But there was a simple answer to that – why not me? I was as choosable as anybody else.

A *what's-this?* look appeared on the customs officer's face and one hand reappeared. In it was a golden coin. The Double Eagle the Zolt had dropped in my swimming pool from a plane! It made no sense whatsoever – how had that gotten in there? The last time I'd seen it, I'd just been relieved of it by two thugs wielding baseball bats.

There was a pretty obvious answer to this question, to so many questions lately – The Debt.

"What is this?" he asked in his perfect English.

"It's a 1933 Saint-Gaudens Double Eagle," I said. "But actually it's a fakeroony."

"A fakeroony?" he said.

"Yes, a fake. There's the eye for a start – there's no way it should be black like that," I said, echoing Eva Carides, Numismatist.

The customs officer held the coin up at eye level, turning it around.

"A real one is actually worth a lot of money," I said.

"Please, one minute," he said.

He took the coin and walked over to a desk where another customs officer was sitting.

This one was sporting more bling, so I guessed she was his superior.

They talked for a while, the more bling-laden senior officer throwing a couple of looks in my direction, before the customs officer returned.

"I'm afraid you need a permit to bring a replica coin such as this into Italy. You can't take it with you," he said.

"That's fine with me," I said, but I wasn't sure I was fine with it at all. The Debt had put it there for a reason; randomness wasn't really their thing.

"We keep it for you until you leave the country and then we give it back," said the officer, smiling at me.

"Okay," I said, reluctantly. I just knew that giving up the coin was going to come back to bite me big-time on the butt.

Mr. Ryan and I had to go into an office then and sign all these papers.

As we did, the customs officer had a running conversation with another officer who was already there. They were obviously talking about the coin, because among all the Italian I could occasionally hear the English words "Saint-Gaudens Double Eagle."

The other customs official started typing on a computer. After a few clicks of the mouse he read from the screen in heavily accented English, "'It is believed that the only example of this coin present in Europe is owned by Ikbal Ikbal, onetime friend of Farouk, King of Egypt.'"

So they obviously had Google in Italy!

He continued, "'The reclusive billionaire is believed to live in Switzerland.'"

But then our customs officer said something to him in Italian and he stopped reading.

Eventually we were able to leave, and as we joined the others getting on the bus that was taking us to the Olympic Village, I figured I owed Mr. Ryan some sort of explanation. "The coin was my good luck charm."

He nodded.

"You won't need it," he said.

Don't you bet on it, Mr. Ryan. Don't you bet on it.

ROMA

It was early evening, and there were cars everywhere and scooters everywhere and people crowding the streets, and everything looked so old, so ancient, especially compared to the Gold Coast. Inside the bus, people were crowding at the windows, desperate to get an eyeful.

It was all "Wow!" and "Ohmigod!" and "Did you see that?"

Not everybody, though. There were a few too-cool-for-Roma types who were flicking through magazines or were focused on their smartphones.

I was feeling pretty excited too – I was the first Silvagni to visit Italy since my ancestor had left all those years ago.

Somehow I ended up sitting next to Dr. Chakrabarty.

"Si fueris Romæ, Romano vivito more; Si fueris alibi, vivito sicut ibi," he said.

“Absolutely no idea,” I said.

“Basically, when in Rome –”

“Do as the Romans do,” I said.

“Exactly.”

Which was pretty much all the learned doctor had to offer, because for the rest of the trip his face was glued to the window. We pulled up at the village, which supposedly was where the athletes stayed during the 1960 Rome Olympics. Waiting for us was a large group of people, including lots of kids around our age. Apparently each of us athletes was to be assigned a buddy whose duty it would be to look after us during our stay in Rome.

But first Mrs. Jenkins gave a rundown of the itinerary. Tomorrow, Saturday, was a free day. Then we had two days before the meet started, during which time mornings were for training and afternoons were free. Under no circumstances was anybody permitted to miss a training. Doing so meant automatic disqualification from the team. If you were eliminated in the heats, or your event was finished, then you were expected to attend other events and cheer on your fellow Aussies.

As she went on, the thought occurred to me, and I felt really dumb because it hadn't occurred to me before: paying this installment would totally get in the way of my running. Because that's what installments did – they got in the way of my running.

And I sometimes thought that this was the "pound of flesh" I was required to pay, that even if I did repay all my installments it would be at the expense of what I loved most in my life: running.

So why even bother trying? I asked myself. Why not just drop out now? Invent some injury or another?

But I knew I wouldn't do that, because that's not what athletes do.

Besides, I'd managed to make it this far, hadn't I, installments or not?

I also knew that the free afternoons gave me the perfect opportunity to go somewhere I'd been wanting to go for a while now. Probably since I'd done that school project on my great-great-great-great-grandfather, Dominic Silvagni, and learned he'd been born in San Luca.

I'd already checked the timetable on the Internet and it was completely doable. Even though Gus's words kept coming back to me: *I'm begging you: please stop digging, Dom. Because if you don't, there's going to be serious trouble.* But the temptation was too great. If I didn't do it while I was in Italy, then when would I do it?

"Time to find out who your buddies are," said Mrs. Jenkins.

She read out an athlete's name from her list and

an Italian official read out the athlete's buddy from his list.

We all applauded and the two people met and then went off to get to know each other.

"Dominic Silvagni," Mrs. Jenkins read, and there were a few titters, I guess because my name was so Italian.

"Antonio Sini," read out the Italian official.

There was no movement in the Italian group.

"Antonio Sini," read the official again.

Eventually a boy detached himself from the group and slouched over to meet me.

He looked about my age. He had messy black hair, but I could just tell that each strand had been artfully arranged to fall over his eyes.

He was wearing Armani jeans and an Armani shirt and something funky around each wrist.

It was pretty obvious, from his body language, from the snarl on his face, that Antonio Sini wasn't here because he wanted to be here.

We shook hands, everybody cheered, and we walked over to the dining hall where the other buddies were sitting. But Antonio Sini pretty much ignored me, not taking his eyes from his phone, a Styxx. One part of me was completely fine with this: the last thing I needed was a third wheel, somebody following me around. But another part of me was outraged at how rude he was.

So after some more of his Styxx-gazing I said, "I guess you don't speak much English."

He looked up at me, snarled some more, and said in a very English accent, "Look who's talking."

"And what's that supposed to mean?"

"You Australians are hardly known for the correctness of your grammar," he said, looking me up and down. "And what are you supposed to be anyway? Some sort of punk. Or is it Goth?"

"It's a long story," I said. "So you're not even Italian?"

"Uh, no," he said. "Who would want to come from this place?"

If he had set out to confuse me, he'd succeeded.

"Okay, I admit: I don't get it," I said.

"I'm half Italian," he said in an oh-so-bored voice, returning to the Styxx. "My father's English."

"So is he the one that made you do this?"

"He thought it would keep me out of trouble," he said.

"So you're not even into running?" I said.

"Running is infantile," he said.

"I'm totally okay if we have nothing to do with each other. In fact, that suits me fine," I said.

He looked up from the Styxx.

"Really?"

"Really, old chap," I said, and I got up to go.

"And you won't complain about me?"

"Of course not," I said. "I really couldn't care less about you."

He actually seemed a bit put out by this.

"Maybe you better give me your number just in case," he said.

"That's probably not necessary."

"Just in case."

So I gave him my number. And he called it just to make sure he'd gotten it right. And then Antonio Sini and I went our separate ways. Never, I hoped, to meet again.

Ω Ω Ω

After dinner, we were assigned our rooms. I was actually very excited to be sharing. Maybe it was because at home I'd always had my own room.

When I got to the room, there was nobody there yet.

Except for the kick-butt plasma, I don't think it had changed that much since 1960.

As I lay on my bed I imagined the conversations my new roomie and I were going to have.

Me: *Imagine, Herb Elliott might have slept on this bed.*

My New Roomie: *Who?*

Me: *Herb Elliott, winner of the Rome Olympics 1500 meters. Maybe Abebe Bikila slept here, too.*

My New Roomie: *Abebe who?*

Me: *Abebe Bikila – the Ethiopian who won the marathon in bare feet!*

And the clincher:

Me: *Perhaps Cassius Clay himself slept in this very room.*

My New Roomie: *Who?*

Me: *Cassius Clay – he won gold in the light heavyweight division.*

A blank look on the face of My New Roomie.

Me: *You might know him better as ... Muhammad Ali!*

It was going to be such great fun.

Except an hour passed and my new roomie still hadn't turned up.

So I watched some TV, mostly *The Simpsons* dubbed into Italian – by the way, *d'oh* is the same in both languages.

My guts were settled by then and I figured that I'd purged every last bug in the airplane lavatory.

It also occurred to me that my little performance, the symphony in D minor in four movements, was the reason my new roomie still hadn't turned up after two hours and was probably never going to turn up.

So what, I told myself. Now I had the place to myself. And with an installment to come, that had to be a very good thing.

I turned off the TV. Turned off the lights.

"Good night, Roomie," I said to the other empty bed.

Good night, Dom, said Herb Elliott, Abebe Bikila and Cassius Clay. *Sweet dreams.*

DEATH IN THE HYPOGEUM

The next morning, after breakfast, I put on the Australian tracksuit and Adidas runners that Mr. Ryan had scrounged up for me.

As I was walking down the corridor I ran into Dr. Chakrabarty.

"When falls the Colosseum, Rome shall fall. And when Rome falls, the world," he said in that hammy way he had.

"Let me guess," I said. "You're going to the Colosseum?"

"We're going to the Colosseum," he said.

I was about to say "I can't come," but the fact was that I wanted to go to the Colosseum, to see the place where men had fought to the death.

And I was also intrigued by Dr. Chakrabarty.

"Are you going to the Colosseum?" came a voice from behind us.

I turned around – just as I'd thought, it was Seb.

"Seems like it," I said.

"Do you mind if I come too?"

I shrugged.

"No, of course not," said Dr. Chakrabarty.

"I just think it would be so cool to stand exactly in the spot were Maximus stuck that blade in the neck of that total scumbag Commodus!"

I cringed.

Dr. Chakrabarty was going to rip him apart, just like those lions ripped apart those gladiators in the film.

"Quite," he said gently. "Actually, history tells us that Commodus was strangled by a wrestler by the name of Narcissus. But the sense of the film is right – he was a member of the ruling class who liked to get, as I believe you young people might say, 'down and dirty.'"

Seb smiled and said, "He sure did!"

"Meet out in front at ten?" said Dr. Chakrabarty, and he added something in Latin, or Italian, or maybe even one of the dialects they spoke on the planet Jupiter, who knows?

But Seb did, because he responded with an "I'll be on time."

And straightaway I remembered the time I'd heard Seb speaking another language on the phone.

Straightaway, a few of the other really suss things about Seb came back to me: him luring me to Preacher's, him in the white van after the State titles.

And what about him and Miranda, what was going on there?

We went our separate ways and then met up at ten, just as we'd arranged, to set off for the Colosseum.

I assumed that Dr. Chakrabarty, being an adult and all, would do the adult thing and take a taxi.

Wrong! About as wrong as wrong can get.

We caught three buses. And not only did we catch three buses, I somehow ended up paying for Dr. Chakrabarty on two of them.

On the third one I sat next to him.

Looking out of the window he said in an excited voice, "The Aventine hill!"

"Is that one of the seven hills of Rome?" I said.

"Indeed it is," he replied approvingly. "According to the Roman version of the Hercules legend, it's where Cacus stole some of the Cattle of Geryon."

I must've been wearing the blankest of blank faces, because Dr. Chakrabarty then added, "But surely you're familiar with the twelve labors of Hercules?"

"Not really," I said.

"Hera drove Hercules mad and in his madness

he slayed his six sons. As a penance he served King Eurystheus, performing whatever labors the king requested."

I was already hooked, and it must've showed, because Dr. Chakrabarty was now off on one of his trademark discourses.

He told me how Hercules slayed the Nemean Lion and the nine-headed Hydra. How he captured the Golden Hind of Artemis. How he captured the Erymanthian Boar. How he cleaned the Augean Stables in a single day, slayed the Stymphalian Birds, captured the Cretan Bull, stole the Mares of Diomedes, retrieved the Girdle of Hippolyta, Queen of the Amazons, and obtained the Cattle of the monster Geryon – the ones Cacus stole.

When Dr. Chakrabarty finally stopped to blow his nose I went through the labors again in my head: *slay the Nemean Lion* ... "But that's only ten labors!"

"Very good, you've been keeping count" said Dr. Chakrabarty, eyebrows dancing. "Eurystheus refused to recognize two of the labors. The cleansing of the stables because Hercules was going to accept payment. And the killing of the Hydra because Hercules's nephew Iolaus had helped him."

That familiar chill danced from vertebra to vertebra. "Hercules wasn't allowed to accept any help?"

"Absolutely not," said Dr. Chakrabarty.

"So he had to perform two more labors?"

"That's right," said Dr. Chakrabarty. "He had to steal the Apples of the Hesperides and he had to capture Cerberus."

If my backbone had been chilled before, it was frozen now.

"C-c-c-capture Cerberus?" I managed to stammer.

"Yes, that's right," he said. "The most arduous of the twelve labors, one in which he had to travel into the Underworld."

By that time we'd arrived.

The Colosseum!

Buses, trucks, cars, motorbikes whirling around it, horns beeping. Like it wasn't just the center of Rome, but the center of the world.

All around it were signs: *The Rolling Stones Rock the Colosseum*. Apparently they were going to play a gig there in a couple of nights.

Dr. Chakrabarty wasn't happy about that.

"Unconscionable," he said.

"Whoa!" said Seb. "Who did that to it?"

Okay, it didn't look much like the Colosseum in *Gladiator,* but Seb probably needed to let go of that film.

"The great earthquake of 1349 had something to do with it. And a lot of the stone was stripped to build other buildings in Rome," said Dr. Chakrabarty.

"Actually, I think we're lucky we still have this much of it to admire."

We joined the line to buy tickets, and what a line it was.

I mean, it probably wasn't the longest line ever – that was probably the line to buy the new iPhone or something – but what it lacked in length it made up in diversity.

There were Japanese, and Chinese and Swedish and Egyptians ...

Okay, you get the picture, there were people from all over the world.

When we reached the ticket booth itself, there was further evidence of Dr. Chakrabarty's stingy nature. Seb and I didn't have to pay full price because we were under eighteen, but Dr. Chakrabarty was determined not to pay full whack either. He had a very long discussion with the ticket seller in Italian until finally they agreed on some sort of fair price.

Dr. Chakrabarty handed over the moolah and we were in.

As soon as I stepped inside I was so pleased that Dr. Chakrabarty had asked me to come along, because it really was pretty incredible to be standing here.

And I don't know if it was *Gladiator*'s fault, but I couldn't help but imagine myself with armor on and a sword in my hand and one of those Darth

Vaderesque masks over my face, about to step into the ring and fight to the death. Even though on the way over Dr. Chakrabarty had told us that the real gladiators didn't usually fight to the death, not unless they'd put up a pretty gutless effort. It was only then that the mob would start baying for their blood.

As we walked along the path, Dr. Chakrabarty didn't stop talking, though again what he was saying was really interesting. He told us that the arena itself, which had been made of a wooden floor covered by sand, was no longer there and what we could see below us was in fact the hypogeum. It was in this subterranean network of tunnels and cages that the gladiators and animals were held before the contests began. He also told us that the hypogeum was connected by tunnels to a number of points outside the Colosseum.

I noticed that a group of people were discreetly following us, discreetly listening.

If Dr. Chakrabarty ever stopped teaching he could be a tour guide, I thought.

We'd reached one of the other entrances to the arena, and Dr. Chakrabarty was telling us how some dude called Trajan celebrated his victories in Dacia in 107 AD with contests involving 11,000 animals and 10,000 gladiators.

I took out my iPhone to take a photo and it was

snatched from my hand. It happened so quickly, so unexpectedly, I took a long time to react. But when I spun around I could see the thief, a kid – he was maybe twelve or thirteen – wearing a gray woolen cap, running full tilt.

I went to take off after him. But he passed another kid, a bit older, this one wearing what looked like a brand-new pair of Nikes.

I didn't see Woolen Cap slip Nike anything, but something told me that he had, that Nike was now in possession of my iPhone. So I made as if to chase after Woolen Cap.

"Hey, that kid just stole my phone!"

But as I passed Nike, I went to grab him instead. Unfortunately Nike squirmed out of my grasp and got free. And now the chase was on.

Nike was small and he was fast, and more than that, he was totally used to running on this surface, these irregular flagstones. As I scampered after him I realized how stupid it was: all I had to do was turn an ankle and I was out of the meet. But you just don't go swiping a person's iPhone.

And then there was the fact that we were at the Colosseum – the Colosseum, for Pete's sakes! It was the last place you wanted to be punked by some kid.

So when Nike suddenly changed direction, ran through a barrier that said *Ammissione Victato* in Italian and *No Admittance* in English and disappeared down some dimly lit stairs, I had no hesitation in following him.

I couldn't see him, but I could hear the sound of those Nikes on the stone. Deeper and deeper into the hypogeum we went. The stairs stopped and there was a passageway and I had his silhouetted figure in my sights again. The flagstones here were even more irregular, and again I questioned my sanity – one mistake and I was out of the meet.

But now that I could see him, I increased my pace.

There wasn't much light here, and it smelled, well, ancient. And, remembering what Dr. Chakrabarty had said, I wondered if the gladiators had been led through here, to and from the arena. And whether the stones beneath my feet were still imbued with their sweat, their blood. The passage ended and there were more stairs going down.

Deeper and deeper Nike went. Deeper and deeper I went.

And another passageway.

There was even less light here, and the flagstones under my feet were broken.

Iron doors on either side led to dingy, dusty cells.

The prison, I thought.

Where the gladiators were locked up at night.

And through all the pumping adrenaline, I was feeling something else now – fear. It was time to stop, to go back the way I'd come. It was only an iPhone, after all.

Right then Nike looked around.

It was only a glance but it was enough, because I could see the amazement in his face: how had the *turista* managed to keep up?

And I knew I couldn't stop now.

I knew I would get him.

The corridor ended at a heavily padlocked iron gate.

He was trapped.

Remembering how slippery he'd been, I kept my distance, ensuring he didn't slide under my arm.

"The phone," I said. "I want my phone."

His hand went into his pocket.

Okay, now he's going to give it up, I told myself.

But when his hand reappeared he wasn't holding a phone, he was holding a thin-bladed knife.

With a flurry of deft moves he diced the air in front of his face. If his aim was to the scare the crap out of me, he succeeded.

Because the stakes had just gotten a whole lot higher – this wasn't about an iPhone, or not making the meet, this was about getting cut here, deep under the ground, slowly bleeding to death because nobody would find me. This was about dying in the hypogeum.

So it really was time to give this up.

It was only an iPhone.

But then I saw it, on the ground, just a meter to my right: a rusted piece of iron. Maybe one of the bars from the padlocked door. I shuffled towards it, my eyes not leaving Nike. Leaned over, picked it up. I tapped it on the ground a couple of times. It was rusted, but it was solid.

The odds weren't so one-sided now.

We were in the hypogeum, not in the arena. There weren't fifty thousand people watching us. There was nobody.

But I was a gladiator.

Not Russell Crowe, he was just acting; this wasn't Hollywood, this wasn't a movie. I was like one of them, the real gladiators.

Men forced to fight for their lives.

I, like them, was scared, but I would not give up now. My sweat would join their sweat. And maybe my blood would join their blood.

He came at me, just as I knew he would.

Delicate steps, his center of gravity low, the knife writing cursive in the air in front of him.

As he did, I reminded myself: the bar was for defense, not attack. Because if I swung at him I would leave myself open and his steel would find a way in. He came out at me low, which I didn't expect.

I'd thought face or guts, but he came much, much lower than that.

And I took time to react. I could see his arm thrusting, the glinting knife, but for some reason I was frozen. The tear of fabric, and steel nicking flesh, my flesh.

Pain, and I stepped back, bringing the bar down hard on his wrist.

But the wrist wasn't there anymore.

And the knife was coming at me again.

Higher this time.

Towards my throat.

A hand on each end of the bar, I brought it up high. New steel hit old iron, sparks flying.

And he rocked back.

Surprise on his face – how had that happened?

And I knew there was a window, the briefest of moments where he was vulnerable.

Two competing voices in my head.

The bar is for defense, not a weapon.

The briefest moment of vulnerability.

I swung the bar, a short arm jab, aiming for his hand.

He moved, but so did I, and the bar caught him flush on the side of the head, and he dropped.

The knife flew out of his hand.

I kicked it so that it flew under the locked gate. Nobody could use it now.

I was on him in a flash, a knee on each shoulder, a hand on each of his hands.

He struggled to free himself but it was useless; I was too heavy for him.

I wondered what the mob would've said.

Thumbs down? Kill him?

And why not?

He'd threatened me with a weapon, so if I killed him, that was about as primal, as gladiatorial, as it got.

And nobody would find out – not deep down here.

It was like he could see what was going through my mind, because his eyes filled with terror and he struggled further.

But there was no mob.

"My phone," I said. "I want my phone."

His eyes indicated his pocket.

I let go of one of his hands.

He understood, prying the iPhone out of his pocket and handing it to me.

I put it in my pocket.

"Okay," I said. "I'm going to get up now, so no funny business, okay? I go my way, you go yours."

"*Niente polizia*?" he said.

I shook my head – *niente polizia.*

The last thing I wanted to do was spend half the day at an Italian police station while an Italian plod pecked away at a computer with two fingers.

One. Two. Three. I stood up quickly and stepped away from him, the iron bar still in my hands.

I watched as he slowly got to his feet.

"*Niente polizia*?" he said again.

"*Niente polizia*," I said, quite pleased with my newfound facility with the Italian language.

He did that thing that I'd only seen Europeans do, like a half shrug, and scampered off down the corridor and up the stairs.

The adrenaline that was still pumping through my bloodstream wanted me to charge back up the stairs after him.

I knew that there was no need to hurry, however. Especially as I could hear Nike's echoing footsteps; he wasn't planning an ambush somewhere.

Finally, when I reached the top, I could see Seb and Dr. Chakrabarty talking to two *polizia*.

"Hey, I'm okay!" I yelled out to them.

When he saw me, Seb came running over, got me in a big old boy-hug.

"Dude, you're okay," he said.

Dr. Chakrabarty was a bit less tactile in his response.

"I was extremely worried."

After giving some details to the *polizia* we were free to go.

SAN LUCA

The next day, it all went according to plan. First training, which was just a light run. A very quick lunch back at the Olympic Village. Then we were free to do what we liked. So I caught a taxi to Stazione Termini, where I bought a ticket on the high-speed train to Siderno on the Calabrian coast.

While I was on the train I googled San Luca. I found out that it was founded in 1592 and for much of its history the town had been extremely isolated with no road to the coast. I also learned that it was considered to be a stronghold of the 'Ndrangheta. During the 1970s and 1980s their main activity was kidnapping rich people and holding them for ransom. By the time the train pulled into Siderno, I wasn't so sure about my trip to San Luca; it didn't exactly sound tourist-friendly. Still, I'd come all this way.

Ω Ω Ω

From outside the Siderno station I was able to catch a bus, the bus that was now rattling up the road, headed for San Luca.

On either side olive trees clutched at the stony ground. I doubted whether this landscape had changed much at all since Dominic Silvagni had done the deal and made his way to Australia. I wondered what had been going through his mind as he passed this way. Was he exhilarated, ready to go out into the world, or was he apprehensive about what he'd just done, the deal he'd made?

I felt a flash of anger: what an idiot he'd been, signing that paper!

But that was all it was – a flash – because I realized that maybe I would've done exactly the same thing if I'd been him.

The bus dropped down a gear; the engine sounded like a singer in a death metal band. The road was getting steeper and the ground even stonier, the olive trees more gnarled.

There were only a couple of other people on the bus – two old women clad in black, and they hadn't lifted their eyes during the whole trip.

We pulled over and the two women got off.

"San Luca?" I said, though I couldn't see a town.

"No," said the driver.

The bus kept going higher.

"*Perché stai visitando San Luca?*" the driver said, keeping his eyes on the road.

"Sorry, I don't speak Italian," I said.

"Why you come San Luca?" he said, his English broken but not so broken that it didn't work.

"My family comes from here," I said.

"What your family's name?"

"Silvagni," I said.

"Silvagni," he repeated, but with the right stresses in the right places.

"That's me," I said.

He turned around; it was the first time I'd really looked at his face, and I wished I hadn't, because there was something scary about it.

Not scary as in scar-down-his-cheek scary, but scary as in intense, as in the way his dark eyes seemed to devour me.

Finally he said, "Yes, you look same Silvagni."

I wasn't sure whether look-same-Silvagni was a good thing or a bad thing.

The driver turned his attention back to the road, which had become even steeper. He changed down another gear. If the engine was a death metal singer before, it was a Mongolian throat singer now.

The barren landscape was host to more buildings; it was starting to look like San Luca town might be around the next corner. I noticed that the driver was talking on his mobile. Okay, there were a million reasons for a driver to talk on his mobile, but I could only think of one: he was telling everybody that there was a look-same-Silvagni on his way.

What was the expression Luiz Antonio had used that first time at the Block? *Carne fresca*, that was it. Fresh meat.

Calm down, Dom, I told myself.

We definitely were in a town now.

And again, it looked like it hadn't changed that much since my grandfather with all the greats had left it.

Cobbled streets, stone houses clinging to the side of the mountain. There was what looked like a checkpoint up ahead. We stopped and two soldiers, guns slung casually over their shoulders, came aboard.

They looked hard and shiny and not to be messed with. They walked up the aisle, checking under the seats. When they came to me they stopped.

"*La fua carta di identità, per favore?*" said one of the soldiers.

The bus driver said something to him in Italian.

"Your ID, please," he said.

I took out my passport, handed it to him.

As he flicked through the pages he said, "And why have you come here by yourself?"

I explained to him how I was in Rome for the World Youth Games and that I had the day off, so had decided to have a look at the village my father's family was from. He nodded as I said this, as if what I was saying was all very reasonable.

"You're Silvagni?" he said, and again the right stresses were on the right syllables.

It was like for the last fifteen years I'd been this other person, this other Silvagni, but now I was Silvagni.

He handed me back my passport and said, "Be careful in this town."

"I will be," I said.

"You cannot be here at night," he said. "It is not safe for you."

Okay, now he was freaking me out.

He said something to the driver in Italian. The driver said something back.

"He is leaving at 5:45 p.m. You make sure you're on this bus when he does."

"No problem," I said. "I'll be here."

He and his comrade left the bus, and as we continued on into the town I was feeling very, very vulnerable.

I looked through the window. I could see what looked like a skate park at the end of an alley. A couple of kids skating.

There weren't many people around, and those

who were seemed to be a variation on the same theme: female, old, dressed in black. Like those cockroaches that scuttled about in the alley behind Taverniti's. But I'd come all this way now, I had to venture outside.

So that's what I did.

When we stopped I ventured down the aisle, ventured a "See you at five forty-five," to the driver and ventured outside. The bus lurched off, and as I watched it disappear around a corner I was sorry I'd done so much venturing. The first thing I noticed was the air – it was crisp, clean, the sort of air you want when you're running.

Well, that's a good thing, I thought.

But that good thought was followed immediately by a bad one.

This is a very creepy town.

There was something about it that made the hairs on the back of my neck come to attention.

I could see what looked like the piazza, the town square, up ahead, so I headed for that. Nothing seemed to be open and I wondered if it was some sort of holiday. There were none of the usual old men sitting at tables, drinking coffee and playing backgammon. None of that. Just the cockroaches scuttling. And when I came close to them, they seemed to scuttle even more quickly.

It was getting frustrating and my thoughts were all over the place. I sat down on a low wall next to a fountain and tried to get my mind into some sort of order.

Okay, what was I here for?

I was here to find out about my ancestor.

Where would be the best place to do this?

A library, maybe?

Okay, where was the library?

I didn't know.

How could I find out?

Ask somebody, one of the cockroaches.

But they probably didn't speak English.

Then ask them in Italian.

But I didn't speak Italian.

No, but my iPhone did.

I took out my iPhone and entered the English phrase, *Can you tell me where the library is?*

Got the Italian translation.

Mi puoi dire dove la biblioteca è?

The next time a cockroach passed me I said, "Scusi."

She looked at me.

"*Mi puoi dire dove la biblioteca è?*" I said, or attempted to say, because she gave me the blankest of blank looks.

So I hit the text-to-speech button.

"*Mi puoi dire dov'è la biblioteca?*" said my iPhone.

This time she understood.

"*Tutti i libri sono lì*," she answered, waving her hand at the church.

And I understood as well: *The books are in there.*

"*Grazie*," I said, and she continued on her way.

The church was a small symmetrical building. And, like the rest of San Luca, it looked closed. But when I pushed at the heavy wooden door, it moved.

I pushed further and the door swung open.

As I'd expected, there was nobody inside. It was the usual churchy setup – pews, altar, various statues of various biblical types. I guess churches are like McDonald's: no matter where in the world you are you're going to get the same basic decor, the same meal.

No books in here, however. So I kept going, moving into another room that had robes hanging up and all sorts of other stuff. But again, no books.

So I kept going deeper, and now I had the feeling I was trespassing.

Okay, the church was open so there was no problem popping in for a bit of casual prayer, but venturing back here?

Along a narrow passage, through another door, and I struck bibliographic gold: floor-to-ceiling bookshelves full of great fat leather-bound books.

So, the cockroach was right.

Tutti i libri sono lì.

But now I had another problem, and it struck me right then that I should be getting used to this, because it was the very essence of The Debt: a solution invariably bred a problem.

Great fat leather-bound books everywhere, but which one was the one for me?

How was I going to recognize it, given that my Italian was pretty much limited to the names of various pasta dishes and the phrase "*niente polizia*"? Right then I wished I'd taken a bit more notice when I'd done languages at school.

I picked up one of the books: *1965 Morti.*

Okay, that I got – all the deaths in 1965.

I went to another shelf and picked out another book.

1972 Matrimoni.

Marriages in 1972.

I started flicking through it. A door creaked open. Footsteps on flagstones, echoing through the empty church. And there was somebody behind me.

I spun around.

The priest.

"*Scusa, posso aiutarti?*" he said.

"Sorry, I'm not Italian," I said.

"Actually, neither am I," he said.

He was short, dark-skinned, Asian-looking.

"I'm from the Philippines," he said. "My name is Father Luciano."

"I'm from Australia," I said.

"Gidday, mate," he said, with an Australian accent so exaggerated it would light a barbie and sizzle a couple of snags.

He smiled at me and said, "I studied at a seminary in Adelaide."

"Cool," I said, though studying at a seminary in Adelaide was possibly the uncoolest thing a human being could do.

"You're wondering how I ended up here?" he said.

Which was a pretty nifty piece of mind reading by Father Luciano, because it was exactly what I was thinking.

"There was an opening here and they thought I'd be suitable," he said, but it was one of those statements that was teeming with what Mr. McFarlane would call subtext.

Why was there an opening?

Why was he thought to be suitable?

"I'm from the Gold Coast," I said, but as I did I wondered whether I should start lying about this, say I was from Sydney, or Melbourne, or even Canberra, because let's face it, what serious person is from the Gold Coast?

"But my father's family is from this village and I wanted to see if I could find out something about them."

"By all means," said the Father Luciano. "What exactly did you want to look up?"

I told Father Luciano about my ancestor Dominic Silvagni. How he'd come to Australia, how'd he'd been part of the Eureka Stockade.

"Amazing stuff," he said when I'd finished. "Let's see what we can find out about Dominic Silvagni, shall we? What year did you say he was born?"

"Eighteen twenty-two," I said. "But I don't have his exact birth date."

Father Luciano scanned the books until he'd found the right one.

He placed it on the table and opened it to the first page.

"There is no quick way to do this," he said, his finger traveling down the column of names.

"No Google?" I said.

He laughed at that.

"No, definitely no Google."

When I thought about it, it was pretty wild: almost two hundred years ago this kid had been born and his parents had come down here and Father Luciano's predecessor had written the name of the newborn in this book.

"Here he is!" said Father Luciano, and he seemed to be almost as excited as I was.

My eyes followed his finger.

Nome: Dominic Silvagni

Nascita: 7 febbraio 1822.

Padre : Guiseppe Silvagni

Madre: Maria Nirta

"Wow!" I said. "That is amazing."

And it was amazing, amazing in a way that no history lesson I'd ever sat through had ever come close to being amazing. But hard on the heels of this amazing feeling was another feeling, equally as strong: disappointment. Because I'd been harboring this hope that there actually wasn't a person called Dominic Silvagni born in 1822. Because if there wasn't a person called Dominic Silvagni born 1822, then there was no debt.

But there was.

Father Luciano offered to photocopy the page for me and then found a plastic sleeve for the photocopy so it wouldn't get damaged.

"And what about your faith?" he said when he'd finished doing this. "Are you a regular churchgoer?"

"I wouldn't exactly say that," I said.

"Well, you live in a wonderful country that has many distractions. But just remember, if you ever need the Lord, He is there waiting for you."

"That's cool," I said. "Father, can I ask you a question?"

"Yes, of course."

"Where is everybody? Why isn't there anybody in the streets?"

"They're at the Sanctuary of Santa Maria di Polsi," he said. "High up in the Aspromonte Mountains."

"Is there some sort of festival?" I asked.

"Yes, a type of festival," he said. "Though the main celebration is a few days away."

Father Luciano was quiet after that, but I could see that he was thinking.

I could tell that he wasn't very comfortable with this line of conversation, so I didn't pursue it. But eventually he said, "You're familiar with the expression 'godforsaken'?"

"Yes, of course," I said.

"Well, I never believed in such a thing. In my country there are some very dark places, but in them you will always find some hope, some love. A candle will be burning somewhere. But this town, San Luca, this is a godforsaken town."

I wasn't big into God, but godforsaken was a pretty scary thought, especially when it came from a person who was totally on God's team.

"Your ancestor did a courageous thing in getting away from here. Because of his bravery, you have a good life. As will your children."

A good life? I thought of The Debt. But I knew what he was saying, and I felt sort of ashamed that

I'd privately dissed Dominic Silvagni. He'd done absolutely the right thing.

"You're leaving on the bus?" the priest said. I nodded. He checked his watch. "Okay, the last bus leaves in twenty minutes. Make sure you're on it."

"I will," I said.

Together we walked into the room with all the robes hanging up. There was somebody there now, sitting on a chair, a chubby boy who looked like he was around twelve.

Father Luciano said something to him in Italian. He replied in Italian.

We continued on to the main door.

Okay, I wasn't big into God but I thought, what the heck? What did I have to lose?

"Can I ask a favor?" I said. "Can you bless me or something?"

"No worries, mate," said Father Luciano in that silly accent.

He blessed me, and as I walked back through the church I was feeling pretty good about everything. But then I stepped outside.

GODFORSAKEN

It's not as if I could see the danger: the streets were now completely empty. Even the cockroaches had stopped scuttling. The only movement was a piece of paper – was it a chocolate wrapper? – that cartwheeled across the flagstones of the piazza. But I could smell the danger. Taste the danger. There was somebody out there. And they were waiting for me.

I could go back into the church, but the bus left at 5:45 p.m. and I had to be on it. The quickest way to the bus stop was straight across the piazza, but there was no way I was going that route – it was too exposed. I could skirt around the edge, from building to building. The trouble with that, however, was that there were lots of little lanes that led into the square and they made ideal hiding spots from which to ambush me. No, I had to get to the bus stop another less obvious way.

I took one final look across the piazza, trying to fix my bearings, before I started off in completely the opposite direction to the bus stop. As I did, I heard a noise behind me. I spun around – there was nothing, but I still sensed danger, that there was somebody out there. I ducked into the first lane I saw, picking up my pace. High stone walls on either side – this hadn't been the best choice. They could pick me off at will.

So when I saw an opening ahead, an iron gate, I knew that was where I was headed. Then I saw what was beyond that iron gate – row after row of gravestones.

"Coimetrophobia" was not just a word written on a piece of paper by a psychiatrist, who smelled like mints.

It was a zombie and it was a banshee and it was a werewolf and it was screaming at me, "Don't you dare come in here!"

But what other options did I have?

I went in there.

Those familiar sensations: heart racing, breath not coming, beads of sweat popping from my forehead. I took off, following one path, then jumping to another, zigzagging my way through all the deceased San Lucans.

Apart from the sound of my own tortured breathing, it was so quiet in there, and I wondered if I'd gotten this completely wrong. Had I imagined the danger?

Eyes flicking from side to side, I saw nobody, nothing. Just gravestone after gravestone. Until, finally, another iron gate.

As I hurried through it, I checked the time: ten minutes until the bus left.

I was back in the village: stone cottages, washing hanging from windows, pretty much standard postcard Italy. Except for the lack of people, the lack of traffic. Again I stopped to get my bearings.

And as I did I heard voices. Okay, maybe they were innocent voices – two Italians talking about the soccer – but that's not how my mind processed them. They were out to get me.

I took off again, spurting up a lane, then another, then another. There were footsteps behind me, coming from several directions.

I checked my watch: five minutes to go.

Another lane and I was on a road.

And there it was: the bus!

I couldn't help congratulating myself on my sense of direction: all that zigging and zagging and I was only fifty meters from my destination.

I gobbled up those last fifty meters with a hungry stride, and I was at the bus stop.

As before, there was nobody waiting to get on the bus.

I could see the driver inside, head back, asleep.

I tried the door.

It was locked.

So I gave a gentle knock.

The footsteps were getting closer, and there were voices now as well.

I knocked harder and the driver woke with a start.

He pressed a button, there was a hiss and the door opened.

As I passed he said something, but the only word I recognized was "Silvagni."

Silvagni, your father was a goat herder?

I didn't care. Once inside the bus I felt safe again. Soon I would be out of here. Just like my namesake had gotten out of here.

I'm not sure what had gotten into me in the first place: why had I ever wanted to come to such a godforsaken – Father Luciano was right about that – place?

I checked my watch – it was five forty-six.

"Isn't it time to leave?" I said.

"We have more passengers," said the driver.

And he was right: a couple of minutes later some people arrived.

I tensed, but as soon as I saw who they were I relaxed – it was just a bunch of kids.

There were five of them, all boys, ranging in age from around twelve to sixteen.

It was such a relief to see some other human beings that I even smiled at them.

They didn't smile back at me, though.

So what, I thought.

The driver closed the door and we took off with a lurch.

I looked out of the window at San Luca.

I knew it was pretty childish, but I couldn't help myself. Up came the digit. I gave San Luca the finger.

As I hoped my great-great-great-great-grandfather had done all those years ago.

The bus lurched down the hill.

And then it stopped.

Time to say good-bye to the kids, I thought.

I was right: they stood up.

The one I took to be the eldest turned around and looked at me.

His right eyelid drooped a bit, so immediately I christened him Droopy Eye.

I know that's not a very nice thing to do, but I didn't have much else to work with.

"We get out here, Silvagni," he said.

He knew my name, he spoke good English: there was a bit to be surprised by.

But the fact that he was also holding a gun sort of trumped these.

We were on a public bus!

What was a kid doing with a gun, let alone pointing it at somebody?

And why wasn't the driver doing anything about it? I looked at him. He gave a resigned shrug.

"You get out here, Silvagni."

"No," I said.

The kid shot me.

I saw him squeeze the trigger and I felt a pain in my leg and I thought, *I'm dead.*

But I wasn't, and it took me a while to realize what had happened: it was an air gun. But as I bent down to rub my leg, the kid jabbed something into my arm, and blackness swallowed me whole.

LA DISPUTA

It was the smell that woke me. Of dust. And human sweat. And old, stale air.

Then followed a series of sneezes, each more violent than the one before. Eventually, when they stopped, I was able to look around.

I was on a thin foam mattress that seemed to float on a sea of garbage: cigarette packs, wrappers, empty beer cans. A coarse blanket was covering me.

And I was underground. But not that deep, because I could see, at the end of a vertical shaft, the distant blue of the sky.

The walls, the floor, the ceiling were all hewn out of the stone – the chisel marks were clearly visible. And at one end of this cell – for that's exactly what it was – were heavy iron bars within a heavy iron door.

I reached into my pocket for my phone – it was gone!

I jumped to my feet, tried the door, but it was locked.

I could feel the panic taking over – I was locked up!

But again I recalled the words of Dr. Chakrabarty, how panic was something concocted by the god Pan in order to confuse the Roman soldiers.

I reined the panic in.

But it unreined itself.

And before I knew it, I had a bar in each hand and I was shaking them as hard as I could and I was screaming "Get me out of here!" over and over.

But my words just bounced, unheeded, off the chiseled walls, back and forth.

I stopped. Got my breath back. When I did I noticed markings on the walls.

Little bars grouped into fives, just like you see on all those prison movies. And people's names. And other stuff written in Italian. I remembered what I'd read about San Luca. How its main industry had once been kidnapping.

Footsteps, and there were suddenly six faces looking at me from the other side of the iron bars.

The kidnappers from the bus, including Droopy Eye. And another kid who I recognized as the chubby boy from the church.

"What is this, some sort of joke?" I said.

"No joke, Silvagni," said Droopy Eye.

Again the right accents on the right syllables,

but there was something else in the way he said my name, something that was sort of sinister.

"Then what am I doing here?" I said.

The boys all looked at each other and grinned like I'd just said something incredibly amusing.

"We are Strangio clan," he said.

You're not wrong, I thought. *Really, really Strangio.*

"And?" I said.

"We are Strangio and you are Silvagni."

Again this didn't shed a whole lot of light on my current predicament.

"*La disputa,*" said the youngest kid.

This I didn't need translated.

"*La disputa,*" I said. "What *disputa*?"

Again that collective amusement from my juvenile captors.

"Silvagnis and Strangios have had *disputa* since 1852," said Droopy Eye.

1852?

Now, why was that date familiar?

Then I remembered: it was when Dominic Silvagni had left Italy to sail to Australia and the Ballarat goldfields.

If this was true, then did that mean that this Strangio family was The Debt?

"Are you crazy?" I said, though I already knew I wasn't taking the right tone here. "This is the twenty-first century!"

The fact that it was 2013 didn't seem to have any importance to these kids.

"No Silvagni has come to this village since the *esecuzione*," said Droopy Eye. "And now you come here to spit in our faces."

Esecuzione? Was that what they called it when my namesake left San Luca? But it sounded more like "execution" to me.

"I was just looking at some stuff in the church," I said.

Their faces said it all: *So what?*

"I'm not even Italian, I'm Australian," I said, grabbing a handful of my green-and-gold tracksuit to show them.

"You are Silvagni," said Droopy Eye in a tone that suggested it wasn't something that was up for debate.

"Let me talk to your father," I said. "I'm sure we can work this out."

"Tomorrow," said Droopy Eye. "Tomorrow the men return from the Aspromontes."

Surely they weren't thinking of leaving me in this godforsaken – Father Luciano had pretty much nailed that – hole for the night?

"But you can't –" I started, before I saw that I was wasting my breath. They were going to leave me in the godforsaken hole until tomorrow when the men returned. I would miss training and get disqualified from the side. What an idiot I was – why had I ever

come to this place?

"Okay, I need some water," I said. "And something to eat."

The Strangio boys exchanged looks – this was a reasonable request.

And then they left.

The first thing I needed to do was urinate. Unfortunately my cell appeared to be very deficient in the places-to-urinate department. There was no bathroom. No urinal. Not even a bucket.

I guess I could've just done it in the corner, but my parents hadn't sent me to the most expensive private school on the Gold Coast to have me pee in the corner of my bedroom. So I utilized some empty beer cans instead. Three and a half of them, to be precise. And I arranged them against the wall so I wouldn't accidentally knock them over.

Now that I'd successfully negotiated that, I figured I should do something about the state of my night's accommodation. I started picking up the garbage, shoving it into an empty plastic bag. Once I'd done that I gave thought to the arrangement of the furniture in the room. The furniture that basically consisted of a skinny piece of foam.

I tried it in four or five different places before I settled on putting it below the vertical shaft.

I figured that way I might even get to see some

stars at night. Okay, it wouldn't exactly be cable TV, but that probably wasn't such a bad thing.

As I made the bed, tucking the blanket in, something at the base of the wall caught my eye. Somehow, it didn't quite look right.

I moved over to it, ran my hands over the roughly hewn surface.

Now I noticed the thin line that ran upwards from the floor for thirty or so centimeters before it turned at right angles and ran for a similar length before turning at right angles again back to the floor.

I tapped the rock inside this line. It made a sort of hollow sound. I tried to move the rock, but it wouldn't budge. I needed to find something to gouge away whatever mortar had been used in the crack. I remembered: in the garbage I'd cleaned up, there'd been the barrel of a pen. I delved into the bag until I found it, and then I started scouring at the crack. White powder dropped to the floor. I'd been right, the rock had been cemented in with something. But gouging it out was very slow going.

After about an hour I'd managed to remove about a centimeter out of the crack. And then there were echoey footsteps, the sound of people talking. I put the pen barrel in my pocket and moved to the other side of the cell. The two youngest kids' faces appeared at the iron bars.

Room service had arrived.

"Is that Evian?" I asked one of the kids as he handed me a bottle of water.

The joke – if you could call it that – was lost on him.

"*Acqua,*" he said.

The other kid handed me a foil container and a plastic fork.

Perfect, I thought. *Now I've got myself a real gouger.*

As soon as I opened the foil container I realized how hungry I was. That I hadn't eaten since lunch. I dug the spoon deep into the pasta and shoveled it into my mouth. The two kids looked at me, seemingly fascinated.

"It's not exactly al dente, is it?" I said, channeling Toby for a second.

This time they got the joke – if you could call it that.

"Al dente," they repeated, smiling.

"Yeah, al dente," I said.

They insisted on staying there, watching, while I finished the pasta. It wasn't exactly al dente, but al dente's overrated anyway, and it tasted great.

Once I'd finished and the show was over, they took off.

It was back to scouring, and I'd been right about the fork – it was perfect for the job. Soon I was able to wobble the rock, the way your tongue wobbles a loose tooth.

Until finally I was able to pry it out.

And see what was behind it.

A notebook. Old, but not ancient.

I removed it from its hiding place and a plume of dust rose up, initiating another sneezing bout.

When I'd recovered I wiped the dust from the cover.

To reveal the letters *DS* written in an elaborate cursive script, letters I was familiar with because they happened to be my initials, and my dad's initials.

I opened to the first page. A poem! In English! And the handwriting: an old-fashioned cursive that looked familiar. I started reading:

Out of the night that covers me,
Black as the Pit from pole to pole,
I thank whatever gods may be
For my unconquerable soul.

In the fell clutch of circumstance
I have not winced nor cried aloud.
Under the bludgeonings of chance
My head is bloody, but unbowed.

Footsteps!

I quickly put the notebook back, and then the rock that hid it.

Stood up.

Tried to look casual. Believe me, not easy when you've just read what I'd read.

Faces at the iron bars again, but this time one belonged to an adult.

"Mr. Silvagni?" he said.

"Yes," I said tentatively, because being a Silvagni didn't seem like such a great career move in this town.

The door clanged open and the man was walking towards me. Telling me that his name was Carlo.

Jeans, leather jacket, cowboy boots – he looked like one of those Italians from Rome, the ones who hang around the cafés being handsome, saying sexy things to the passing girls.

"I am so very sorry about this," he said, his English rapid-fire with the tinge of an American accent. "This has been a terrible terrible mix-up."

Carlo put his arm around my shoulder. "Come on, let's get you out of this rat hole."

"It's not that bad," I told him.

And I almost – almost! – said, "Actually, I wouldn't mind spending some more time here," before I realized how ludicrous that would sound.

Nobody in their right mind would want to spend more time here.

So I followed him out, and he kept talking in his rapid-fire American-tinged English.

Mamma Mia, did he talk.

"Yes, there was a dispute," he said. "But that was an ancient thing. The boys, they just got carried away, as Italian boys often do …"

After a while I stopped listening, concentrating instead on the complicated route we were taking out of there. Tunnels leading to other tunnels leading to other tunnels – a whole underground network.

Eventually we reached a door that Carlo unlocked with a huge key and then we were inside a building, a simple hut. Carlo locked the door behind him.

"Those tunnels are incredible," I said.

"Yes," said Carlo. "During the war this is where the resistance fighters hid."

Possibly true, I thought.

But they'd also had other uses.

We walked across a stony field, through a gate with white posts, and onto a road where there were some cars parked, some people waiting.

Among them was Droopy Eye.

Carlo said something to him in Italian.

Whatever it was, I could see that Droopy Eye wasn't happy with it.

"*Sbrigati*, Francesco," said Carlo.

So Droopy Eye's name was Francesco. But there was no way I was going to give him the dignity of a real name, not after how he'd treated me.

"I am sorry for what we did," Droopy Eye said to me.

That was what came out of his mouth, but what was coming from his eyes, from his whole body, was something very different.

"That's okay," I said.

And then Droopy Eye said a few words in Italian and suddenly Carlo's arm shot out and Droopy Eye was lying on the ground.

Something told me that Carlo wasn't just one of those handsome Italians who said sexy things to the passing girls. Something told me that he was much more dangerous, that this, that he, was 'Ndrangheta.

He moved over to one of the cars, a Mercedes SL, and opened the door for me.

"My driver will take you back to Siderno in time for the train to Rome."

"Can I get my phone back?" I said.

"Of course!" he said. "Why didn't you say?"

He yelled something in Italian and my phone appeared out of the gloom.

It even had charge!

I got into the car and he shut the door behind me. Just as it took off I had a thought: I went to the Maps app and stored my current location.

Soon I was too busy being terrified to think of anything else but how ridiculous it would be if I died in a car accident. It didn't seem possible that the driver could take these tight corners at such a speed. That he could pass other cars like this. In the end I had to close my eyes.

And when I eventually dragged them open again we were outside the Siderno train station.

The driver held out a wad of cash.

"For ticket," he said.

"I have money," I said.

But he gestured – *take them* – so I figured I may as well. I got out of the car and hurried towards the station.

Inside it was light and warm – such a contrast to the underground cell. Soon I would be sitting in a comfortable seat drinking a coffee.

Who was I kidding?

Out of the night that covers me,
Black as the Pit from pole to pole,
I thank whatever gods may be
For my unconquerable soul.

In the fell clutch of circumstance
I have not winced nor cried aloud.
Under the bludgeonings of chance
My head is bloody, but unbowed.

They were my and my dad's initials on the front of that notebook. The handwriting was familiar. And

I'd heard him use something like that line: *My head is bloody, but unbowed* before. Had my father really spent time incarcerated in that hellhole?

I had to find out. I had to get that diary, confront him with it. I had to go back.

BACK TO SAN LUCA

Getting to San Luca had been straightforward: buy a bus ticket, get on a bus.

But getting back there?

Again, I had to question my sanity. This wasn't The Debt. My leg, my life weren't at stake, so why was I hell-bent on returning to that godforsaken place?

A battered taxi passed and I thought, *What the heck* and put out my hand.

The taxi stopped and I opened the front door.

The driver looked like Luiz Antonio.

Actually, he didn't look like Luiz Antonio at all – he was much skinnier, much darker, but there was something about him that reminded me of Luiz Antonio. And it wasn't just the fact that both of them drove cars that were equipped with meters.

"How much to get to San Luca?" I asked.

The driver rubbed his thumb across his fingers – universal language for heaps.

"Do you take cards?" I said.

He shook his head – no cards.

I showed him the wad Carlo's driver had given me. Again, he shook his head – not enough.

I added what I had in my wallet. Again, he shook his head – still not enough.

"You Americano?" he said.

"No, Australiano," I said.

He broke out into a broad grin. "Maybe you know my cousin Giovanni Toscano? He big man in Proserpine."

I wasn't even sure where Proserpine was, let alone a big man called Giovanni Toscano.

"Why you go San Luca, Australiano?" he asked.

"To see a girl," I said.

"A girl?"

"Yes, a beautiful, beautiful girl."

If you asked a taxi driver in the Gold Coast for a considerable discount because you needed to see a girl, he – or she – would probably make several anatomically impossible, or uncomfortable, suggestions.

But fortunately for me, and my anatomy, this was Italy, not the Gold Coast. This was where Romeo and Juliet came from. And a whole host of other ridiculously romantic beings.

The taxi driver nodded towards the backseat.

Get in.

So I got in.

He took off and the lecture started immediately.

"I tell you all about the *ragazza*," he said. "Tell you all young man like you need to know."

For the next half an hour that's exactly what he did. There were *ragazza* who just wanted your money. And other *ragazza* who just stole your sperma to make the babies. And other *ragazza* who were vampiro who just wanted to suck the blood out of you.

I was beginning to wonder, with all these money-grabbing, sperma-stealing, blood-sucking *ragazza* out there, why he was so willing to convey me to one at such a cut-price rate.

But finally, just as we entered San Luca – looking even scarier at night – he said, "But there are other *ragazza*, like your *ragazza*, they are angels of the top order."

Angels of the top order wasn't exactly Shakespeare or even Walt Whitman 1819–1892, but I had a fair idea what he was getting at.

"You can drop me off here," I said when we reached the edge of the piazza. "It's better if I walk to her house."

I offered him the wad of money, but he waved it away, saying, "Next time you're there, you say hello to my cousin Giovanni Toscano in Proserpine."

I promised that I would do exactly that.

As I watched the red taillights disappear, I again questioned what on earth I was doing here.

A thin rain had begun to fall, and somewhere nearby two cats were caterwauling.

Hands in pockets, head down, I made towards the piazza. There were more people around now, not just the cockroaches. As I passed the skate park, illuminated by a couple of lights, I could see the shadowy shapes of five or six skaters. But I wouldn't say that the residents of San Luca were what you would call friendly. They all seemed to have the same guarded look. They all seemed to know that I was an intruder. A Silvagni.

I stopped by the fountain, took out my iPhone and went to the location I had previously stored into Google Maps. The entrance to the tunnel didn't seem that far away, just out of town a bit. I needed a couple of things before I ventured back there, however. Thankfully the supermarket was open. I slipped inside, grabbed a shopping basket.

Five minutes later and it had an assortment of objects in it: a box of matches, a cheap screwdriver set, a flashlight, water and a bag of chocolate cookies.

I put my basket on the counter and the girl serving said something to me in Italian.

But I couldn't answer.

And it wasn't because I couldn't speak Italian. It was because I was totally dumbstruck.

The girl looked like my mother in the photo, the black-and-white one she carried in her purse.

She even had a mole near her chin like my mother.

"*Questa torcia elettrica è senza batteria,*" she said as she took the matches from the basket and zapped the barcode.

Finally I managed to find some words. "Sorry, I don't speak Italian."

"No ... have ... *batteria,*" she said.

Now I understood.

"Okay, can I have batteries for the flashlight, please?" I said.

It was just a coincidence, that was all, I told myself as she got the batteries. People look like other people, it happens. I even read somewhere that Saddam Hussein used to have, like, a dozen doubles, none of them related to him. The Queen of England, too, doesn't mind sending a doppelganger out when she gets sick of all that waving.

"Where you from?" she said as she zapped the batteries.

"Australia."

A change came over her face.

"Australia?" she said.

"Yes, you know, kangaroos?" I said, making some really pathetic kangaroo paws with my hands.

She opened her mouth again, as though she was going to ask another question, but she seemed to change her mind.

After I had paid her I hurried out of the shop, and across the piazza. Following the directions given by Google Maps, I was soon out of town.

There were no lights out here and it was very, very dark. But it didn't take long before I was at the gate with the white posts.

It was now locked, but I had no problem climbing over it and continuing on to the hut. Once inside I switched on the flashlight. As I did I thought of how grateful I was to the girl. I also thought of how much she looked like my mum in that photo. But there was no time now to think more about that.

I drank some water.

Ate a couple of cookies.

Holding the flashlight in one hand, the smallest screwdriver in the other, I set to work picking the lock to the door Carlo had locked. Or trying to pick the lock, because it just didn't seem to want to be picked. I wondered if locks were radically different in Italy, if all the stuff I'd learned about lock picking from the PDF I'd downloaded from the Internet didn't apply here.

Okay, the instrument I was using wasn't ideal, but I couldn't blame it.

Just as I was getting really frustrated with the lock, with its foreignness, I recalled what it had said in that PDF: *Project your senses into the lock to receive a full picture of how it is responding to your manipulations.*

I took a couple of deep breaths and tried doing that. I soon realized that there was nothing foreign about the lock at all. Slowly, methodically, I set to work, keeping that picture of the lock inside my head.

Click!

I was in.

I wondered about locking the door behind me, but decided against it. Yes, it would indicate that somebody was inside. But if I had to make a hasty exit, the last thing I wanted to negotiate was a locked door.

As soon as I started walking I realized that I had another problem – even my runners sent great echoey noises down the tunnel.

I took them off, tied the laces together and slung them around my neck.

That was better.

Now that I wasn't making much noise, I could hear all the other noises.

There were rumbles.

And creaks.

And groans.

The subterranean San Luca certainly was a whole lot livelier than the aboveground one.

I kept on going, retracing the way I'd come with Carlo.

Once again, I wasn't sure how I did this – it had been a complicated route – but my internal GPS was spot-on as usual.

Eventually I reached the cell.

It was still unlocked.

Excitement growing, I lay down on my stomach so that my eyes were at the level of the hole and positioned the flashlight so that I could work.

I removed the rock.

There was nothing inside!

No, it couldn't be!

But no matter how much I shone the flashlight into the hole, it was still empty.

"No!" I screamed, not caring who heard me.

No! No! And more no!

And when I'd finished, out of the darkness came a voice. "Silvagni."

Right stresses in the right places.

Droopy Eye.

But how did he …?

As soon as I'd asked myself that question I knew the answer – he'd had my phone for hours, more than enough time to put some tracking software on it.

What an idiot I'd been.

An idiot for coming back here.

An idiot for not checking my phone.

I shone the flashlight in the direction of the "Silvagni" and there he was; there they were, three of them, the three eldest kids.

One of them was carrying a lamp.

"Maybe you're looking for this," said Droopy Eye, holding up the notebook with the initials on the cover.

Droopy Eye obviously wasn't stupid – his English was fluent – but what did he want from me? Money? They couldn't possibly believe in some crazy feud that had been started more than a hundred years ago, could they?

"Maybe," I said, shuffling away from the wall, getting closer to the cell door so they couldn't close it on me.

As I did, I remembered how Zoe had alerted me that she'd been kidnapped that time, how she'd surreptitiously dialed my number.

One hand reached into my pocket. Trying to remember how the icons were arranged, I went to Phone, then Recent and hopefully dialed a number.

"Your father killed my father," said Droopy Eye.

His words echoed back and forth along the tunnel, the words colliding with each other ... *killed my father ... killed my father ... killed my father*.

"I don't think that's possible," I said, choosing my words carefully.

"He killed him like a coward, stabbed him in the back, and then he ran back to Australia."

"I'm not sure you've got that right," I said. "My father has never even been to Italy."

"You think I am an idiot – everybody in this village knows what Silvagni did. But they are not men anymore."

He looked at his two accomplices and they nodded their agreement – *not men anymore*.

"All they think of is this, the money," he said, rubbing thumb and finger together.

There goes my money theory.

"But not me, for me it is this."

As he said "this," he thumped his chest with his fist.

And that's when I saw the glint of steel.

He had a knife.

And what did I have? A cheap screwdriver.

"This is crazy," I said. "I'm sure we can work something out."

"There is nothing to work out, Silvagni," he said. *"Occhio per occhio, dente per dente."*

That I got: an eye for an eye, a tooth for a tooth.

He stepped closer to me.

A crappy screwdriver, that's all I had.

But then I remembered: maybe not all.

I shuffled back to the wall, my hands feeling behind me.

Until I had a can.

He kept coming towards me, slicing the air with the knife.

And when he was about three meters away, I took careful aim and threw with a snap of my wrist.

As the can spun through the air, his eyes opened wide.

He tried to dodge, but he was too late and the can smacked into his chin. The contents flew upwards, into his face, up his nostrils.

I ran straight at him.

The knife came up, but I easily knocked it out of his grasp with a sideways chop of my arm. He went to grab me, but another chop of my arm and I was free.

As for his two accomplices, they were hardly worthy of the name. They cowered as I made towards them, saying something pathetic in Italian.

But visiting violence on them was the last thing on my mind – I just had to get out of here.

Obviously, when the barefooted Abebe Bikila won that gold medal in the marathon he was a lot tougher than I was, because as I scampered back along the tunnel, my feet were seriously letting me down.

It seemed like I'd stubbed each of my ten toes.

I'd definitely sliced my heel on something sharp and nasty.

And I would've stopped and put my shoes back on, except somehow we'd become separated from each other.

So I had no choice but to attempt a Bikila, to run like an Ethiopian.

But when I stopped to get my bearings, there was no sign of pursuers, no footsteps or voices.

Maybe that pee bomb had done its job and taken the sting out of him, I thought.

And I knew that without Droopy Eye, the others were nothing. They didn't have his appetite for vengeance, as misguided as it was.

So now I was thinking ahead: how to get back down the mountain?

It was pretty much downhill all the way – so all I needed was a bicycle, or even a skateboard.

I stopped again.

Still no sound of pursuers.

Weak, I thought.

And I couldn't help laughing.

I hurried back through the door.

Out through the hut.

And right into the very teeth of the 'Ndrangheta.

THE TEETH OF THE 'NDRANGHETA

Carlo had changed his clothes since I'd last seen him, but he still had that same look, like he belonged in a café in Rome, saying sexy things to the girls.

The men with him – there were about a half dozen – wouldn't be in Rome with him, though.

They were more the sort of men who ate girls. Al dente.

They were ugly and they were mean and I could smell the violence on them the same way you can smell the lab on a chemistry teacher.

Droopy Eye was also there, the front of his shirt soaked.

I looked around for possible escape routes, but there didn't seem to be any.

There was even a man standing, legs planted wide, at the entrance to the tunnel, making sure I didn't scamper back in there.

One of the men said something angry in Italian.

Another responded with something even angrier in Italian.

Which set them all off, angry Italian flying all over the place.

Until Carlo said, "*Tranquillo!*"

Immediately they were quiet and I had some indication of Carlo's high standing – if he wasn't the boss, he was pretty close to him.

"You are a very silly boy," he said, and I wasn't going to argue with him. "I give you money to go back to Roma, but you insist on coming back here."

"I had to find out about my great-great-great-great-grandfather Dominic Silvagni," I said.

At the mention of his name, all the angry Italian started again.

Which became even angrier Italian.

And again Carlo had to do his *tranquillo* thing.

There was a sweep of headlights and a car pulled up nearby.

A door slammed.

Footsteps.

Obviously Carlo and his men weren't expecting anybody, because they started talking excitedly among themselves.

I saw a gun go into a pocket.

A man appeared: small, dark-skinned, Asian.

It was Father Luciano.

"This is no place for you, Father," said Carlo.

Father Luciano moved closer to me.

"I am taking him with me," he said.

More angry Italian.

"Get in front of me," said Father Luciano.

I wasted no time in doing what he asked.

"Make sure you stay there as we walk," he said. "Even these men will not shoot a priest."

It was maybe two hundred meters across the stony field, but it was the longest two hundred meters I'd ever covered.

Every second I expected the sound of a gun, the slam of a bullet.

We came to Father Luciano's car and I allowed myself a look behind.

The men had followed us.

"Get in the front and keep low," he said.

Again, I did exactly as he asked.

Father Luciano hurried around to the driver's seat and we were off.

I couldn't help but feel disappointed: I'd come all this way, taken all these risks, and had nothing to show for it. But maybe that wasn't the way to look at it, I told myself. Maybe I was lucky to be getting out of this unharmed.

"How did you know?" I asked Father Luciano.

"Divine intervention," he said, a smile playing on his lips. "Actually, my altar boy told me."

I thought of the chubby boy.

"So what do we do now?"

"Go back to the church and then figure out a way to smuggle you out of here."

I looked behind: there were no cars following us yet.

We passed the skate park I'd seen earlier where there were still a couple of shadowy figures practicing stunts.

An idea flashed across my mind.

"Can you let me off here?" I said.

"But –" said the priest.

"With all due respect, Father, if I stay with you they will eventually catch me. But if you let me out now, they'll think I'm still in the car and they'll follow you, and then I can find my way out of this town."

"How?" said Father Luciano.

It was a fair enough question, but I wasn't going to give it a fair enough answer.

"I just will, okay," I said. "Trust me, this is the best way."

Father Luciano pulled up quickly and I didn't even have time to offer him a real thank you.

I snapped the door open, got out, and he took off with a very unpriestly squeal of the tires.

SKATE+HITCH = SKITCH

Yes, I had ridden skateboards – I don't reckon there is a kid, boy or girl, on the Gold Coast who hasn't. I'd even ridden one downhill a couple of times. Yes, I was an athlete with an athlete's excellent reflexes, an athlete's excellent balance. Yes, I needed to get out of here. Yes, gravity was on my side. Add all these up and what did I have: a pretty straightforward ride down from San Luca all the way to Siderno on the coast.

Yeah, right!

For a start, there were the people who were after me, mean murderous men who would not think twice about passing a knife across your throat. There was the skateboard, the one I'd exchanged for my wad of cash. It was short, made for doing tricks, not for tooling down a mountain. There was the road, which was poorly maintained, with

potholes and swathes of gravel across it. There was the fact that the darkness was only relieved by the occasional streetlight. There was my lack of shoes, because on a skateboard your shoes make pretty good brakes. And finally there was me – did I have the skill, the courage, the audacity to pull this thing off? Basically, did I have the guts?

On YouTube I'd seen downhill skaters use their gloves with bits of plastic stuck to them to brake, so I figured that I'd do something similar.

So as I made my way out of town I scrounged around in trash cans until I found a plastic Coke bottle.

It didn't take long before I was at the start of the descent. I threw the board down, pushed off, and I was away.

The skateboard quickly gathered speed, too much speed, but there wasn't much I could do about it as it hurtled down the mountain.

I went into a half crouch, making sure my weight was mostly on the front of the board.

A car approached from the opposite direction, its headlights on high beam. I was immediately blinded.

I covered my eyes with one hand, and the skateboard went into a wobble. *Relax,* I told myself. *Relax. Relax. Relax.*

Because I knew that if I tensed up, the wobble would become a death wobble.

The wobble stopped, the car passed and my eyes readjusted to the darkness once again.

Black tar flew under me, the wheels screaming, and there it was: the first corner, a radical dogleg to the right.

As I careered into it, I crouched down lower, throwing the board into a slide, maintaining balance by pressing the Coke bottle on the road.

The effect was instantaneous – I slowed down, enough so that I could coax the skateboard around the bend.

Then, as I came out of it and onto straight road, I quickly picked up momentum again.

Ahead I could see the twinkling lights of the coast.

This stretch I remembered from the trip down: it was quite a long straight, with an even more radical hairpin at the end of it.

I put my hands behind my back like I'd seen the longboarders do on YouTube.

I've said before, you can't be a runner and not enjoy speed. And this speed was about as raw as it gets. As thrilling as it gets. As terrifying as it gets.

Then ahead, some taillights.

A car.

But why were they going so slowly?

This is Italy, I wanted to yell. *You're supposed to drive like a lunatic.*

But they obviously didn't conform to the national stereotype.

Or maybe they were Germans. Or Dutch. Or whoever it is who are supposed to drive really, really slowly.

Whatever they were, I had no choice. I had to pass them.

If it had been terrifying before, it was beyond that now.

As I got closer, the taillights getting brighter and brighter, I crouched down as low as I could.

Then I hit the car's slipstream, and got sucked even closer.

Now! I told myself, the car's rear filling my vision. *Now!*

Making sure my feet were planted, I threw all the weight in my upper body to the left.

The board changed course, I broke out of the slipstream, and was alongside the car, level with the back window.

On this narrow road, if a car came from the other way, I was front page of the *Gold Coast Times*.

Australian Runner Killed in Italy While Skateboarding down Mountain at Night

I was level with the driver's window.

And the driver – funnily enough, he did look a bit German – was staring at me, a mixture of shock and miscomprehension and outrage on his face.

He did have the courtesy to touch the brakes, however, and I was able to duck in front of him.

Now the road ahead was illuminated by the German's headlights. Which was pretty fortunate, because I was coming up to the mother of all hairpins.

Once again, as I moved into the curve I went into a slide, pressing the Coke bottle onto the road for balance.

This time I was going much faster and the plastic began disintegrating.

But again I was able to negotiate the corner and barrel into another straight.

And that's when they caught up to me.

The same Mercedes SL that had taken me down the mountain, the same madder-than-mad driver at the wheel.

Carlo was in the front seat and the backseat was full of ugly meanness or mean ugliness; whatever way you looked at it, I was a goner.

What possible chance did I have against the 'Ndrangheta in their own hood?

They had a car, I had a skateboard, and a busted Coke bottle.

They had guns, I had nothing.

Why not just give up?

But while one part of me was surrendering,

another part considered other, less cowardly options.

Run the skateboard off the road and then try to escape by foot?

The problem with that was we were on a serious mountain, not just some hill, and trying to escape by foot, at night, would probably end up with me falling. To my death.

The Mercedes made its first move, and it was a pretty obvious one.

It swerved across the road, trying to force me off.

I was ready for it, though.

I threw the skateboard into a huge slide, using what was left of the Coke bottle to keep my balance.

The asphalt tore up the plastic, flesh met road, but I gritted my teeth.

And it worked – the skateboard lost enough momentum and the Mercedes whooshed past me, missing by centimeters.

But now I was on gravel, and gravel and skateboards aren't a great mix.

The board was wobbling, wobbling, wobbling.

Relax, I told myself.

But I knew I was going to lose it.

So I bailed.

Just rolled off the board, making myself as small and compact as possible.

I bounced once, twice, before I came to rest.

A quick inventory: everything was hurting like

crazy. My feet, my hands, my left hip, and the side of my right buttock was on fire – road rash! – but I couldn't feel anything broken.

I unballed myself, looked up to see my board smash into the guardrail and fly into the air, wheels spinning.

For an agonizing second it looked like it was going to go over the rail and over the mountain.

But it came down on top of the rail, bounced into the air again, and then came down on the right side – for me, anyway – of the rail.

I rushed over and grabbed it.

Now I noticed how incredibly quiet it was up here. The only sound was my heart drumming in my chest.

The Mercedes was about twenty meters ahead of me.

Just sitting there, all black and ominous.

They knew, like I knew, that they had me. That there was no escape route.

But then, below the silence, a low rumble.

My bare feet could feel the vibrations on the road: a truck was coming. If I had a chance, this was it.

The Mercedes stayed where it was, playing the waiting game.

Maybe they hadn't heard the truck. Or felt it like I had.

There was a sweep of headlights. The truck was on the straight.

It would turn the corner and it would be upon us.

But I needed to be going, to have momentum, when it reached me. But I also had to wait, to wait, to wait.

Because if I went now, they, the 'Ndrangheta, would eat me.

The rumble became louder, then deeper as the truck changed down gears. The driver must be negotiating that hairpin bend.

Get ready!

I threw down my skateboard. The Mercedes was still there. Still waiting.

Then powerful headlights.

Just as I'd hoped, the truck was coming down the straight, heading towards us.

It changed up gears.

My eyes flicked between the oncoming truck and the waiting Mercedes.

Now!

I pushed off hard with my bare foot, trying to ignore the red-hot pain that shot up my leg. Trying to ignore my burning buttock.

Again I pushed.

The truck was almost on me, but I'd misjudged it, I didn't have enough momentum.

The truck was passing.

Passing too quickly.

But I knew I had no choice.

I set myself low, and I reached out and grabbed at one of the straps that held the truck's load on.

The strap stretched.

The skateboard went into a wobble.

And then it stopped stretching, springing back, jerking me forward; it felt like my arm was going to pop out of its socket.

Back leg, front leg, whole body, working furiously, trying to keep the board stable.

And now the truck was trying to suck me under, crunch me.

I pushed off it hard with my elbows.

And somehow all those forces that had been working against me came into alignment.

The truck and I were now moving at the same speed.

Skating. Hitching. Skitching.

The Mercedes flashed past.

I crouched lower, expecting a gunshot. Something.

Nothing came.

Hadn't they seen me catch a ride?

Didn't they know I was here?

Or having scared several different types of poo out of me, were they satisfied with that?

Relax, I told myself. *Enjoy the ride.*

Yeah, right!

Still, I skitched the truck all the way down the mountain. Although I didn't see the driver, I had an overwhelming love for him.

Never again, I promised myself, would I bad-mouth a truckie.

When the road leveled out and the traffic started to build up, I let go of the truck and coasted until my skateboard ran out of momentum.

For a second I considered taking the skateboard with me, but I knew that I no longer needed it.

It had served its purpose, I could now set it free.

"Go, little skateboard! Go!" I said as I gave it a gentle push.

It rolled along the footpath for a while before it came to a stop against a fire hydrant.

Now I had to find the train station.

"*Stazione?*" I asked a woman passing by.

She gave me a serious once-over and pointed down the street.

"*Grazie*," I said, and headed in that direction.

The station was only ten minutes away.

"Roma?" I asked the woman in the ticket office.

"*Senza ntorno?*" she said. One way?

"*Si*," I said.

I handed her the money, she gave me a ticket, I gave her a "*Grazie*" and she gave me one back.

I had thirty minutes until the train left, so I went to the *caffetteria*.

Inspired by my previous successes, I tried some more Italian on the woman serving "*Spaghetti e Coca Cola*."

"*Arrivo subito*," she said.

The only empty table was right under the television.

I sat down and suddenly everything hurt, and hurt a lot. I'd treated my body badly and now it was letting me know.

The road rash on my buttock was stinging.

One arm felt longer than the other.

I tried to ignore the pain, focusing on the television instead.

Any illusion that I had achieved some proficiency in the Italian language was soon dispelled – I didn't have a clue what the reporter was saying.

But then a photo of an older man came up, and underneath it the caption, *E. Lee Marx*.

He had craggy weather-beaten features: an outdoors face.

Of course, I knew who he was: the world's most famous underwater archaeologist. There had even been that television program about him: *The Treasure Hunter*. And I'd seen Eva Carides, Numismatist, reading one of his books.

And then another photo, a younger man.

Now some shots from a funeral.

Ohmigod! Was it the man's funeral? Had he died in some sort of diving accident?

The item finished with some shots taken at an Italian airport and I got the sense that E. Lee Marx was now in this country.

So what? I told myself. It was just a random piece of news.

What! I told myself. It wasn't random at all. The Zolt, the Double Eagle, Yamashita's Gold, E. Lee Marx – were they connected somehow?

I finished the spaghetti and the Coke and went to stand up – but I couldn't. My body was on strike.

We reached an agreement – if it got me out of the cafeteria, I would find it some Tylenol.

Once on the train, in my seat, the Tylenol doing exactly what it was supposed to do, I put my head back and was ready to drift off to sleep when I remembered something: Droopy Eye had bugged my phone.

So I took it out and ran Miranda's anti-tapping app.

Bingo!

Warning! Unauthorized location tracking software detected! Remove?

I tapped "yes."

Software successfully removed!

Great, I thought.

But then another message came up.

Warning! Unauthorized location tracking software detected! Remove?

Had Droopy Eye bugged it twice?

Surely not.

But if he hadn't, then the only other conclusion was that somebody else had bugged my phone.

But who?

I was too tired to try to grapple with this right now, so I just tapped "yes" again.

Software successfully removed!

Now I could put my head back. Now I could drift off to sleep.

THE HEAT IS ON ...

My slow train descended on Roma at five-thirty in the morning and I wasn't feeling much like Alaric the Goth, ready for a day of pillage.

My body felt so stiff, so sore; even if they let me race in today's heat – which I doubted – I was pretty sure I would have to pull out.

As I caught a taxi to the Olympic Village, I thought *here we go; I'm going to be in more trouble than Maximus.*

But I wasn't; apparently some shot-putters had snuck out last night and gotten drunk and brought disgrace upon themselves, the team and their whole nation, so the emphasis was pretty much on them.

Nobody seemed to take any notice of a bruised and battered middle distance runner.

After a very long, very hot shower, and some

stretching exercises, I realized that I wasn't in such bad shape after all.

I found a first aid kit and cleaned up the cut in my heel.

It was deep, but not deep enough to warrant stitches, and it wasn't on a part of my heel that would make running difficult.

Painful but not difficult.

By the time I'd boarded the shuttle bus to Stadio Olimpico I was excited: in less than an hour I would be running!

"Good luck in your heat," said a girl sitting in the front seat.

She was dressed from head to toe in green and gold. She had an Australian flag painted on each cheek. And she was holding a huge Australian flag.

Aussie! Aussie! Aussie! Oi! Oi! Oi!

I knew that she was on the team, but I'd forgotten her name and I was too embarrassed to ask, so I just said, "Thanks."

I took out my iPhone, sent a couple of excited texts to Mom and Dad.

I'm running!

I'm running!

But when I went to put my iPhone away, my mail application started downloading message after message after message.

Weird, I thought. *I'm not even connected to a Wi-Fi network.*

I checked the settings.

Cellular Data was off, so it wasn't somehow getting data from my Italian phone carrier and charging me some crazy rate.

Eventually it stopped downloading; I had a hundred new messages.

Exactly a hundred – it was getting even weirder.

I scrolled through them – it seemed like I had the same message a hundred times.

Okay, something had gone screwy with the server, I told myself.

What was more, according to the subject line, it was a Google alert and I didn't even have any Google alerts set up!

I read it anyway.

News **1** new result for **E Lee Marx**

Treasure Hunter Bunkers Down

GlobeNews

After the recent tragic death of his nephew in a diving accident, E. Lee Marx, renowned marine archaeologist, abandons search for the Portuguese wreck Las Cinque Chagas *and returns to his base in Maremma in Italy.*

At once, alarms were going off everywhere. For a start, this so called "news" was dated a month ago.

I opened Safari intending to google E. Lee Marx, but I didn't have to, because E. Lee Marx came up anyway.

Eventually I managed to get an empty Google screen.

I entered the string *gold coast football team*.

I got taken to E. Lee Marx.

I entered *world youth games*.

I got taken to E. Lee Marx.

It was starting to freak me out, but then the screen went black and the words *Fetch The Treasure Hunter* were written across it.

They dissolved to nothing to be replaced by the words *Bring him to the Gold Coast*.

The Debt had spoken: this was the fourth installment.

I was both surprised: it's not often your search engine of choice gets hijacked like that. And not surprised: I'd suspected that there'd been nothing random about the news I'd seen on TV the day before.

Still, The Debt had spoken, and that now familiar sensation – a mixture of excitement and dread – took hold of me, sunk its teeth into me and shook me like I was the raggiest of rag dolls.

Ω Ω Ω

Half an hour later I was trackside and Coach Sheeds was saying, "You shouldn't have any trouble getting through this and into the final. Nobody in this group has got a PB anywhere near yours."

She was right: on form, I could still run at half rat pace and come in the top four, which was what I needed in order to qualify.

But I wasn't going to come in the top four.

I wasn't even going to come in the top eight. Or the top twelve.

I wasn't going to even finish the race.

Around the second lap, if all my injuries hadn't already caused me to pull out, I was going to pull up lame, anyway.

I was going to clutch at my calf or my hamstring – I hadn't decided which – and roll around a bit.

And then I was going to limp to the finish line, a distraught look on my face, maybe even a few tears rolling down my cheeks, because my World Youth Games was over.

I was going to do this because for the last half hour I'd been wondering how I was going to fit them both in: the running and the installment.

But as I'd walked onto the track I'd realized what the solution to my problem was: *lose the running, Dom.*

It was as simple and straightforward as that.

Lose the running and my time was my own. Or The Debt's.

And more than that, if I lost my heat none of the officials would take the least bit of notice if I wasn't around, because they would be too busy concentrating on the athletes still competing, those still in the hunt to bring back gold, and glory, to Australia.

"Kick with two hundred to go, not a millimeter more, not a millimeter less," said Coach Sheeds.

"Okay," I said to Coach. "I've got that. Sit and kick."

"Exactly, sit and kick."

"And, Coach," I said.

"Yes, Dom?"

"Thanks for everything, for being such a cool coach."

Coach Sheeds looked a little perplexed.

"Well, thanks, Dom. But we've still got lots to go here. This heat. And then the final itself."

It had been a dumb thing to say, but I was glad I'd said it.

The announcer called the runners to the starting line, and Coach slapped me on the back and said, "Go get 'em, champ."

As I walked onto the track I could feel the warm Italian sun spilling onto my shoulders.

It should've been one of the highlights of my running career – my very first overseas race – but all I could feel was this huge sucking emptiness.

I looked around at the other runners, black

runners, white runners, Asian, Caucasian, and I could see it on their faces: they were here to compete, to do their best.

Except for me.

I was here to throw the race.

"All the best, mate," somebody said from behind me, mimicking Rashid's Aussie–Afghani accent.

I turned around.

Rashid was standing there, in his running gear.

My brain refused to believe it was him – how could it be?

But then it started processing the visual information it was receiving: Rashid wasn't wearing Australian colors.

He was wearing red, black and green – Afghani colors.

Was Rashid running for Afghanistan, was he representing the country of his birth?

How was this possible?

But the proof was irrefutable: Rashid was running in this race.

And a huge feeling of relief surged through me – I hadn't kept Rashid out of the Games after all.

"On your marks," said the official, and I didn't have a chance to say anything to my former teammate.

"Get set."

"Go!"

There was even more jostling than usual as we all

took off, and I automatically found myself looking for Rashid's big frame.

He was where he usually was, striving for front position.

So I tucked in behind him – why not?

In the beginning I felt incredibly stiff and incredibly sore, but with each step I could feel myself loosening up and by the first lap I actually felt pretty good.

And as Coach Sheeds had predicted, there wasn't much pace on.

By the end of the second lap Rashid and I were in a leading pack of six runners.

The pace had increased considerably, but I was still feeling great.

Characteristically Rashid was starting to falter; the locomotive that had pulled the carriages through two laps was now running out of steam.

Why not help him? I thought.

It wasn't as if I needed to keep anything in the tank, because any second now I was going to fall over, clutching my leg.

I sprinted in front of Rashid.

That little surge was enough to drop two runners; there were only four of us left.

Bell lap, and I had never felt so good in a race.

Nothing to lose.

Nothing to win.

Now, I told myself. *Do it now!*

But I couldn't.

I just couldn't throw a race.

And maybe more than that, I couldn't waste this feeling I had, which an athlete gets maybe only once or twice in a whole career.

I could feign injury tonight, or tomorrow at training. There was plenty of time, and opportunity, to pull out.

I increased the pace, jumping up not one but two gears.

Nobody could go with me.

With three hundred meters to go, I had the heat done and dusted.

All I had to do now was stroll over the line and I'd qualified.

But this would be the last race of my meet – who knows, maybe of my career.

I thought of yesterday, hurtling down the mountain, the 'Ndrangheta after me.

I found some more energy.

I increased the pace.

I could hear the buzz from the sidelines – *It's a heat, what in the blazes is this kid doing?*

I was kicking like I'd never kicked before.

Head up, arms pumping.

I lunged across the line like a 100 meter runner.

It was the best race I'd ever run, and it was for nothing.

Coach Sheeds was making towards me, stopwatch in her hand. “You’ve done a bloody 4.00!” she said, with both amazement and anger in her voice.

4.00 was 2 seconds better than my personal best. 4.00 was only 1 second outside the world record for my age group. And I’d done it in a heat.

“I’ve got to go,” I said, and I really did have to go.

Running, world records, PBs; all of that suddenly seemed incredibly trivial now that I had an installment to repay.

PIMP MY RIDE

When I came out of the locker room Antonio Sini was standing there, hair over his eyes, smoking a cigarette.

It was such a studied pose, I'm sure he'd spent hour after hour practicing it in the mirror. Or maybe he even recorded himself on webcam so he could play it back, see what needed adjusting.

"What do you want?" I said.

"So you can run a bit, eh?" he said.

"How would you know?" I said, and then I threw his words right back at him: "Running is infantile."

"Well, my father saw you run today," he said. "And he *is* Scott Hurford."

The winner of Olympic silver and three Commonwealth gold medals. The first man to run the 1500 meters under 3 minutes and 30 seconds.

"But –" I started but he'd already anticipated my

question. "Sini is my mother's name," he said. "I got sick of people asking me if I was a runner just like my dad."

I had a thousand questions, but I couldn't articulate one of them.

"What is this?" said Antonio, holding up his Styxx, hitting a button.

From it came Droopy Eye's voice: "... killed my father ... killed my father ... killed my father."

I got it: it was Antonio I'd managed to call from the cell in San Luca.

"I went to San Luca, where my father's family comes from. And there were these crazy Mafia types there."

Antonio scoffed at that. "That's what you people think Italy is: pizza and Mafia."

"I thought you didn't even like Italy."

"I don't, but that doesn't mean I can't resent the way it's stereotyped."

For the first time it occurred to me that beneath that bratty exterior there was actually somebody who was pretty smart.

"But what was all that stuff about your father killing somebody?" he said.

"Like I said, they were crazy Mafia."

I could see that Antonio didn't buy this, not for a second. But I could also see that suddenly the kangaroo had become interesting.

So why not use this?

"Have you ever been to Maremma?" I said.

"Maremma?" he said, giving it the correct pronunciation.

I nodded.

"As far as I know, nobody has ever been to Maremma."

"Why not?"

"Because it's just not that sort of place. You go to Puglia. Or you go to Ravello. Not a dump like Maremma."

"So let's go!" I said.

"What for?"

"See a man about a dog," I said, borrowing one of Gus's phrases.

Antonio laughed at that – the first time I'd heard him laugh – and he had one of those great machine-gun laughs, the *ha-ha-has* spitting like bullets from his mouth.

"Yeah, why not? Let's go to a dump like Maremma and see a man and his dog."

"So any idea how we could get there?"

Antonio smiled. "Not really, I don't think there are any buses that go there. But we could go see another man about another dog."

Suddenly I realized that I was totally jumping the gun here.

I couldn't just rock up to Maremma, I had to make sure I was welcome first.

"I have to do some stuff," I said. "But I can meet you in a few hours if you like?"

"Sure," said Antonio. "Text me when you're ready and we can meet at the McDonald's next to the station."

Ω Ω Ω

The man and his dog worked as far as Antonio Sini went, but I was pretty sure it had now outlived its usefulness. I couldn't see myself knocking on E. Lee Marx's front door and telling the world's foremost treasure seeker that I'd come to see about a man and his dog.

But I did have a lead: Hound de Villiers knew E. Lee Marx. According to him, they went "way back," to "army days," and they still talked "every now and then."

If he was telling the truth, then could he give me some sort of introduction to the great man himself?

Immediately, I could see a problem here.

Hound owed me nothing. In fact, he had every right to be really, really angry with me, given that I'd snatched the Cerberus from under his very nose.

Though, I have to admit, when I'd called him before to see if he'd kidnapped my brother and was now *snap-snap-snapping* his fingers, he hadn't seemed angry at all. Drunk, but not angry.

A favor, then?

Hound wasn't really into favors.

Actually, that wasn't strictly true – but the favors he was into were the sort that were repaid with even more favors.

So what did I have for him?

All the way back to the Olympic Village on the shuttle bus, my mind was in turmoil. What carrot could I dangle in front of Hound de Villiers?

I went up to my room and my imaginary roomie was stretched out on his bed.

"How'd you do?" I said. "You fight today?"

Float like a butterfly, sting like a bee, said Cassius Clay.

"Nice," I said.

It's hard to be humble, when you're as great as I am, he said.

"Nobody's arguing with that," I said. *Or with you*. Imaginary or not, I'm sure he could beat me to a pulp.

It's just a job. Grass grows, birds fly, waves pound the sand. I beat people up, he said.

I was thinking it was just about time to lose my roomie, that maybe he was a tiny bit too self-involved, when he turned to me and said, *The man with no imagination has no wings*.

Cassius Clay was so right; I needed some imagination, I needed some wings.

It's easy to say that, but how do you actually do it: get imagination, grow wings?

I took off my clothes except for my undies, and lay on the bed. I concentrated on my breathing. I closed my eyes. I maybe even fell asleep for a second or two.

When I woke there was one thought, one question, in my head: why did The Debt want me to entice E. Lee Marx, the world's greatest treasure hunter, to come to Australia?

For the same reason King Eurystheus got Hercules to slay the nine-headed Hydra, to capture the Erymanthian Boar, to clean the Augean Stables? As a test of my ability, my courage, my strength, my determination?

Was I their little Hercules?

As I considered this, I could feel my wings growing, my imagination soaring.

What if the answer was "no"?

What if the installments, the labors, weren't Herculean? What if they were all part of a bigger whole?

But what bigger whole?

One answer kept presenting itself, golden and gleaming in my head: Yamashita's Treasure.

If this was true then something else was apparent. The Debt wasn't some semi-mythical semimystical organization. They were like pretty much everybody else in the world; they were just plain old money-grubbers.

And this thought was so incredibly liberating, I kept revisiting it – they were just plain old money-grubbers, they were just plain old money-grubbers, they were just plain old money-grubbers.

But if this was the case then how did the pieces fit together?

I started from the first installment.

That wasn't so difficult. They wanted to catch the Zolt because they wanted to know what he knew about Yamashita's Gold.

And even though they didn't get the chance to question him, they must've somehow found out where the treasure was.

The second installment hadn't been about turning off the lights, but about proving that the Diablo Bay Power Station was vulnerable, and thereby getting it decommissioned. And because of this the previously no-go waters around Diablo Bay had been opened up for recreational use. For fishing. And diving.

Which meant that The Debt must be pretty certain that the treasure was somewhere on that seabed.

Which reinforced my theory that they'd found a map or something.

I was getting excited here, my wings had grown swan-like in their size and splendor, powering my imagination into the stratosphere.

But then I came to the third installment, Bring back Cerberus.

Swan wings became gnat wings. I plummeted earthward.

What did getting a phone have to do with the search for underwater treasure?

I looked over at my roomie's bed. Cassius Clay had gone, maybe to win the gold medal he later threw into the Ohio River. I wasn't going to be getting any inspiration from him.

So maybe this task was Herculean, while the others weren't.

No, that didn't make sense: pieces in a puzzle, part of a greater whole.

Think, Dom!

Wings. Imagination.

Thanks, Cassius, but not needed anymore. iPhone!

Excited, I grabbed my phone, went to mail, scrolled through the email messages until I came to the one I wanted, the one from Miranda.

I clicked on the link.

Please don't be expired, please don't be expired, I begged.

It wasn't.

"Cerberus – Too Smart for its Own Good?" the article was titled.

Miranda had been right – it was very, very technical, with terms like "preconfigured SIMD" and

"Thumb Execution Environment" and "Advanced Architectural Plasticity," but I persevered.

And in the last very last paragraph I struck gold, maybe even Yamashita's Gold.

"A concern of the authorities was that the Advanced Architectural Plasticity made the device eminently adaptable," I read. "There was even suggestion that it could be configured into a very sophisticated handheld sensing device, useful in both the terrestrial and marine environment."

I didn't read any further; I didn't need to – *a very sophisticated handheld sensing device, useful in both the terrestrial and marine environment.* Herculean, my Erymanthian Boar! Because, the third piece of the puzzle had just slotted neatly into place.

And it was like that bit in *Star Wars* when Darth Vader says to Luke "I am your father," because suddenly the past and the present and the future all came zooming in on each other, colliding with each other. What resulted was this perfect atom of understanding, of comprehension.

If you're going to get somebody to head up your search for treasure – why not the best in the world? Why not E. Lee Marx?

I wanted to lie on the bed, and revel in the perfection of it all – it made sense, it made sense, it made absolute sense.

But I didn't have the time.

Hound didn't owe me any favors but I now had the solid-gold carrot that was Yamashita's Gold to dangle in front of his double-bent nose. And given how much effort he'd already put into searching for that particular treasure, I'm pretty sure he was going to look favorably on me and my endeavors.

As for the fallout of that – I would just have to deal with it down the line.

I called Hound.

He answered straightaway. "*Buongiorno,* Youngblood."

"How do you know I'm in in Italy?"

"It's my business to know."

"You still in Vegas?"

"Nah, they kicked me out."

I knew there was an appropriate response to this, something really, really blokey, but I didn't know what it was, so instead I just said, "Vegas, eh?"

"Yeah, Vegas," said Hound. "Anyway, what can I do for you?"

"You know E. Lee Marx?" I said.

"We go way back," he said.

"Back to army days?"

"You got it, Youngblood."

"I'd really like to meet him," I said.

"You and a million other people."

It was time to dangle the carrot.

"It's about Yamashita's Gold," I said.

Silence from the other end and I could picture Hound with that characteristic look he had when he was thinking hard.

Eventually he said, "I'll make some calls."

There was no doubt that Hound had many faults: he was violent, he was ruthless, he was basically amoral, but once he decided to do something, he certainly didn't muck around.

Five minutes later he called me.

"It's sorted," he said, and he proceeded to give me the details.

After he'd finished, he said "Yamashita's Gold, eh?"

"That's right," I said. "Yamashita's Gold."

"We'll talk," said Hound, and I had no doubt that we would.

Ω Ω Ω

I texted Antonio, and half an hour later we met at the McDonald's.

From there we went to see the other man about the other dog. He was a Tunisian by the name of Slim, and we found him in a café that was full of other Tunisians drinking mint tea and playing backgammon.

They all seemed to know Antonio, and I wondered what sort of trouble he'd been getting into.

Antonio and Slim talked in Italian for ages until finally Antonio turned to me and said, "He'll take us."

"How much?" I said.

"Don't worry about that," said Antonio.

"But who is –"

Antonio wouldn't let me finish the sentence.

"I said don't worry about that."

Slim's car was parked around the corner.

"Wow!" I said when I saw it and I really meant it, because it looked like something straight out of *Pimp My Ride*.

"Seventy-five Chevy. Monster hemi. All alloy," said Slim proudly.

"So how long did it take you to get it all together?" I said.

He looked at me blankly.

Slim's English, it seemed, was pretty much confined to car specs.

He got behind the wheel. Antonio got into the front passenger seat and I sat in the back.

Slim started the engine and the stereo kicked in, the car filling with bass-heavy rap.

As we negotiated a number of backstreets, Antonio and Slim started talking, yelling over the rap.

I wondered why they didn't just turn the music down.

But I also noticed something else: they weren't speaking Italian anymore.

"You speak French?" I asked Antonio.

"Sure," he said. "We were in Paris before here. And his Italian is terrible."

"So what does your father do now, exactly?" I asked.

"He works for the IOC," he said. "Though don't ask me what it is he does."

The International Olympic Committee! No wonder he'd wanted to get his son involved in the World Youth Games.

We passed the Colosseum.

"Kid tried to rip off my phone in there," I said.

"Yeah, good place to keep away from during the day," said Antonio. "All those tiresome tourists. We only ever go there at night."

"At night? I thought it was closed."

"It is," said Antonio mysteriously. "But there are ways around that problem, if you know what I mean."

It was hard going, talking above the music, so I kept quiet after that.

We'd soon left Rome behind and were heading down a very impressive freeway.

Despite the loud music, I found my eyelids getting heavier and heavier.

Yesterday I'd skated down a mountain. This morning I'd run a PB. Now my aching body was demanding some shut-eye.

And who was I to deny it?

Ω Ω Ω

I woke to the sound of silence, to a pimpmobile that was rap-free, to Antonio gently shaking me.

"We're here," he said.

I looked out of the window. We were next to the sea, on a sort of promenade.

But there were no people around, and it had a windblown, sinister look about it.

"What now?" he said. "I don't see too many men with dogs around."

A man about a dog had gotten me this far; it was probably time to elaborate a bit.

So I told Antonio and Slim – though I'm not sure how much Slim understood – that I'd found a golden coin while I was diving off the coast in Australia.

How I believed that coin belonged to a treasure.

And now I wanted to show it to E. Lee Marx, the world's preeminent marine archaeologist, to see what he thought.

When I'd finished, Antonio emitted a low whistle and said, "That is probably the most preposterous thing I've heard in my life."

Just I was about to react to this he added, "But nobody would make something like that up, so I guess it has to be true."

"It's true, alright," I said.

"So what now?" he said. "How do we contact this treasure hunter dude?"

I took out my iPhone and showed Antonio the map that Hound had sent to me.

Antonio in turn showed it to Slim.

"When we get there, I send a text and he'll pick me up," I said.

Slim studied the map for a while before he started up the pimpmobile, and the rap. We were off again.

E. LEE MARX

We turned off the main road onto a poorly maintained dirt track. As we progressed, the track got even worse, more rutted, with bigger potholes.

And there was no sign of human life, just a sort of thin, ugly scrub.

I'd never thought of Italy being like this; I thought it was all Leaning Towers of Pisa and Colosseums, vineyards and olive groves.

But I guessed it had to have scrub as well.

"*Merde*," said Slim.

I knew absolutely no French, but I had a fair idea what this meant.

And I couldn't argue with him, either – this was really, really *merde*.

Finally, there was no more track.

We all got out of the pimpmobile, and I could hear the sound of the water.

"Beach must be down there," I said, pointing to a walking track.

Antonio and Slim talked – Slim agreed to wait for us here – and Antonio and I started walking.

It didn't take long for us to reach the beach, though "beach," with its suggestion of waves collapsing on white sand, probably wasn't the right word for this place.

It was sort of muddy, and mangrovey, and didn't smell very good.

"My God!" said Antonio, pinching his nostrils.

It didn't take me long to see the source of the stench – a dead dolphin, its belly swollen, a cloud of flies hovering above, was lying nearby.

I sent a text – *we are here* – to the number Hound had given me, but already I was thinking that something was wrong.

Why would you meet in such a desolate, stinky place?

Was this a setup? An ambush?

"There," said Antonio, pointing out to sea.

I followed the line of his finger.

A Zodiac was making its way towards us, a figure standing in the stern, steering. As the boat pulled into the beach I could see that the figure belonged to a kid, a girl who was maybe eleven or twelve.

"Okay, jump in," yelled the kid in an accent that was all over the place: American, Italian, but other stuff as well.

"Mr. Marx?" I said.

Nobody had said anything about a kid in a boat.

"That's my dad," she said. "I'll take you to him."

I hesitated, looking back at Antonio.

"I'll wait here for you," he said. "Me and dead Flipper."

"Okay," I said, and I waded into the water and scrambled into the boat.

"Not there!" said the kid in her mongrel accent. "Sit in the bow!"

I wasn't that used to primary-school kids ordering me about, but I got into the bow. The girl reversed the boat, swung it around and we were off. The sea was much rougher than it had looked from the shore and the boat was bucking around quite a lot, spray flying in the air. The girl was still standing up, though. Her knees bent, absorbing the buffeting.

With all this bouncing around, my injuries started up again. Especially the road rash; it had been burny, then stingy, but it was now achy, really, really achy.

"You've obviously done this before," I said.

She looked at me, her eyes the palest blue in her tanned face, and said, "You're not full of crap too, are you?"

That's nice, I thought.

"I hope not," I said. "What's your name, anyway?"

"Sal," she said.

"As in Sally?" I said.

"As in Salacia," she replied. "The Goddess of the Sea."

Bag. Vomit. Need.

"I'm Dom," I said. "As in Dominic."

"I know," she said.

As we got further from the shore the water became calmer and the boat stopped bouncing around so much.

Up ahead, what looked like an island was now visible. Beyond an arc of dark sand I could make out a splash of vegetation and some buildings.

And then, as we got closer, two figures standing on a small jetty.

I was starting to get excited: I was about to meet E. Lee Marx, a mythical figure in the treasure-hunting world, a real-life Indiana Jones.

There he was, only twenty or so meters away!

But as we got closer, my excitement took a nosedive – he wasn't there.

Instead, there was a woman and another girl, younger than Sal, both with the same Goddess of the Sea looks.

With them were two bouncing dogs, Labradors by the look of them.

"Let me guess," I said. "That's your mum and your sister?"

Sal nodded.

Where was E. Lee Marx, I wondered. I must've wondered it aloud without realizing, because Sal said, "He doesn't like to be disturbed when he's working."

She cut the motor and we glided in to the jetty.

I'd been right, they were Labradors. And they sure were excited as I got off the boat, jumping all over the place.

"Settle down," said the woman.

Instead of her daughter's long, untamed hair, hers was cut short, spiky short.

"Dominic?" she said, her accent American.

"That's me," I said.

"I'm Trace," she said.

She was probably around the same age as my mum, but my mum probably wouldn't have liked that comparison.

Because the sun and the sea had written on Trace's skin, especially her face.

We talked a bit and she was really nice, but I couldn't help thinking: *Where in the blazes is E. Lee Marx?*

She gave me a tour of the "compound," as she called it.

There were photos everywhere, incredibly beautiful underwater shots of sharks and whales and swarming fish.

And then she served lunch: mackerel that the Goddess of the Sea had apparently caught that

morning with salad that was straight from their garden. It was delicious, but all I could think was: *Where in the blazes is E. Lee Marx?*

After lunch Trace talked about diving and shipwrecks and all the great work E. Lee Marx had done. How he'd gone from somebody who, in his youth, had plundered shipwrecks, to somebody who now believed in the sanctity of the shipwreck. Again, it was pretty interesting stuff, but all I could think of was, you guessed it: *Where in the blazes is E. Lee Marx?*

When she stopped to ask me whether I'd like some tea, I figured this was my chance.

I wanted to say, *Would I be able to see Mr. Marx now?* but that other phrase had been spinning around my head for so long that it came out instead.

"Where in the blazes is E. Lee Marx?" I blurted.

Trace gave me funny look and I couldn't blame her.

But she stood up and said, "Follow me."

I did just that, trailing her through the compound to a hut right at the back.

She tapped lightly on the door, but there was no reply.

She tapped again, harder this time, and there was a response from the other side of the door, a muffled, "Wait a moment."

After a while the voice said, "Okay, you can come in now."

We entered, and E. Lee Marx was sitting at a desk on which was piled papers, journals, old maps.

It's pretty weird when you meet somebody who is really famous, somebody you've seen on television, and in books, and in the papers.

My first reaction was: *This man is a fraud!*

He couldn't actually be E. Lee Marx, because somebody like me didn't get to meet really famous people.

I quickly snapped out of that: no, this was E. Lee Marx alright.

Though maybe not the E. Lee Marx who was the star of *The Treasure Hunter*. That E. Lee Marx was larger-than-life, bouncing all over the plasma. And this one seemed much more subdued, less colorful, much sadder. Like a photocopy of a photocopy of the original.

I also got the sense that he'd just sat down at his desk. And when I glanced over at the leather couch on the other side of the room, I noticed a couple of telltale depressions. I was pretty sure that E. Lee Marx had been having a good old-fashioned snooze when his wife had knocked.

E. Lee Marx peered at me.

As he did, I noticed a framed photo of him on the desk with two men who looked like pirates. Miranda would've been outraged, because it actually took me a couple of seconds to recognize Johnny Depp dressed

up in his *Pirates of the Caribbean* outfit. And the other pirate, the one with all the wrinkles? It was one of the Rolling Stones, but which one? Not Mick Jagger. Keith Richards, that's right. Now I remembered reading somewhere that Johnny Depp had based his look on Keith Richards. I guessed that E. Lee Marx had been some sort of consultant on the film.

"Dominic?" said E. Lee Marx.

Seriously, the most famous treasure hunter in the world, a man who had completely out-Indiana-ed Indiana Jones, knew my name!

"Yes, that's me," I replied.

"Take a seat, young man," he said.

Unfortunately, all the seats were covered in papers.

"Just move that lot out of the way," he said, pointing to the nearest chair.

"So, son," he said, his voice as deep as some of the Spanish galleons he'd discovered. "You know Hansie?"

"Hansie?" I said, before I realized he could only be talking about one person. "Oh yes, of course. Hansie. Except we all call him Hound."

E. Lee Marx seemed to find that amusing. "Can I ask you what is the nature of your acquaintance?"

"I've done some work for him," I said. "Computer stuff."

E. Lee Marx raised his eyebrows; I wasn't sure if he was impressed or not.

"Anyway, let's get down to business, shall we?" he said, though I had the sense that he was going through the motions, that business was the last thing on his mind. "What do you have for me?"

Here we go, I thought. *I have to be absolutely on my game here, I have to convince him that Yamashita's Gold is worthy of his attention.*

"I know somebody who knows where Yamashita's Gold is," I said.

There was no change in E. Lee Marx's face. Nothing.

Eventually he said, "I once met Rogelio Roxas in Baguio City. He told me how he'd seen the gold bullion, stacks and stacks of bars. There was a gold Buddha, too. He removed the head and it was full of uncut diamonds. And he saw precious coins of every denomination." But his voice, when he said this, was almost emotionless.

"He's the man who found Yamashita's Treasure in a cave near Manila," I said, reiterating a line from the Wikipedia entry for Yamashita's Gold that I must've read a thousand times.

"Exactly. Marcos, the President of the Philippines, had him killed, you know. Poisoned," he said. "And then the treasure disappeared."

He seemed lost in his thoughts after this and wondered if The Debt had this wrong, if E. Lee Marx was still the man for their job.

For a second I even thought about trying to contact them to voice my concerns. But I soon realized how crazy this was – I wasn't on their side! It didn't matter what state he was in, I just had to get him to Australia.

"So, Mr. Marx, would you be interested in coming to Australia to look for Yamashita's Gold?" I said.

The look on his face said it all – it was like I'd just asked him to accompany me to Mars.

I could feel my opportunity slip, slip, slipping away. "I have a 1933 Double Eagle," I blurted. "It came from the treasure."

"Ah, the mystical 1933 Saint-Gaudens Double Eagle," said E. Lee Marx, smiling in a sort of patronizing way that told me this wasn't the first time somebody had mentioned this coin to him. "Let me ask you, young man, do you know how many were minted originally?"

"Four hundred and forty-five thousand," I said.

"And how many ended up in official circulation?"

"None, officially. Supposedly, they were all melted down," I said, and I knew I was undergoing some sort of exam here. "But some escaped."

Again he smiled. "Some escaped – that's a nice way to put it. But tell me, how could one of these escaped coins have possibly found their way into Yamashita's Treasure?"

Definitely some sort of exam, and this was the toughest question by far.

"A collector in Singapore – sorry, I forget his name – was thought to have some of these escaped Double Eagles in his possession when they were looted by the Japanese."

"Kwek Leng Hong?" he said.

"Yes, that's him!" I said, cursing myself – why hadn't I remembered his name?

"I've met him, too. Lovely old rogue," said E. Lee Marx. "But I believed him when he told me that the Japanese had taken six Double Eagles from him."

For the first time, the E. Lee Marx in front of me was something like the larger-than-life E. Lee Marx from *The Treasure Hunter*.

"You have this coin on you?" he said.

"Customs took it," I said, taking my wallet out, showing the receipt they'd given me.

"It says 'replica' here," he said, and sighed.

I could feel the disappointment coming from him, waves of it.

And I couldn't blame him – why hadn't I remembered that they'd written "replica"?

He looked over at Trace, and though he didn't say anything he must've conveyed something to her, because she said, "Well, Dom, we better get you back before it gets too late."

As Trace, Sal and I walked back to the jetty nobody said anything, but as I went to get in the boat

Trace said, “You’re not joking about the treasure?”

“No, of course I’m not joking,” I said.

“But the Double Eagle?”

“What if I brought him the real thing, would he believe me then?”

She looked at me, her face all lines, a road map of worry.

“My husband needs to get back to sea,” she said. “As soon as possible.”

I thought of the nephew who had died.

“Come back,” she said. “Bring the coin with you.”

“I will,” I said.

As I went to leave, she said, “Just make sure it’s not a phony. Lee can pick a phony from a mile away.”

So can Eva Carides, Numismatist.

This time, as we skipped back across the bay, Sal seemed to be doing everything she could to avoid making eye contact with me.

We glided into the beach, and I said, “Thanks.”

She sort of grunted at me, and I said, “What’s the problem, are you angry with me?”

“No, not angry,” she said. “It’s just that I don’t really trust you that much.”

“Don’t trust me?” I said, feeling wounded.

“Yeah, that’s right,” she said. “I reckon you’re up to something.”

Okay, she was right: I was up to something.

But she was a twelve-year-old kid!

I expected Antonio to be in filthy mood – he'd had to wait for three hours with nobody except a dead dolphin for company.

"It's been nice here," he said as we walked back towards the pimpmobile. "So quiet, so calm."

As soon as I was back inside the pimpmobile I got to work.

Lee can pick a phony from a mile away, Trace had said, so there was no use rocking up with my Double Eagle.

I had to get hold of the real thing.

FOREIGN CUSTOMS

The shuttle bus, as it made its way to the training ground, was full. Everybody seemed to be in a pretty good mood, too.

I caught Coach Sheed's eye across the aisle and she smiled at me.

Obviously she'd forgiven me for smashing my PB yesterday.

I smiled back, but I felt like a complete fraud.

The bus pulled up and we all piled out.

I hurried through the entrance to the arena, hurried through one door of the locker room, hurried out of another, and hurried through the arena exit.

I was pretty sure nobody had noticed me.

I had now missed a mandatory training season. I was now out of the games.

"Bugger!" I softly said, but that was it. That was

all the mourning I was going to allow myself. Out on the main road, I hailed a taxi.

"Airport, please," I told the driver.

Once there, I made for the customs office.

As I handed the customs official my receipt my iPhone rang.

I wasn't surprised when I saw that it was Coach Sheeds calling.

I knew I should've answered it, told her some crazy story, but I just couldn't.

As the official read, her reptilian eyes flicked between the receipt and me. If her intention had been to scare the bejesus out of me, she'd succeeded. Because there was me, and there was the bejesus, now two separate entities.

"Ticket?" she said.

I handed her the computer printout.

"Why are you going to Switzerland?" she said.

That's none of your business, I wanted to say, but I couldn't, of course.

"I'm going to meet my father there," I said.

She raised her eyebrows.

I took out my iPhone and scrolled through the messages until I came to one that was – supposedly – from my dad.

Dom, it said. *I've booked us into a nice hotel in Geneva. Will pick you up at the airport. Love, Dad.*

"Okay," she said. "Wait here."

Five minutes later she returned with my coin enclosed within a plastic bag, like it was contaminated with Ebola, or one of those flesh-eating viruses.

I had to sign a couple of forms, and then I was free to take my reclaimed possession and go.

I went to the bathroom, locked myself in a cubicle and slipped the Double Eagle into my shoe, just under my heel. It wasn't too comfortable, but I couldn't afford to have it confiscated again. As I did, I couldn't help but think of all the other people who'd secreted something on their body just before they boarded a plane. There was even a word for people like us: smugglers. I also couldn't help thinking of what had happened to a lot of us. Imprisoned. Dead. But I was being dramatic – it was a coin, not a baggie full of cocaine. It was under my heel, not in my stomach.

By that time the flight was ready to be boarded.

It was only about quarter full and the other passengers were business types: suits, briefcases.

Again, I took out my piece of paper and went over my meticulous plan. No, it wasn't exactly James Bond – Agent 007 never seemed to write anything down – but putting it on paper seemed to make my outrageous plan more real, more achievable.

The flight seemed to take no time at all, however.

"Please fasten your seat belts for takeoff," was

followed, it seemed, a few minutes later by, "Please fasten your seat belts for landing."

As I shuffled off the plane and headed for customs I knew I was in trouble, knew that already I was exhibiting suspicious behavior, behavior that customs officers are trained to detect.

I was sweaty and I was twitchy.

It wasn't as if I was a real smuggler. In fact, I had nothing illegal on me. But my body seemed to think that I did, that it should sweat and that it should twitch.

I stopped to drink some water from a fountain.

Several liters of it.

Okay, pull yourself together!

Somehow it worked, because by the time I was in front of the passport dude I was in better shape.

He said nothing to me, just checked that my face was the same as the one in the passport, before he stamped the page and handed it back to me.

I had no luggage to pick up, so I walked straight past the carousels.

But now my body was up to its old tricks again: sweating, twitchy.

The Nothing to Declare exit looked very inviting – just a few more meters and I was free. But I guess that's what every one of my fellow smugglers tells themselves.

Just a few more meters.

I joined a group of what looked and sounded like American college students, in the hope that I would blend in.

Just a few more meters, that was all.

And I was there.

There was a tap on my shoulder, and I got ready to run, run, run.

I knew all that sweat and twitching had given me away. I knew there were squadrons of customs officers peering at screens looking for people behaving just like me.

But I put on the brakes, turned around to see who the tapper was.

"Oh, I'm sorry," she said, her voice southern American. "You're not one of ours, are you?"

"No, I'm not," I said, and I was away, not running, but walking very, very quickly towards the train station.

As I did I took out the piece of paper, my plan. Now, I had to catch the 10:42 a.m. train to Neuchâtel.

I checked my watch – it was only 10:12 a.m. and the station was an eight-and-a-half minute walk – I had plenty of time.

I allowed myself the tiniest pat on the back – *You're doing okay, Dom. You're doing okay.*

IKBAL^2

Lake Neuchâtel looked like something you'd see depicted on the wrapper for a brand of expensive Swiss chocolate: an expanse of silvery water with snowcapped mountains rising up behind. All very scenic, all very seventy-per-cent-pure cocoa, but I didn't have time to ponder its beauty; it was straight into the boat-hire shop for me.

"I'd like to hire a speedboat for the day," I said to the bored-looking man with the salt-and-pepper beard behind the counter.

He gave me an up-and-down look before he said, "You can't."

"Why not?" I said.

"Because you are of an insufficient age," he said.

"And what is a sufficient age?"

"Eighteen."

I was really kicking myself – I mean, who goes to Europe without some phony ID?

"So I have sufficient age to hire what?" I said.

"A pedal boat," he said.

Pedal boat? The choice of getaway vehicle for criminals the world over. But I guessed, given the insufficiency of my age, I didn't have much choice. According to Google Maps, there was no other way to get to Schwarzwasserstel, my improbably named destination.

"I'll take it," I said.

So after I'd given him my details and a ridiculous amount of euros, I was the proud renter of pedal boat number fourteen.

"You must bring it back on time," was the last thing he said to me.

I bought some supplies, also ridiculously overpriced – water and chocolate – and boarded my vessel.

I took out the map of the lake I'd printed off Google Maps. According to it, if I headed two hundred and seventy-eight degrees west from my present position, then I would hit Schwarzwasserstel. I took out my iPhone, opened the compass utility, and placed it on the seat in front of me so that I could see it.

As I started pedaling, it soon became apparent to me why the pedal boat has not figured hugely in the history of waterborne locomotion. Why Matthew Flinders did not use one when he became the first man to circumnavigate Australia.

Basically, they're useless. Even for somebody like me, who probably has much better than average leg power, they're useless.

The ratio of effort to result was pitiful. I pedaled and I pedaled and I pedaled and the water churned and it churned and it churned, but I hardly seemed to move at all. It was depressing. It was tiring. I ate some chocolate. I drank some water. And I churned even more water.

But after two hours I could make out Schwarzwasserstel on the far shore. It looked pretty cool, just like a castle out of a Disney film. Behind it the mountain rose up sharply, a wall of smooth bare stone. So Google Maps was right: there was no land access. Closer and closer I pedaled, and I could see that Schwarzwasserstel, Disneyesque from a distance, was actually pretty dilapidated. The turrets were crusted in birdlime. The lake's waters lapped walls that were shaggy with algae.

A terrible thought occurred to me: there was nobody living here anymore, Schwarzwasserstel was abandoned. The closer I came the more likely this seemed, because the castle was pretty much falling down. But as I pedaled into the little stone pier a dog barked.

I tied up the pedal boat and stepped out and onto the flagstones. Weeds sprouted up through the cracks, like the hairs out of Dr. Chakrabarty's nose.

Surely nobody lives here, I told myself.

But again the dog barked.

Time to put this part of my plan into action. I set my shoulders. Rearranged my face. I was now a fanatical numismatist, so fanatical that I would come all the way from Australia to Switzerland, pedal a boat across a lake, just to, perhaps, get a glimpse of a Saint-Gaudens Double Eagle.

I set off in the direction of the dog's bark.

The doors were enormous: wood slabs, iron fittings, like something made to withstand the biggest of battering rams. I knocked, but the resulting noise sounded pathetic; I doubted whether it had gone any further than where I was standing. So I put my shoulder against the door and I pushed and it gave way – the doors weren't locked!

They slowly creaked open and I was able to step inside Schwarzwasserstel. I couldn't remember actually having been in a castle before. But I had seen lots of movies, lots of TV shows about castles, and because of that I guessed I had a pretty clear idea as to what they should look like.

And let me tell you, it definitely wasn't this. This was Miranda's room after a seven-girl sleepover. This was the locker room after the football team had been in there. People, this was trashed!

There were piles of crap everywhere. Bundles of newspaper tied up with string. Black garbage bags, lumpy with stuff. And the smell was appalling. Like one of Bevan Milne's paint peelers.

Again my thought was: *Surely there's nobody living in this dump.* But almost as if it'd read my thoughts and wanted to tell me how wrong I was, the dog barked again.

And the bark was definitely from upstairs.

So I took the staircase, one of those winding types that princesses like to sweep down in fairy stories. And then I was in a corridor. The dog was barking pretty much continuously now – obviously it could sense that I was here.

I followed the corridor; on either side portraits of severe-looking people in high collars gave me disapproving stares.

I came to another of those medieval doors. The dog must be on the other side, I figured, because I could hear paws scrabbling against the wood.

I knocked.

No reply.

"Hello, is there anybody there?" I yelled.

Again, no reply, so I pushed at the door.

Again, it wasn't locked.

The dog's head appeared: it was one of those breeds with the squashed-up faces. Mrs. Grinham from down the road has one. What were they called again?

Of course – pugs!

To say that the pug was excited is probably understatement of the year; this pug was almost wetting himself.

So when I pushed the door open further and the pug was able to squeeze through, it came at me. It licked my ankles. It licked my feet.

This was the most grateful dog I'd ever met, like gratefulness had decided to take canine form.

A voice came from behind the door: "Who is our visitor, Montgomery?"

On the posh scale from one to a hundred, with a hundred being the Queen, this voice was up around the ninety-eight mark, maybe even ninety-nine.

Montgomery yapped some more.

"Well, show him in then," said Posh Voice.

I followed Montgomery through the open door and into the room.

There was a lot to take in.

Unlike the rest of the castle, the room itself looked modern, with carpet on the floor and paneling on the wall. Music was playing: lots of mournful cello, mournful violin, like the instruments were having a competition to out-mournful each other. And then there was Posh Voice himself: as soon as I saw him he ceased being Posh Voice and became Jabba the Hutt.

It was hard to work out what was chest and what was stomach and what was legs: it just seemed like one mass of amorphous body.

Above that was a head, which was pretty much the same head I'd seen on the net, with the heavy eyelids and curled-up moustache.

So he'd gotten fat but his head hadn't.

Now I noticed something in his hands. And that something was an old-fashioned pistol and it was pointed in my direction.

"Montgomery seems to have taken a liking to you," he said.

I was hoping this was a good thing, that the famously reclusive billionaire Ikbal Ikbal, one time friend of Farouk, King of Egypt, took notice of his canine companion.

"He's a really nice dog," I said.

"Now that accent, we had a chap at Eton who talked like that. Rilly noice dawg," said Ikbal², mimicking my accent.

Did I really sound like that?

"If my memory serves me correctly, the chap's name was Robert. Australian?"

"That's right," I said. "I'm from the Gold Coast."

"Well, jolly good for you," he said, his laugh a sort of seismic rumble.

"I didn't come to rob you or anything, Mr. Ikbal Ikbal," I said, nervous eyes on the pistol.

"Young man, as you can probably see, there isn't much to rob anymore," he said with a wave of his hand.

My heart sunk: he no longer had the Double Eagle that, according to the Internet, he'd acquired from King Farouk!

Why hadn't I factored in that possibility?

"So what brings you to me?" he said, and it was a pretty fair question.

Fanatical numismatist? Really, was that going to work? Probably not, but so what, he didn't have the coin anyway. So I went with fanatical numismatist. Told him how I'd always been interested in coins, especially the Double Eagles. How I'd read that he'd purchased one from King Farouk. And as I talked, I realized that "fanatical numismatist" wasn't altogether a performance: I really, really, really wanted to see what a genuine Double Eagle looked like.

Finally I said, "So I thought that maybe, just maybe, if I came all the way here I could see one."

"By what means did you get here again?" he asked in that posh voice.

"In a pedal boat," I said.

"You pedaled all the way across the lake?"

"Yes," I said. "And I would've pedaled across the Pacific to see a Double Eagle."

Ikbal^2 was slowly stroking Montgomery, who was now sitting on his lap.

"Do you know something, living here hasn't been

cheap. Yes, the Swiss offered me refuge, but they're a nation of bankers; they've made me pay for it."

Ikbal[2] paused there and when he continued talking again, there was no mistaking the sadness in his voice.

"Of all the things I've owned, the Fabergé eggs, the diamonds, the Double Eagle has always been my favorite ..."

There was a flush of color around his neck and my heart climbed back to its usual place in my chest – he still had it!

"It's the most beautiful coin," I said. "The most beautiful coin that was ever struck."

"My last wish is that I be buried back in Egypt. Then, at least, I can spend eternity in my homeland, the land they banished me from. The current administration is, shall we say, sympathetic to my wishes."

I figured that now was not the time to talk: I said nothing.

"Of course, their sympathy waxes and wanes, depending on how much money I can promise them."

"You will sell the coin?" I said.

"Yes, I will sell the coin. In fact, I'm expecting somebody later on this week. They, unlike you, will probably arrive by helicopter."

The gun, I noticed, was no longer pointing at me.

"So you would like to see the Double Eagle?"

"Yes, I would," I said.

"Well, young man, come here before I change my mind."

I wasted no time and hurried over to where he was sitting. Now that I was closer I could smell Ikbal^2: a mixture of the fragrant and the pungent.

He reached inside his shirt and came out with a bunch of keys on a chain, which he slipped over his head.

He leaned to one side, until he could reach a set of drawers.

"It's probably better if you don't see this," he said.

I looked the other way, but what Ikbal^2 didn't consider was that right in front of me was an enormous gilt-edged mirror which enabled me to see everything he was doing.

He slid down a small panel, behind which was a hidden drawer. Using one of the keys, he unlocked the drawer and took out a red box.

He closed the drawer, slid the panel back.

"Here we are," he said, which I took as permission to turn around again.

A flick of his thumb, a click; the box sprung open and there it was, nestled on blue velvet, the Double Eagle. Not a fake, not a phony, the real thing.

"Isn't it glorious?" he said.

Glorious was the right word.

"Can I hold it?" I asked.

A look of consternation passed across his face and I noticed his other hand tightening its grip on the pistol.

"Just for a second," I said.

Ikbal^2 plucked the coin from its nest with his long, manicured fingernails, placing it on his plump hand.

I held out my right hand.

He placed the coin on the palm.

My left hand crept into my pocket, where my Golden Eagle was.

How to swap them?

What I needed was some sort of distraction.

"It's incredible!" I said. "It's amazing!"

Behind Ikbal^2, Montgomery had jumped up onto a chair, and his front paws were scrabbling on the top of a table.

He wasn't in any danger, but I sensed that this was my opportunity.

"Montgomery, watch out!" I yelled.

Ikbal^2 twisted around – not a straightforward process.

"Montgomery, get down from there!" he said.

By the time he turned back to face me, his genuine coin was in my pocket and my phony coin was on my palm.

I couldn't quite believe how simple it had been. And when I handed the coin back to him, I was sure I was going to be found out, that he would

immediately spot my coin as a fake.

But he took it and placed it carefully back in its box.

"Well, I hope it was worth all that pedaling," he said.

"Without a doubt," I said, feeling the weight of his coin in my pocket. "That was incredible."

I thanked Ikbal[2], patted Montgomery, and I got the heck out of there.

I didn't run, I didn't rush, but I got the heck out of there.

Once back in the pedal boat, I pedaled hard. If ever pedal-boat racing becomes an Olympic sport – and what a sad day that will be – then I am sure to medal. The sun had disappeared behind the snowcapped mountain range; the water had turned glassy, and I pedaled. I actually hadn't thought how much the coin was worth, but now that I did it made me a bit giddy. A Double Eagle had been auctioned in 2002 for US$7.59 million.

I could see the town now, the dinky little pier where I had hired the boat.

I pedaled and I pedaled and I pedaled.

One last revolution and I glided in to the shore.

There, waiting for me, was the police. Shiny badges, stern faces – the usual constabulary thing. I'd been crazy to think I was going to get away with it.

I stepped out of the boat and onto the wharf.

Make a run for it?

No, probably not.

Dive into the water and swim for it?

Also, probably not.

Now I noticed that as well as the two cops there was another person: the man from the hire shop, he of the "insufficient age" line.

What was he doing here?

He said something to the policeman in French.

The policeman looked at me and said, "You have a contract to hire the boat for four hours?"

At first I wasn't quite sure what was going on: would somebody really get the police because somebody had kept out a pedal boat longer than they should?

Okay, I was a bit late bringing it back.

Two hours late.

But I figured that probably happened all the time, that they just did a run around the lake every morning and picked up all the abandoned pedal boats.

I mean, it wasn't as if anybody would actually steal a pedal boat, was it?

"I can pay the extra money," I said.

The cop looked at the pedal boat man and said something in French.

The pedal boat man said something back.

I'm pretty sure, despite my insufficient age, he wanted me to go to jail.

Eventually the boat man said, "You owe me sixty euro."

Sixty euro was outrageous, but I happily paid.

And, coin bouncing in my pocket, I hurried to the railway station.

Safely in my seat, I moved the coin into my shoe for smuggling again and sent Trace a text message.

Her reply came just before the train pulled into Geneva: *that's gr8!*

I sent her another text: *when can I come?*

Her reply didn't take long: *we're in rome tonight for stones concert*

It took me a while to make sense of this: *stones concert*?

But then I remembered the signs I'd seen all around Rome: *The Rolling Stones Rock the Colosseum*.

I remembered the photo I'd seen in E. Lee Marx's office. E. Lee Marx was coming to Rome to go to the Rolling Stones concert.

I started typing a reply text, *so maybe*, but then stopped.

Sometimes it's easier just to do it the old-fashioned way.

I called Trace. She answered straightaway.

"Well, I've gotten him out of the compound," she said.

"That's great," I said.

“And Keith wants to see him after the gig.”

Keith? Who was Keith? And then I got it: Keith Richards!

“That’s awesome!” I said, and I really meant it.

Okay, the Rolling Stones were about a thousand years old, and they hadn’t put out a good album since before I was born, but they were still the Rolling Stones, they were still my dad’s all-time favorite band.

“So I can meet you before the gig?” I said.

“No, we won’t have time.”

I figured that after the gig wouldn’t be possible, not if he was going backstage.

“Can I come to Maremma tomorrow, then?” I said.

“Oh, Dom, didn’t I tell you? Lee is flying out tomorrow, back to the States. He’s looking to set up some sort of charity there, in Trent’s memory.”

Trent must be the nephew who died, but still, what?

No, she hadn’t told me, and I was starting to wonder about Trace, nice as she was: she seemed to enjoy making me jump through as many hoops as possible.

But when I thought about it just a little bit more, it seemed only fair and reasonable that she did.

Some kid rocks up, reckons he knows where Yamashita’s Gold is, why wouldn’t you give him a hard time?

“So what about at the gig itself?” I said. “Maybe I could meet you there?”

“Sure,” she said. “Meet us there.”

It was only after I’d put down the phone that I realized I’d left out a few important details, like how on earth I was going to get into the concert and how on earth I was going to find them when I did.

THE ROLLING STONES ROCK THE COLOSSEUM

By the time I got back to Rome there was less than two hours before the concert started.

In the taxi from the airport I tried to buy a Stones ticket online, but with no luck – apparently it had been *esaurito* – sold out – for weeks already. If I couldn't get in legally, I'd have to resort to other, less legal methods. I was a pretty resourceful sort of kid, after all.

A quick reconnoiter, that's what I needed.

"Can we go past the Colosseum?" I asked the taxi driver.

"Many, many roadblock," he said.

"Yes, but I'd still like to go."

He sighed heavily and said, "You're paying the meter, *amico*."

He was right: there were many, many roadblock with many, many security guard manning these

many, many roadblock. Security guards so big and hairy they made the gorillas we had working on the Gold Coast look like lesser primates.

Can't go through it.

But what about under it?

I remembered what Dr. Chakrabarty had said about the hypogeum being connected to different parts of Rome by underground tunnels.

"Where to now, boss?" asked the taxi driver.

"The Olympic Village," I said.

The taxi driver seemed to think that we were now on familiar enough terms for him to offer me a whole lot of his opinions about a whole lot of different subjects.

"This pop concert, it is disrespectful of *il Colosseo*," he said.

Would that be the same *Colosseo* where men used to get their heads chopped off?

"The Rolling Stones are more rock than pop," I said.

"Rock. Pop. Same thing. Disrespectful."

After he'd dropped me off, I hurried through the entrance, keen to find the doctor and take advantage of all the awesome stuff he knew about the subterranean Colosseum.

I didn't have to look very far.

Dr. Chakrabarty was waiting for me. Along with Mr. Ryan. And Mrs. Jenkins. Coach Sheeds. In fact, a whole gaggle of officials.

And I could tell from the collective looks on their faces that, again, I was in more trouble than Maximus.

Behind them, sitting on one of the couches in the foyer, I could see Seb.

I looked at Dr. Chakrabarty, repository of all that information, and I knew it was no longer available to me.

"Dominic, a word," said Mrs. Jenkins, chins wobbling in all directions like some mad physics experiment.

Really, would one word be enough to tell me what a disappointment I was? How I'd let the team down and myself as well? How their hands were tied, how rules were rules and they had no option but to suspend me from the team?

All that, in one word?

It would have to be a big one, something along the lines of antidisestablishmentarianism or pseudopseudohypoparathyroidism.

Right then I had two choices.

My first choice was to let them have that word, to take in that word, to promise them I would knuckle down, and maybe, perhaps, possibly, perchance, they would let me stay on the team.

But if I did this I didn't like my chances of getting out of the Olympic Village tonight.

My other choice?

"I have to go," I said, making what I hoped was a serious I-have-to-go face.

Obviously not serious enough, because Mrs. Jenkins said, "Go where?"

"To the bathroom. But I'll be right back."

"If you have to," said Mrs. Jenkins, who obviously had memories of me on the plane.

I ran inside the bathroom, into a cubicle, my mind racing.

How to get out of here without them seeing me?

A door opened and I figured it was Mr. Ryan or maybe even Mrs. Jenkins come to check on me.

"I haven't finished," I said, making a wet farting noise with my mouth.

"Not very convincing," said Seb

"Crap!"

"Exactly."

"No, I meant crap crap, not poo crap," I said.

"So what's happening with you, dude?" said Seb.

"I totally need to get to the Rolling Stones concert," I said.

"Totally?" he said.

"To-tal-ly," I said.

"Okay, I dig that," said Seb. "They're, like, my favorite heritage band."

"You actually like the Rolling Stones?"

"'Like' is a bit puny for how I feel about them," he said.

A fifteen-year-old kid liking the Rolling Stones that much was pretty whacko, but Seb was a pretty whacko fifteen-year-old kid.

"So maybe you'd be keen on getting into the gig, too?" I ventured.

"'Keen' is a bit puny for how –"

"Okay, I get it."

"And I got knocked out in my heat, so it is getting a bit boring around here," he said.

"The question is: how do we get out of here without being sprung?" I said.

"That's easy," said Seb, pointing to a high-set window.

"You think we could squeeze through that?"

"I know we could squeeze through that."

I gave Seb a quizzical look – how could he be so certain?

"I've done a fair bit of caving, and caving is all about squeezing through tight spaces," he said. "You just need to make sure you get one arm and one shoulder through to begin with."

"Me first?"

By way of an answer Seb linked his fingers to make a step with his two hands.

"Here, I'll give you a hoist."

With Seb's help I was easily able to get on top of the partition.

The window still looked too small, though, and I wondered whether Seb had misjudged it.

"Are you sure?" I said.

"You want me to go first?"

"No, I've got it," I said.

Taking his advice, I put my left arm through first, followed by my left shoulder.

And then, by tucking my head under my left arm, I was able to get the top of my body through.

The problem was that now I was facing downwards and there was probably a three-meter drop to the ground.

On my present trajectory I was going to end up with a broken neck.

I twisted myself around so I was facing up, my hands feeling for holds on the smooth brick.

Bingo!

A slightly protruding brick provided just the purchase I needed. Using this to steady myself, I was able to shuffle my bum out through the window. Then, somehow, I was able to get my feet under me and stand up. Now all I had to do was turn around. Doing this necessitated letting go of my brick and then gripping either side of the window frame.

I had no choice.

One. Two. Three.

I let go of the brick and shuffled around, hands finding the frame.

I'd made it!

Sort of.

There didn't see any way to clamber down from where I was. I had to jump. Fortunately there was a flower bed just to my right. But if I missed that and hit the stone, I'd probably break something. Like an ankle. Or a leg.

One. Two. Three!

I jumped, both feet landing in the soft soil. I rolled to the left, squashing a bunch of the flowers. By this time Seb had appeared at the window.

What had been so difficult for me, he seemed to do easily, and quickly. He jumped, he landed, and was immediately up on his feet like a cat. I wondered about the caving explanation. Not for long, though. Because we were both running, giggling as we did.

It'd been a pretty excellent escape.

And it also felt a bit like old times, when we used to run together, before The Debt had come into my life, into our lives.

I hailed a taxi.

This driver also spoke pretty good English, but unlike the other one he thought that the Rolling Stones concert was a good idea.

"It will put Rome on the map," he said.

Actually, I thought Rome was already on most maps.

He dropped us as close as he could get to the Colosseum.

Already a big crowd had gathered.

There were the usual tourists doing the usual rubbernecking, but other people as well. Maybe they had tickets, maybe they didn't, but it certainly had the sense of a big event.

But I guessed the Colosseum had been doing big events for a while now – since at least 107 AD when Trajan and his 10,000 gladiators had totally rocked it.

Among them I saw a bald man standing on a milk crate, with what looked like a sheaf of tickets in his hand.

As we got closer I could hear him say, his accent like something out of that film *Lock, Stock and Two Smoking Barrels,* "Tickets to the Stones. Who wants tickets to the Stones?"

"I need two," I said as I came up to him. I didn't have much cash on me but I figured that if the price was right I could go get some out of the ATM.

He looked me up and down and said, "It's not Justin Bieber on tonight."

"No kidding," I said. "How much is a ticket?"

"Seven fifty," he said.

"Very funny," I said, thinking he meant seven euros and fifty cents. "Really, how much is a ticket?"

"You heard me, seven hundred and fifty euros."

Seven hundred and fifty euros was crazy, nobody was going to buy a ticket for that price. And it was much more than I could get out of the ATM.

But as soon as I had this thought a man in a suit approached the scalper.

They talked for a while, euros changed hands, and the man in the suit walked off with a ticket.

I didn't like Justin Bieber that much, but somebody had to stick up for him.

"Have you thought that the Rolling Stones were just the Justin Bieber of their time?"

The scalper gave me a look, also from *Lock, Stock and Two Smoking Barrels* and said, "Rack off, kid, and stop wasting my time."

It seemed like pretty sound advice.

"No luck," I said to Seb.

"What now?" he said.

Couldn't go through it.

Couldn't go under it.

But hadn't Antonio hinted that he and some of his friends had once climbed over the Colosseum?

I called his number and fortunately he answered straightaway.

"Kangaroo," he said.

I tried to think of an animal that was representative of somebody who was half English and half Italian, but I couldn't, so I just said, "Antonio, my man!"

"What can I do for you?"

"You know how you sort of suggested that you and your mates climbed into the Colosseum?"

"Sure," he said, but I detected a note of uncertainty in his voice that hadn't been there the other day.

"How did you do it?"

Silence, and that note of uncertainty had become a whole symphony of uncertainty.

"You lied to me," I said.

"Yes, I lied to you."

"You didn't go over."

My heart sank, dropping into the bottom of my chest, where it rolled down one leg, coming to rest in my foot.

"I didn't, but some people I know did."

"Do you have any idea where they went over?"

"Give me a minute, okay?"

I gave him a minute. And another minute. And another minute.

And just as I was about to start hating him again, a text arrived.

start from small park opposite oppio cafe be careful

That was it, *Climbing the Colosseum for Dummies*?

Still, I guessed it was better than nothing.

The crowd had swelled even more. Limos were pulling up, dropping people off.

Apart from the occasional faded T-shirt from

years gone by, there wasn't anything particularly rock'n'roll about the audience. They could've been going to the opera or the theatre. There were a lot of sexy dresses and flashing jewelry.

Oppio Café was crowded, people getting their last overpriced drink before they hit the gig.

From here the Colosseum was pretty much intact, the full fifty meters high, equal to a twelve-story building. My first thought was that Antonio, or his friends at least, were crazy: why would you go over here when there were parts of the wall that weren't as intact and were therefore much lower? But after another walk around, it was obvious why: this was the least busy area of the Colosseum, the part that was furthest from the entrances. It was also the darkest part; there were plenty of helpful shadows.

"You still game?" I said to Seb.

I followed his gaze up and up and up until it came to stop at the very top of the Colosseum. For an agonizing second I thought he was going to pull out. And it was agonizing because I really didn't want to tackle this thing by myself. His gaze returned from the skies and a smile appeared on his face.

"Loose as a goose on the juice," he said, which I took to be an affirmative.

"I think we should wait until the concert starts," I said.

"So do I," he said.

While we waited, both sitting on the ground, I noticed that the security guards patrolled at regular intervals.

I timed them – three minutes, twenty-five seconds.

So that gave us about three minutes to start climbing and find some cover.

Oppio Café was emptying now, its customers joining the people streaming towards the entrance. Obviously they couldn't all fit inside, but I guessed they were going to sit outside. So what if they couldn't see them, at least they could hear the Stones.

I had the same feeling I had before a big race: butterflies in my stomach, but not those delicate fluttery types. These were big brutes, and they were smashing into each other.

We could hear the stage announcer: "Ladies and Gentleman, the Rolling Stones!"

And then a tremendous roar that seemed to lift the Colosseum off the ground. I wondered if it was the same sort of roar as hundreds of years ago when the gladiators clashed.

The opening riffs of a song.

"Start me up," said Seb.

"Start you up?" I said.

"That's the song," he said. "'Start Me Up.'"

Now I recognized it, and it seemed pretty appropriate, too. Start me up, and get me over that monster.

Two security guards walked past. One of them looked our way, so I started doing a bit of heavy-metal head shaking in time to the music. *Hey, man, we're here to dig the music, not to break into the Colosseum.*

When I looked up again, his gaze was elsewhere.

"Okay," I said to Seb. "Let's go."

He didn't need any more prompting than that, and scampered across the concrete. I followed. But once we'd reached the base of the Colosseum I hesitated.

Were we crazy?

This thing was twelve stories high!

But Seb was already on his way.

So I followed his lead.

Last year, at school, we'd done some indoor rock climbing and, if I do say so myself, I'd been pretty good at it. I have a long reach and a good power-to-weight ratio.

But climbing in an indoor gym and climbing on an exposed wall: not much comparison, I'm afraid.

There you have a harness. Make a mistake, fall off, and you dangle around for a while until the instructor makes a dad joke and lets you down.

Here I had no harness.

Still, because it was so worn, so damaged, with so many cracks and crevices, there was no shortage of footholds and handholds.

It was actually pretty straightforward climbing and, harness or not, it didn't take very long until we'd reached the first level.

From here we could see through the gaps into the amphitheatre itself.

At the far end was the purpose-built stage, with four figures on it, three of them moving about, the other's arms lifting high as he drummed away.

The skinny figure of Mick Jagger out front.

And then the crowd, a sea of bodies, all moving to the song.

The sound seemed to just swell up, like a wave at Surfers when the wind was offshore and the tide was just right.

Forget the scalper's seven hundred and fifty euro tickets, right now Seb and I had the best seats in the house.

There was only one drawback – there was no easy way to get down into the amphitheatre from here.

It would involve climbing down and I didn't really like that idea. For a start it would be much more dangerous because we wouldn't be able to see the footholds. And for sure somebody would see us. Probably one of those big hairy security guards.

But if we kept climbing up to the top, there seemed to be a series of steps that led down from there.

"We need to keep going," I said to Seb.

I couldn't have blamed him if he'd just stayed

where he was. Like I said, there were no better seats in the house.

But he nodded and said, "Let's go!"

Technically, the climbing wasn't very difficult. But we were higher now, much higher.

Each year during spring break when some kid falls off a balcony at Surfers, it doesn't seem to matter what floor they fall from – sixth, eighth, twentieth – because they always end up dead.

A wrong move, a fall, and death seemed the most likely outcome for us too.

I stopped to get my breath, and watched Seb. He was so fluid, each action so economical. *Is there anything this kid can't do?*

And fast on the heels of that question, came another question. *Why is he so eager to help me?*

Surely it couldn't be because he wanted to see a rock band who hadn't put out a decent album in thirty years?

No, it was pretty obvious that Seb was involved in The Debt.

The opening riff to "Miss You" had started – a song even I knew – and the crowd, the mob, was going crazy, Italian-style.

I started moving again and soon caught up to Seb. We climbed together, hand for hand, foot for foot, until we arrived at the second level.

The view from here was even more spectacular.

The crowd, down below, looked like a sort of heaving protoplasm, undulating in time to the music.

Lights flashed onstage, lasers sweeping this way and that way. And then suddenly they were on us. But they were gone again.

"That was close," I said.

"Let's keep moving," said Seb.

I didn't need any more prompting, and once again we headed skyward as the lasers kept sweeping across us.

The third level now.

Don't look down, I told myself. *Whatever you do, don't look down.* I looked down. It was a long, long way to the bottom.

I tried to move my hand. It wouldn't move.

I tried to move my arm. It wouldn't move.

I was scared and I was stuck.

What had I been thinking?

All this, just to see E. Lee Marx before he left the country? Surely there were other more sensible ways I could've done this.

I wondered if I'd become some sort of adrenaline junkie, always looking to get my next fix.

Because of that I'd become delusional: I wasn't thinking stuff all the way through, I was totally overestimating my capabilities.

Seb, who had already started moving again, stopped to look down at me.

"You okay, Dom?" he said.

"Not really," I said. "I can't seem to move."

The song had ended and a new one had started, a slow song.

The amphitheatre was bathed in dark and people had their phone screens lit up, waving them in time to the music.

"We're almost there, mate," said Seb. "Just a few meters more."

"We are?"

"No crap. It's just a process, that's all. Find a handhold. Find a foothold. Drag yourself up. Little by little. Loose as a goose on the juice."

He was right: it was just a process. It was a goose. It was on the juice. It was loose.

Handhold. Done.

Foothold. Done.

Lift myself up.

Just a process.

Handhold. Done.

Foothold. Done.

Lift myself up.

And then I was on the top, straddling the Colosseum, the stars my headband.

The whole of Rome spread out in front of me, and down below, that heaving protoplasm. I felt a

rush of pure emotion – excitement, triumph, thrill – that seemed to lift me up even higher.

It was Seb who brought me back down to earth.

"Let's get off this baby," he said.

"Let's."

It was obvious what we had to do.

Just below the lip of the wall was a ledge. It was small but it looked solid enough to hold our weight.

So, holding on to the top, we made our way around this ledge, heading for the steps that would eventually take us down to the hypogeum.

Again the lasers swept back and forth over us.

Almost there, just a couple of meters to go.

The song ended and there was the usual tumult of applause.

Another laser swept by.

And another one.

A meter to go.

Another laser.

Except it didn't sweep by.

It stopped right on me.

I looked to my left – a laser was focused on Seb.

We'd been spotlighted.

Down below, the crowd stopped cheering.

There were audible gasps.

And then a booming voice, Mick Jagger's voice: "Looks like we've got ourselves a couple of gate-crashers, people!"

Seb started moving again, and so did I, but the lasers kept with us.

He finally reached the end of the ledge.

I hadn't noticed before, but there was a two-meter gap between here and the stairs.

A gap that could only be traversed one way – by jumping.

Seb hesitated.

One part of me thought: *Thank God, he's human after all.*

But another part thought: *If he can't do it, then how can I?*

The crowd was chanting. *"Saltare! Saltare! Saltare!"*

Seb looked back at me. Opened his mouth as if to say something but then seemed to think better of it.

He turned back, he crouched, and he jumped up and out.

It was soon pretty obvious that he'd misjudged it, that he'd gone too high.

That he was going to miss the stairs and drop to his death.

But somehow, mid-jump, he managed to change his trajectory.

His feet hit the edge of the stairs, but his momentum carried him forwards and onto the stairs. One roll before, catlike, he was back on his feet.

Huge applause from below.

My turn.

Seb beckoned with his hand – *Come on, Dom.*

Having learned from his effort, I knew exactly what to do. I shuffled to the end of the ledge, I crouched, and I jumped. Not too high, I'd told myself.

It worked, and I nailed the landing, both feet hitting the stairs at the same time.

Even more applause from below.

And now I could see them coming from every direction: security guards, loping up the stairs towards us.

"I'd say that's the end of our gig," said Seb.

I scanned the Colosseum, my brain working hard. It was a bit like one of those Escher drawings that Miranda liked so much – which stairs went where? But I quickly worked out a possible escape route.

"Maybe not," I said. "Follow me."

I ran down one set of stairs, taking them three at a time.

Then across onto another set.

Down another set.

The security guards were running all over the place, but I figured that as long as we stayed high and kept moving they'd have trouble zeroing in on us.

Across some more steps.

Now I could see it clearly: our one chance of avoiding capture.

"Let's go," I said. "All the way down."

Seb could see it too.

The security guards would have to go up and then across and then down to get to us.

We went flying down those stairs.

One wrong move and we were gone. Busted ankle, busted leg, busted life.

And then the stairs ran out.

We were on a small stage, which I guessed was where the emperor or the caesar would've sat to watch the spectacle below.

But there was no way out of here except the way we'd come.

I looked back.

A scrum of security guards was converging on us.

I looked down at the crowd, which was perhaps four meters below.

Somebody said something, and soon there was yelling, arms raised, fingers pointing, thrusting, at us.

I looked at Seb standing next to me.

"You done much crowd-surfing?"

"Oh yeah," he said.

We stood on the lip of the platform and adopted the crowd-surfer pose: chest out, arms up.

And as we did, arms reached up. They were ready for us.

Behind us arms reached out; the security guards were almost on us.

"Let's go!"

Seb and I dived off.

Not too deep, I kept reminding myself as I soared through the air.

And then *oomph!* the air was knocked out of my chest.

And double-*oomph!* I copped an accidental hand right in the knurries.

But then I was being passed along, people screaming stuff at me in Italian.

And then, when we were well away from the security guards, right in the thick of the crowd, they put us down and Seb and I became just like them, ticket-paying concertgoers.

I looked up – we were about two meters from the stage.

And I swear Mick Jagger, all ribs and wrinkles, winked at me as he launched into "Jumpin' Jack Flash. You're a gas gas gas."

After that was "Satisfaction" and, though Mick apparently was having trouble getting any, I was feeling just about as satisfied as a human being can get, as this human being had ever gotten, anyway.

A couple more songs and then the obligatory encore.

When that was finished and the lights went on, people started streaming towards the exits.

Okay, what now?

I'd been so focused on getting into the gig, I hadn't given much thought about getting backstage once I was here.

Once the crowd had thinned out, I could see that not everyone was leaving.

Some people, conspicuous by the red passes dangling from their necks, were headed towards another door manned by two security guards.

After inspection of the passes they were let through the door.

Backstage, I reasoned, was on the other side of that.

"What's up?" said Seb.

"I have to get backstage," I said.

"You have to?" he said, hitting hard on the "have."

"Have to," I replied.

He looked around, scratched the side of his face a couple of times and then said, "Give me ten minutes."

"Okay," I said.

It was pretty much what I'd expected.

Seb was part of The Debt. The Debt really wanted me to do this. So that cardinal rule, nobody was allowed to help, had been done away with.

I was one of the few people left inside now and I figured that any minute I would be asked to leave.

Or maybe even be arrested if they recognized me as the gate-crasher.

There were no more people getting their passes checked before they went backstage.

I checked my watch.

It had been almost fifteen minutes since Seb had left, so I figured that whatever his plan had been, he'd failed.

I'd have to come up with something else.

What, I didn't know. It felt right then that I'd pretty much run out of both motivation and imagination.

I looked over at the two security guards and one of them was showing the other something on his phone.

Could I bribe them?

But then I remembered that I didn't actually have much cash left.

And if you're going to go down the bribery path, it's usually a good idea to have something to bribe with.

I could just hang outside and hope to get E. Lee Marx as he came out.

Problem with that was I didn't know where he would come out.

Or if he'd be taken somewhere directly by car.

So that wasn't really a plan; that was just pure hope.

I could feel despair starting to claw at me.

And then the noise, a guitar on full volume, screeching.

My hands immediately went for my ears – it wasn't just earsplitting, it was brain-splitting, the sort of noise that would give you lifelong tinnitus.

Somebody stop that!

The two security guards were already running, trying to find out where this appalling racket was coming from.

Thank God, I thought. I was so relieved that they were going to stop this god-awful noise that I didn't take in the implications of this.

The two security guards!

Which meant that they'd abandoned their post and there wasn't anybody guarding the door.

As they passed me I took off full-pelt in the opposite direction.

I tried the door. It was unlocked.

I pushed it and slipped through.

I'd done it: I was backstage at a Rolling Stones concert!

A very big hand clamped my shoulder.

The very big hand belonged to a very big man.

He was dressed in black jeans, black T-shirt, black boots, and he had a bald head that looked like it belonged on Easter Island.

"Not so friggin' fast, Sonny Jim," he said with an accent he'd borrowed from Hound de Villiers. "And, where do you think you're going?"

"Backstage?" I suggested.

He didn't say anything. He didn't have to – the look he gave me said it all – *No, you're not, Sonny Jim.*

"How did you get this far anyway?" he said.

You know what, I was getting pretty sick of men – mostly very big men – getting in my way.

"If you must know, Sonny Jim, I climbed over the top of the friggin' Colosseum," I said.

"That was you?" he said, and I could detect something else in his voice now.

"Didn't I just say it was me?" I said.

"And you did that because?"

Okay, I figured the truth, as good as it had been, wasn't going to serve me any further.

"Because it was always my father's dream."

"To climb over the Colosseum?"

"To see the Stones live."

"And, what, he didn't have the guts to do it himself?"

"He passed away," I said.

The bald man looked me in the eyes.

"Kid, I'm not sure if you're lying or not. But, what the heck, if you're that desperate, then who am I to say no?"

Absolutely, I thought.

"Hold your arms out, Sonny Jim."

Sonny Jim held his arms out.

He frisked me, and then he pulled one of those red passes from his pocket and hung it around my neck.

"If anybody asks you, Lem had nothing to do with it, okay?"

"Okay, Lem," I said.

BACKSTAGE

Not sure what I expected: maybe a whole lot of old people sitting around, sipping champagne, talking about all the stuff they did when they were young.

But it was actually a bit livelier than that.

Even if there were a whole lot of old people sitting around sipping champagne.

There were lots of photographers taking lots of photos.

And reporter types getting exclusive interviews.

But all this was wallpaper, because I had eyes for one person and one person only.

The person I couldn't see.

I'd come all this way. I'd risked my life several dozen times. And he hadn't even made the concert?

"Dominic!"

I turned around.

It was Trace, dressed in a figure-hugging dress, looking rock'n'roll glam.

"You made it?" she said.

No, Trace, this is a hologram you see before you. Of course I bloody made it.

"Your husband?" I said.

"Oh, he's been talking up a storm with Keith!" she said, and I could hear the lightness in her voice.

"Do you think I should ask him about Yamashita's Gold?" I said.

"Absolutely. Now would be the perfect moment," she said. "Come with me."

I followed Trace into another room.

There were five or six people sitting around on sofas.

Two of them I recognized.

E. Lee Marx, of course. And Trace was right, he did look different, larger rather than smaller-than-life.

The other person was Keith Richards. Who actually looked a lot like Johnny Depp in *Pirates of the Caribbean*.

And I had that same feeling I had before, that he must be a fraud, because people like me don't get this close to famous types like him.

Trace said, "Sorry to interrupt, but Dom's here. He came to see us at the compound, remember?"

E. Lee Marx looked me up and down.

The world's greatest treasure hunter!

So did Keith Richards.

Okay, the Rolling Stones were about ten million years old, but they were still the Rolling Stones and this was still Keith Richards and he was still looking me – me! – up and down.

"You the stage diver, then?" he said.

There was really no use denying it.

"That was me," I said. "How'd it look from where you were?"

For a second I thought my joke had fallen flat, but then he smiled a lopsided smile, held out his hand and said, "Ten out of ten from the English judge, son."

So I shook Keith Richard's hand. As you do.

We talked a bit more about the mechanics of stage diving, and I thought this was as good a time as any.

"Mr. Marx?" I said.

"Yes?" he replied.

"Remember I was telling you about Yamashita's Gold?" I said. "How I had proof?"

E. Lee Marx raised his eyebrows.

I looked over at Trace – she smiled encouragingly at me.

I reached into my pocket and brought out the Double Eagle and handed it to E. Lee Marx.

He took it, weighed it in his hand.

He gave a sort of nod of approval – obviously it was the right weight.

He took out a one-euro coin and gave the Double Eagle a rap with it.

There was a resultant *ding!*

Another nod of approval – obviously it sounded right.

Then he looked at it closely.

When he'd finished he handed the coin back to me, an enigmatic smile on his lips.

"It's a fake," he said. "A very good one, but a fake nonetheless."

"How do you know?" I said.

"Not many people are aware of this, but the real 1933 Double Eagle has got a black eye," he said.

Eva Carides, Numismatist, my fat butt!

Technically, I guess you could say that I fainted.

The blood drained from my face, my blood pressure plummeted and I crumpled onto the floor. And when I came to, that's certainly the term everybody was throwing around.

As in, "Can we have some water here, this poor boy has fainted." And, "Dom, do you faint very often?"

But I knew that it was no faint, it was my body's way of saying *No!*

Had I really swapped the real thing for a phony?

Well, according to E. Lee Marx, the world's greatest marine archaeologist, I had. And that was good enough for me.

BACK TO LAKE NEUCHÂTEL

E. Lee Marx was leaving for the States tomorrow at six in the evening.

I had no time to lose.

I had to get back to Switzerland tonight.

I got out my iPhone, brought up the Skyscanner app. There were no more ROM-GEN flights tonight, and the earliest one I could get a ticket on tomorrow wasn't until the afternoon – not enough time.

I brought up Google Maps. Typed in *Rome to Neuchâtel*.

There were nine hundred and fifty-seven kilometers between them, a distance that would supposedly take nine hours and four minutes to drive.

But Google Maps was a pretty slow driver, I reckoned.

And I knew somebody who wasn't.

And what's more, he was for hire.

I called Antonio and twenty minutes later the pimpmobile pulled up outside Oppio Café.

"Neuchâtel?" queried Slim when I got into the front seat.

I nodded, and showed him exactly where I wanted to go on my iPhone.

"*Pourquoi?*" he said.

My French wasn't up to explaining why. And certainly not my Italian. Actually, I didn't think even my English was up to explaining why.

"*Pourquoi* not?" I said.

Slim smiled and put the pimpmobile into first gear.

As we traveled out of Rome and headed north I made an attempt at the conversation thing.

Not that easy when (a) we didn't have a common language and (b) I was really, really tired.

Eventually Slim, who was either sick of my pidgin French or my constant yawning, pointed to the backseat and said, "*Dormez.*"

That much I understood – sleep – and it seemed like just about the best idea I'd ever heard.

So after putting my iPhone on Slim's car charger I crawled into the backseat and I dormezed.

I woke a few times – once when we'd stopped for fuel and another time when we were winding through the Alps, but mostly it was dormez.

When I woke it was daylight and the pimpmobile was stationary.

I cracked open the door.

We were at the lake.

I checked my watch – it was just after eight.

We'd done the nine-hour-and-four-minute trip in seven and a half hours.

Wow!

Slim was squatting on his haunches, smoking a cigarette, looking out over the water. He smiled when he saw me.

"*Dormez?*" he said.

"Yes," I replied. "Lots of great dormez."

"Same my country this," he said, and it had the sound of a phrase he'd been practicing for some time.

I realized, with some shame, that I'd forgotten what country Slim was from. I knew it was in Africa, but that was all.

But then it came to me.

"In Tunisia?" I said.

"Tunisia," he replied, giving it the correct pronunciation.

And what did I know about Tunisia? Slim was from there. It had a lake. Apart from that, not much.

Okay, that was something else I had to look up. So little time. So much to google.

"*Beaucoup texto*," said Slim.

That's right, I'd put my iPhone on his charger.

I unplugged it.

He was right: beaucoup texto.

Twelve, to be exact.

The first was from Seb.

I'm okay cops held me for five hours then let me go because no charges.

Well, that was a relief.

Then a whole lot of messages from Mr. Ryan and Coach Sheeds. They could wait, I figured. It wasn't as if I could get into any more trouble. Looming over everything was E. Lee Marx's six o'clock departure time.

I told Slim that we would meet up later, that I would send a *texto* when I was ready to leave. He didn't seem so happy with that, though. Eventually, using a mixture of sign language and Google Translate, I worked out what was wrong: he thought I was too young to be left alone in a foreign country. I told him, using a mixture of sign language and Google Translate, that I'd be okay and if I got into trouble I would contact him. He seemed satisfied with that and got into the pimpmobile and rumbled off.

How to get back across that lake? This early in the morning, the boat-hire place wasn't open. And even if it was, I'm not sure the owner would rent me one of his precious pedal boats anyway, despite my sufficient age.

Steal one?

It seemed to me that as far as criminal activities went, stealing a pedal boat was about as desperate as you could get.

But I didn't see what choice I had, as a hasty survey of this part of the lake revealed nothing else suitable.

Adopting what I hoped was a nonchalant air, I strolled down the little pier to where the pedal boats were tied up.

I should've guessed – not only were they tied up, they were locked up. A great fat chain that linked all the boats was padlocked to a steel ring on the pier.

But now I noticed something I hadn't seen before: as well as the more conventional pedal boats, there were a couple shaped like swans.

There was nothing subtle about them, either: they had huge curving swan necks, extravagant swan wings.

They were chained up, too, but the chain looked older, rusted, and nowhere near as heavy-duty as the other one.

There was no one around, so I grabbed the chain with both hands and yanked as hard as I could.

It snapped easily, too easily, and the momentum caused me to topple backwards. I picked myself up and clambered aboard a swan.

I felt pretty conspicuous – how could I not, pedaling a giant bird? – but the swan was actually faster than the other pedal boat I'd used.

Maybe it was the wings that gave it some aerodynamic advantage, but whatever it was I was glad for the extra speed as I flew across the water.

It was probably just my imagination but Schwarzwasserstel looked even more dilapidated than it had yesterday.

Exponential decay, I thought.

And then I got the shivers – did I really want to see Ikbal² with his fragrant/pungent smell again? No, of course I didn't, but I had no choice.

Just as I was tying up the swan, the tranquility was rent by the high-pitched screech of a speedboat. I checked the lake. It was coming this way, and coming quickly.

Merde! They were on to me.

Where to hide?

Nowhere outside, it was too exposed.

So I hurried towards the front door of the castle, the sound of the speedboat getting louder and louder. As before, the heavy front door wasn't locked.

I carefully pushed it open just as the motor cut out.

Where to hide?

Footsteps, and voices.

Not French.

Not English.

Another language I knew but didn't know.

Maybe it wasn't me they were on to, after all.

I crouched down behind a huge pot containing a dusty palm, making myself as small as possible. The men hurried past – I saw three sets of feet, Adidas, Nike, Converse. And now I got it: they were speaking Arabic, the same language spoken by the men who worked in Cozzi's café back home.

Up the stairs they swarmed.

I took a deep breath.

Stay here or find somewhere more secure?

Just as I'd decided that I was better off staying where I was, there was the sound of a gun going off, followed by another gun going off and then another one.

There was yelling, all of it in Arabic, and the sound of furniture being overturned.

One final gunshot and then men running back down the stairs.

I shrank behind the pot, too scared to look.

The speedboat started up and took off.

It was only when the sound had attenuated to nothing and all I could hear was the percussion of my heart that I looked up.

I knew something evil had happened.

I could feel it.

Smell it.

And every particle of my being told me that I had to get out of this terrible place.

But the weight of the phony coin in my pocket told me something else.

I had to go up those steps.

Slowly I stood up.

So far, so good.

I shuffled around the edge of the plant.

Dom! Pull yourself together.

You've had the inside of your thigh seared four times.

You've almost been run down by a supertanker.

You've been punched in the guts.

You've been shot at.

You've been knifed.

And now you're acting like a big old scaredy cat.

I pulled myself to my full height and forced myself to walk normally, to march up the stairs.

"Ikbal Ikbal," I said in a loud, clear voice as I neared the door. "It's me, Dominic."

The only reply was Montgomery's.

Not his customary yap, however. This was more like a whimper.

"Ikbal Ikbal, it's me, Dominic," I kept repeating as I walked through the door.

More whimpering from Montgomery.

But when I was inside, when I saw Ikbal^2, I stopped talking.

Words are wasted on the dead.

Not so long ago, I'd thought that Brandon had been dead. But now that I was looking at a real dead person I knew how wrong I'd been then. Ikbal Ikbal, friend of King Farouk of Egypt, was slumped in his chair, his eyes open, unmoving. And blood was coming out of him.

At his feet was Montgomery. He look at me with his squashed-up pug face and then back at his dead master.

I could feel the bile rising in my throat. And I wanted some water. And I wanted to retch. And I wanted to get out of here.

But first I went over to the overturned dresser.

The panel, thank God, was still in place.

But now I needed the key he kept around his neck.

No, this was too much.

Too much.

Too much.

I wanted my mum to stroke my forehead and tell me that everything was going to be okay.

I wanted Imogen to hold my hand like she had that night in the minibus after the state titles.

I walked over to the body.

I'd never seen a dead person before.

Never touched a dead person before.

It was a day of firsts.

"Sorry, Ikbal Ikbal," I said as I went to feel around his neck.

Montgomery yapped at me.

"It's okay, Montgomery," I said, hoping he would remember my voice and calm down.

Again he looked at me with that squashed-up face.

What has happened? he seemed to say.

Again I went to feel around Ikbal Ikbal's neck, and this time Montgomery did nothing.

My hand dug into the still-warm flesh.

And then I could feel metal.

Nearby, a phone rang.

I ignored it.

I dug one finger in, getting it under the chain. And slipped it around until I could feel the keys. My fingers went around the keys, holding tight. I couldn't bring myself to slip the chain over his head – what if I touched his face? – so I yanked.

The chain bit into the flesh but didn't break.

I readjusted my grip and yanked harder, as hard as I could.

This time the chain broke, and I had a handful of keys.

I hurried back to the dresser and slid the panel across, revealing the locked drawer.

From memory it was a silver key.

I tried one of those first.

No luck.

Then the next one.

No luck.

The third one worked and the drawer slipped open.

The case was there.

I opened it.

My coin was sitting there on its bed of velvet.

I swapped coins.

But then I remembered about fingerprints and forensics and DNA – this was a murder scene.

I took the coin, wiped it on my shirt, then put it back.

I closed the drawer. Slid the panel across. Gave it a wipe with the edge of my T-shirt.

As for the keys, I hastily wiped them and threw them on the floor.

I made for the door, but just as I was about to disappear through it I took one last look behind me.

Montgomery had found his way onto his master's lap and was looking up at him, waiting to be stroked.

As I ran downstairs, taking the steps three at a time, I realized that tears were cascading down my cheeks.

Through the door.

Onto the landing.

And *thwocka thwocka thwocka* – a helicopter was coming this way – I could see the white speck on the horizon.

And so were two police boats.

The swan was not an option.

I ran around the side of the building. Scrambled through the unruly garden. Until I reached the cliff, a solid wall of smooth stone.

Impossible, I thought.

Even a rock climber with all the rock-climber paraphernalia would have trouble getting up this thing.

I had to go back, face the music.

I would just tell the truth. It wasn't as if I'd done anything wrong. I'd swapped my real Double Eagle for a fake one, but then I'd realized my mistake and come back to replace the fake one with the real one.

I imagined explaining that to a roomful of Swiss cops.

I turned to face the cliff again.

Yes, there were some cracks I hadn't noticed before. And there were some minor protuberances that could be used for purchase. And there, about four meters up, was a definite ledge.

If I managed to reach it, surely it would be easier going after that?

All I had to do was get there.

And I'd scaled the mighty Colosseum, hadn't I?

Who was I kidding? The Colosseum was a doddle compared to what I was confronted with.

Again, I thought about turning back and giving myself up. But again I decided against it.

The crack was actually more like a crevice, and several of the protuberances were chunkier than I'd first thought.

I worked out a route in my mind. I tightened my backpack, spat on my hands and set off.

The rock was cold, much colder than I thought it would be.

But it was easier going than I'd expected.

Right handhold – done.

Left foothold – done.

Stretching up and my left hand had purchase.

No obvious footholds from here, but this was where the crevice came in.

I was able to jam my right foot into it. I pushed against it and got just enough lift for my right hand to find another chunk of rock. I swung my left hand around so that it, too, had a piece of this rock.

Now the trick was to get at least one foot onto this chunk as well. The only way to do this was to boost myself upwards.

I remembered the instructor at the climbing gym showing us how to do this, how easy it had looked when he demonstrated it. But not one of us kids had been able to pull it off. Every one of us had dropped off the wall, ending up dangling in the harness.

I'd realized then what amazing upper body strength climbers have.

Negative thoughts found their way into my head: *If you couldn't do it then, what makes you think you can do it now?*

You're a runner, not a climber; all your strength is in your lower body, your legs.

But the cool rock seemed to be saying something else: *You can do this, of course you can.*

I set my shoulders, dug my toes in, crouched and then pushed up with all my might.

At first it was my legs propelling me upwards, but then my arms took over, pulling up.

Until the pulling up became pressing down, pushing my body weight higher and higher.

Arms burning, then shaking as muscles fatigued.

Just a little bit more.

I brought one knee up, jamming it into the chunk of rock. To get my hands off the rock, I spread them against the wall, fingers out wide.

I was up there, but I was balancing on one knee.

How to get to my feet?

With my face pressed against the rock, I couldn't see above.

So first my left hand crept across the rock, feeling for some purchase.

It found nothing.

The rock was biting into my knee, the pain increasing.

Now the right hand moved, feeling for something.

A small crack, but enough to jam three fingers into.

Now I had to swing the other leg around, put it where my knee was.

I dug my fingers in deeper, tearing the skin.

One. Two. Three.

Leg around. Toe on rock. Fingers twisting. Pushing up.

I was standing on the chunk now.

And the ledge was about half a meter higher than my hand could reach.

A "dyno" the instructor had called it, and we'd all known he was showing off, because there was no way any of us could have done it. He'd jumped up and grabbed a handhold with one hand and, for a second or so, he'd just dangled there, showing us how amazing he was.

It seemed to me that the only way I'd get to that ledge was by doing a dyno.

The sun had appeared from behind the cliff and its rays spilled onto my face.

It was like Mother Nature, despite the obstacles she was putting in my way, was encouraging me.

I thought of how easily the instructor had done it.

Yes, he was an experienced climber. But I was an experienced athlete.

Thwocka! Thwocka! Thwocka.

Another helicopter was making its way to Schwarzwasserstel.

And was that a dog's bark I could hear? A guttural bark, so different from Montgomery's it may have well belonged to a different species.

Were there tracker dogs on my trail now?

A day of firsts; it was time to do my first dyno.

I flexed my knees.

One. Two. Three.

I pushed up out of the semi-squat, pushed up hard.

The momentum carried me up, my arms up, and I was floating in space, no contact at all with the rock.

Then rock at my fingertips. Both hands grabbing.

But I knew this wasn't enough.

I needed to utilize what momentum I had left.

I swung my left foot up, willing it higher and higher until the heel was on rock too.

And now gravity had hold of me and was trying to drag me back down.

But, using my heel as a fulcrum, I dragged myself onto the ledge. Into a sitting position, my back against the rock, my legs dangling.

Schwarzwasserstel below, all its turrets visible, again looked like some sort of Disney castle. The police boats were pulling in at the wharf.

I could see two men with a dog on a leash.

If I could see them, then of course they could see me. I had to keep going.

I twisted around, got to my feet.

There was a crease in the rock, in some places quite deep, in others shallow. If I could wedge myself into that crease, then I could use my whole body – legs, bum, arms – to shimmy upwards.

And there was no time to lose.

The dog and its handlers had disappeared from view and the barking was getting louder. I figured that they were in the garden on their way to the cliff.

I shuffled along the edge until I reached the crease.

It wasn't elegant, every move scraped more skin off my body, but it was effective and I clawed myself incrementally upward.

After about twenty minutes, I started to cramp, my legs complaining about being kept in such an awkward position.

But I kept going, willing everything upward.

Don't look down, I told myself.

But when I heard voices, I ignored my own advice.

I looked down.

And they'd seen me.

Tiny figures were down there, pointing up.

And I wondered whether there'd be a welcoming party for me if I did manage to make the top.

I kept going, pushing myself harder.

I could smell the vegetation before I reached it.

And then the first tufts of grass came into view, so green against the rock's gray.

Then there was no more rock, no more wall, only air. I scrambled over the edge and got to my feet, stretched out my body.

There was no time to waste, the *thwocka thwocka thwocka* was getting closer.

I ran with stumbling steps into the forest. Lots of tracks, crisscrossing, going in all directions. Which one to take?

The cross-country runner I once was had the answer: the most worn, of course. The most used.

I ran down this, stumbling on the occasional exposed tree root. But after all that climbing this felt like home, this felt right.

Running; arms, legs working together. Air in. Air out. Oxygen-rich blood pumped to muscles.

The track led to a clearing. A cluster of buildings. The Gebirge Café.

Now I had a landmark.

I took out my iPhone. Thank God, there was coverage.

I went to compose a text to Slim. But how do you say "Can you pick me up" in French?

I looked around.

There was a group of kids about my age sitting on the grass, eating their lunch.

I approached one of them, a boy with curly red hair.

"Excuse me?" I said, speaking slowly, enunciating each word. "Do you speak English?"

"Pretty well," he said. "I'm from Idaho."

I'd gone and picked a group of American college students!

But then I had another thought.

"Do you speak French?"

"Not really," he said. "But Gillian over there is pretty good."

Gillian was lying on the grass reading a book called *Les Enfants Terribles*. It looked very French, so I figured if she could manage that she could manage a few lines of text.

"Hi," I said. "I wonder if you can help me."

I explained my predicament to her. Well, as much of my predicament as she needed to know. I made no mention of legs lopped off, for instance.

"Give me your phone," she said. "It's probably easier if I type it in for you."

She did just that and passed me back the phone. I hit send.

A reply came back almost immediately.

Je suis sur mon chemin.

I showed it to Gillian.

"He's on his way," she said.

"Great," I said.

Gillian said, "Can I ask you something?"

"Sure," I said, figuring I owed her.

"How did you get so banged up?"

"Banged up?"

I'd been so busy that I hadn't had time to consider my appearance, but even a cursory glance revealed that Gillian was right: I was totally banged up.

And, weirdly enough, now that I knew that, I was starting to feel banged up too. Starting to hurt all over.

"It's just been one of those days," I said.

"Tell me about it," said Gillian, and turned back to *Les Enfants Terribles*.

It was a relief when the pimpmobile rolled in. Slim looking cool behind the wheel.

"Well, that's my ride," I said to Gillian. "Thanks again."

I got into the passenger seat.

"Où maintenant?" said Slim.

"Roma," I said. *"Aéroport."*

He nodded, as if this was the most usual of requests.

"And we need to get there by five," I said, indicating the time on my watch.

At this he raised his eyebrows.

I didn't blame him – seven hours for a nine-and-a-bit hour trip. Google was a slow driver, but it wasn't that slow.

We pulled in for fuel and I rushed in and bought some food for us.

As Slim slalomed the pimpmobile through the traffic and we ate the sandwiches I tried to keep cool.

It was no good, however – the anxiety was coming at me.

I almost wished I was back on the rock face, desperately scrabbling for handholds, because at least then I was – how did that poem go again? – *master of my destiny*.

Here I was a passenger, master of nothing.

BOARDING PASS

Slim, the world's best driver, dropped me off at the airport and after paying him I scampered for the entrance, cursing all the slowpokes pushing their trolleys with their tottering towers of luggage.

Inside, I checked the departures board.

Flight 21 LAX 6:00 p.m.

Just when you want a plane to be delayed, it isn't.

I took off to the check-in counter in the vague hope that even now, forty minutes before the flight, they would still be checking in.

Of course, they weren't. There were no passengers there at all.

So I had to get to the departure gate.

But how do you get to the gate when you don't have a ticket?

I mean, that's the sort of question terrorists usually concern themselves with, not fifteen-year-old kids.

Just act like you own the place, I thought. *That's the way to do it.*

So I strolled up to the entrance, just like I owned the place, and the guard said, "*Biglietti, per favoré,*" holding out his hand.

"Sorry?" I said, though I had a pretty good idea what he was after.

"Boarding pass, please," he said.

I patted my pockets, did what I thought was a very good oh-no-I've-lost-my-boarding-pass routine, but to no avail.

"If you lose it, just get them to make a new one," he said, not unkindly.

"But my flight's leaving soon," I said.

"Then you better hurry."

I hung back after that, tried to think of another strategy.

It didn't take long before I found one.

And it involved large groups of people, because having watched what looked like a soccer team go through, it seemed possible that not all their boarding passes had been checked.

So I had to find a big group and I had to find one soon.

If I'd had more time I probably wouldn't have

chosen Jews for Jesus, but I didn't, so that's the group I joined.

I didn't have a clue why they were for Jesus, and I didn't really care.

As they made for the entrance, I joined them, trying to make myself look as pro-Jesus as I possibly could.

We were there now, the security guard was checking passes.

I kept changing my position in the group, keeping my back to him so he couldn't see my face.

And somehow it worked: I managed to shuffle through.

Having gotten through, I immediately discarded my excellent Jews for Jesus disguise and hurried towards customs.

I chose the electronic option: the machine scanned my passport, took my photo.

A quick glance revealed that the boarding light for the flight was now flashing. I ran towards departure gate 42.

And when I got there, disappointment kicked me, Tristan-style, right in the knurries.

There were only five or six people who still hadn't boarded, and none of them was E. Lee Marx.

But I hadn't gone through what I'd gone through to give up there: I joined the line.

"Your boarding pass, please," said the flight attendant when it was my turn.

I pointed ahead and said, "I have to get it from my mum," and continued walking.

"I'm afraid you can't –" she said, but I ignored her, pushing past the people waiting to board.

"Boarding pass, please," said the exhausted-looking flight attendant standing at the plane's entrance.

"It's okay, I know where I'm sitting," I said.

I pushed past some more people.

"*Scusa!*" a woman said.

"Manners!" said somebody else.

And when I looked behind I could see the flight attendant making for me, not so exhausted anymore.

But now I could see E. Lee Marx up ahead, putting his bag into the overhead bin

"Mr. Marx," I said.

He looked up at me and I could tell that he was having a real problem placing me, that I was totally out of context.

"Dominic Silvagni," I said. "The boy with the coin."

"Oh, the fake Double Eagle?"

"Not this one," I said, reaching into my pocket, bringing the coin out. "Not this one."

I could feel the flight attendant behind me, feel her breath on my neck, but I managed to remain focused on the world's most famous treasure hunter.

E. Lee Marx looked at the coin. At an eagle that

was almost lifelike, as if it was struggling to free itself from the coin's lustrous surface.

His hand reached out, almost as if it had a life of its own, and gently plucked the coin from my outstretched palm.

He weighed it in his hand.

He brought it up to his face.

And he said, his voice tremulous with excitement, "Son, this is no fake."

A hand touched me on the shoulder.

"So you'll come to Australia?" I said. "You'll look for Yamashita's Gold?"

"I'll come," he said, and now there was something gold-like in the gleam in his eyes.

"You promise?" I said.

E. Lee Marx gave me a look that made me feel about two centimeters tall, like I belonged in a Happy Meal. He'd just said he'd come; E. Lee Marx was a man of his word.

And if we'd all been in a movie, or on a TV show, right then there would've been some serious sound track, some major da-de-da-da music.

He went to give me the coin back but I said, "You keep it for now."

"Excuse me," said the flight attendant behind me. "May I see your ticket?"

I turned around to face her.

From the deep black rings around her eyes, she was even more exhausted than I first thought.

"Actually, I just realized I'm on the wrong flight," I said, looking her straight in the eye.

She hesitated: as far as excuses went, it was pretty flimsy. And I had no doubt that there was some procedure she was supposed to follow that would involve officials and a delay in takeoff and lots of complaints from lots of passengers.

She sighed, and said, "Then maybe we better get you deplaned."

"I reckon that's a good idea," I said.

After I'd been deplaned, I collapsed into a seat in the departure lounge. A lot of stuff had happened to me, but I hadn't had the time to process it, because even more stuff had happened. Well, it was like the floodgates were now open: memory after memory coming back at me, demanding my attention.

Toby at Palazzo Versace. The demonstration outside school. Visiting the Labor Party office. Saving Brandon from drowning. The crazy ride with PJ to the airport. Getting my iPhone stolen in the Colosseum. My trip to San Luca ...

Again, my phone beeped. This time, instead of ignoring it, I checked the message.

It was from Mr. Ryan: *Dom, we need to talk to you asap!*

My phone beeped again. Another message, this

one from Coach Sheeds: *Dom, we need to see you urgently!*

I had no doubt that a whole world of pain awaited me at the Olympic Village, but I figured I would have to face the music eventually, so why not get it over and done with? Besides, I did owe Mr. Ryan and Coach Sheeds some sort of explanation. Not the truth, of course – that was too outlandish, nobody would ever believe it, but maybe I could cobble something together that sort of made sense. Maybe.

So I sent a text to Mr. Ryan: *love to meet*

And he sent one back: *9 pm at hq* ☺

I replied ☺

He replied ☺

But when I arrived at a little past nine Mrs. Jenkins, Mr. Ryan, Coach Sheeds and another official were seated around the table in the official's room and I didn't see too many smiley faces.

More like ☹ ☹ ☹ ☹.

"Sit down, Dominic," said Mrs. Jenkins, indicating a chair directly opposite her.

I hadn't even settled in my seat before she launched into one of her tirades.

"In all my time as an administrator I don't think I've encountered an athlete with such a blatant disregard for the rules as yourself!" She followed

this up with a thermonuclear glare that, I guessed, was supposed to reduce me to cinders.

Just as Mrs. Jenkins was about to launch into another tirade, Coach Sheeds butted in, "Dominic, you're racing tomorrow."

"Yeah, sure," I said.

"It's true," said Mr. Ryan.

I looked over at Mrs. Jenkins, the boss of everything.

The chins wobbled. The lips pursed. And she said, "I'm afraid they're right."

But how could that be? I had broken the team rules; I deserved to be disqualified from competing.

"The IOC has taken an interest in this," said Mr. Ryan.

"Somebody by the name of Hurford," said Mrs. Jenkins.

"Given that you are by far the fastest qualifier, they've asked us, in the interest of the race, to waive our rules," said Coach Sheeds.

"So I really am racing?"

"You don't deserve to, but you really are racing," said Coach Sheeds.

I looked at Mr. Ryan.

"You're racing," he said.

Finally I looked at Mrs. Jenkins.

"Tomorrow," she said. "You're racing."

I thought of what they said – *get on the wrong*

side of her and your career's ruined.

And maybe mine was. But tomorrow, I was racing!

"Who else made it?" I asked, feeling embarrassed that I had to even ask this question.

The officials exchanged looks.

"You're the only one," said Coach Sheeds.

"So how about you go to your room and you get into your bed and you stay in your bed for the whole night?" said Mr. Ryan.

"The whole night!" added Coach Sheeds.

"That sounds like a good idea," I said.

And, after firing off some emails, that's exactly what I did.

THE FINAL

I woke to the sound of my phone ringing.

I checked it.

Gus calling …

No, how could that be possible?

Gus is one of those old people who thinks that calling somebody while they are overseas is about the most expensive thing a human being can do. That the whole American military budget is less than the cost of a five-minute call to Europe.

I answered it.

"I got your email," he said. "So you're definitely running?"

"Definitely," I said.

"You know they're going to give you a hard time."

"They are?"

"Don't be naive. Run a heat time like that and you set yourself up as a target. If you sit in the pack they're going to smash you."

"But that's what I am, a sit-and-kick runner."

It's what Gus had told me a million times.

It's what Coach Sheeds had told me a million times.

It's about the only thing they agreed on.

"It's not going to work this time," said Gus.

It didn't seem fair – I was going to get punished for running the best race of my life.

"Okay, so what do you suggest?"

"You've got access to YouTube there?"

"Yes, of course."

"Nineteen seventy-two Commonwealth Games, a runner by the name of –"

"Filbert Bayi. Gus, I've seen that race, like, a thousand times."

"Okay, you know what to do, then."

"You want me to run from the front?"

"Believe me, it's the only chance you've got," said Gus. "And this bloody call is costing me a fortune. I've got to go."

And with that he hung up.

I kept it low-key that morning: no climbing over the Colosseum, no skating down mountains, just kept my still-aching body in bed and flicked compulsively from one news channel to the next, looking for something, anything, on a killing in Switzerland.

Nothing.

I searched on the Internet as well.

Nothing.

Had I imagined it all?

No, of course I hadn't, but already yesterday was taking on a sort of cinematic quality.

There was a knock on the door.

Immediately, I imagined a squad of Swiss Guards, or gendarmes, or whatever they call themselves, come to drag me back to Neuchâtel to face some serious questions.

"Who is it?" I said.

"It's me, Mr. Ryan," answered one voice.

"And me, Coach Sheeds," answered another.

"Come in," I said.

They may not have been gendarmes, but they were wearing some pretty serious cop-like faces.

"The shuttle bus leaves in an hour," said Mr. Ryan. "We're here to make sure you're on it."

Coach Sheeds was more concerned about other matters.

"What the blazes is that?" she said, indicating my bare legs.

I looked down at them, and even I was surprised at what bad shape they were in: they were scratched, they were bruised, they looked more like a war zone than the legs of a supposedly elite athlete.

I just shrugged.

"I'll be right back," said Coach Sheeds.

"And I have some matters to see to," said Mr. Ryan.

Coach Sheeds returned by herself, a bottle of massage oil in her hand.

As she set to work on my legs, I said, "Aren't you going to ask me any more questions?"

She said nothing, but she hit some sort of knot in my left hamstring.

I screamed. "That hurts!"

Again she said nothing.

Now I understood the game: she was going to interrogate me with her thumbs, not her voice.

And that was going to be much, much more painful.

Ω Ω Ω

By the time I boarded the shuttle bus to the stadium my legs felt almost normal again.

That girl whose name I should've known but had forgotten was sitting in the front seat.

Again, she was dressed from head to toe in the green and gold of Australia.

I sat across the aisle from her.

"Good luck with your race," she said as the bus neared Stadio Olimpico.

"Thanks," I said. "How'd you do, anyway?"

"I was only in one event, the 100 fly, and I got disqualified in the heats," she said.

That's right: she was a swimmer.

"Disqualified?" I said.

"Jumped the gun," she said, giggling.

"That's a bummer," I said.

"Not really," she said. "It means I've been able to go along and cheer everybody else on."

The bus pulled up outside the entrance. We both thanked the driver, and got out.

The girl-whose-name-I-didn't-remember said, "I'll be cheering for you," and made for the general entrance.

"Thanks," I said as I walked towards the athletes' entrance.

As I got changed I kept expecting some official to come up to me and tell me that there had been a mistake and I wouldn't be running after all.

But no official came; there'd been no mistake.

Outside the locker room, Coach Sheeds was waiting for me.

"How are the legs?" she said.

"Much better," I said.

Then it was time for her pep talk.

With no other runners in the race it was for my ears only.

She's going to say what she always says, I told myself. *She's going to tell me to sit and kick.*

But instead she said, "That heat run's going to make it tricky."

"They'll be gunning for me, you reckon?" I said.

"I'd say so."

I made out as if this was all news to me. "So sitting in the pack's not going to work?"

Coach Sheeds shook her head.

Again, I made out as if I was giving this some pretty deep thought.

Eventually I said, "Why don't I just go for broke then?"

"No guts, no glory," said Coach, slapping me on the shoulder.

I could tell from the predatory looks on the other runners' faces as we waited trackside that both my coaches were right: they were gunning for me.

Only one of my competitors said anything to me.

"Mate, good luck," said Rashid.

I still wasn't used to him wearing the Afghani colors.

"Good luck to you too," I said, smiling at him.

Even as we took our positions I copped a couple of elbows in the ribs.

So when the starter gun went off, I bustled past Rashid and shot to the front.

No guts, no glory.

And I piled on the pace.

At the end of the first lap I was still there, the other runners strung out behind me.

As far as tactics go, it had been simple but effective.

Nobody had expected it, and they hadn't had time to regroup, to work out tactics of their own.

It all pretty much depended on me now, whether I had the stamina, the endurance – the guts – to keep this going.

Right now, I felt as if I did. Yes, I was hurting, but it was the sort of hurt you could push through.

And that's exactly when the girl-whose-name-I-didn't-remember yelled out, "Go, you good thing, Dom!"

When you're running, you think a lot. Mostly it's about how much it hurts, or when exactly you're going to kick.

At other times, however, you do other types of thinking, unconnected to running.

It's like the physical strain releases something into your bloodstream that makes the synapses in your brain spark in different ways.

When the girl-whose-name-I-didn't-remember yelled that out, I didn't think how much I hated that phrase – which I did – or what a bummer it was that she'd been disqualified for jumping the gun – which it was.

No, what I thought was: *Dom, you're a prize a-hole.*

Every day the girl-whose-name-I-didn't-remember had dressed up in that hideous green-and-gold outfit and yelled her heart out for her teammates.

Me, I didn't even know who had come where in what event. In fact, I hadn't even been to any other events.

Hey, I didn't even know her name.

Yes, there was The Debt, but could I keep blaming everything on The Debt?

Coming up to the third lap, I was still out front.

I looked behind.

They'd organized themselves into a pack now.

There were Kenyans, Ethiopians, a Spaniard maybe, and – no, it couldn't be – an Afghani.

"Aussie! Aussie! Aussie! Oi! Oi! Oi!" yelled the girl-whose-name-I-didn't-remember.

If I hated "go, you good thing" I detested "Oi! Oi! Oi!" but I looked up at the stands and I caught a glimpse of her. It was hurting like crazy now, but I still managed to keep up the pace.

The pack was nearing, but I still had fifteen or so meters on them as we approached the bell lap.

"Go, Dom, you good thing! Aussie! Aussie! Aussie! Oi! Oi! Oi!" yelled the girl-whose-name-I-couldn't-remember.

My eyes searched for her in the stands, and when I found her, a blaze of green and gold, I considered acknowledging her and her support somehow: a big old thumbs-up, maybe.

I didn't, of course – no runner does that.

But somehow the trailing runners had managed to catch up and I was engulfed by the pack.

It was rough going in there, elbows flying everywhere.

But we were on the home straight and I was still in the hunt for a medal.

I just needed to find some space, and kick.

But every time I went to move out, another runner blocked my way.

And by the time I did eventually kick, I had nothing left to kick with. Nothing. The tank, finally, had run out of fuel.

Ω Ω Ω

The official placings:

Gold medal to Nixon Kiplagat of Kenya.

Silver medal to Mohammed Gebremedhin of Ethiopia.

Bronze medal to Rashid Wahidi of Afghanistan.

Fourth place to Dominic Silvagni of Australia.

Coach Sheeds was coming towards me and I thought: *Here we go!*

"You almost pulled that off," she said.

I shrugged.

"If only you'd had a bit left."

I thought of everything I'd been through – the chase through the hypogeum, the skate down the mountain, the scramble into the Colosseum, the pedal boat across the lake, the climb up the rock face – it's a wonder I'd had anything in the tank to start with.

"But the fact is that you still ran the fastest fifteen hundred meters in these games," she said, her voice brightening.

I hadn't even bothered to look up at the winning time, but when I did I realized that she was right: it was a full five seconds slower than my heat time.

"We've got something to work with in the future."

I realized what Coach Sheeds was doing; she was asking me for a commitment, she was asking me if I was going to continue running.

"We sure do," I said.

As she moved away, she passed Mrs. Jenkins coming in the opposite direction.

Laminated passes jiggling, chins wobbling, tracksuit swishing; she was a woman on a mission.

"Your behavior at these games has been unprecedented," she said. "You are a disgrace to your country."

Here we go, I thought. *Next she's going to say my behavior was un-Australian.*

"Your behavior was un-Australian."

I knew she was just doing her job, but right then I really wanted to visit some ultraviolence on Mrs. Jenkins.

If I was a shot-putter I would've put a 7.26 kilo shot in her mouth.

If I was a discus thrower I would've inserted a discus into each of her lips so she ended up looking like a member of one of those African tribes.

If I was a javelin thrower I would've jammed a javelin into her neck, shish-kebabing some of those laminated passes in the process.

But I was none of these, I was a runner and I had only one weapon.

So I used it.

I ran.

Very slowly, but I ran.

Away from her, off the arena, out of the Stadio Olimpico and onto the Viale dei Gladiatori.

I ran past the Pantheon.

I ran through the Piazza di Spagna.

And when I'd finished running I sat down and I realized there was one more thing I had to do before I could leave Italy.

BACK TO SAN LUCA – AGAIN

My mind kept changing: Droopy Eye was lying, Droopy Eye wasn't lying.

As for my mother: she was American, born and bred.

She'd auditioned with the great Pacino.

But what about that girl serving in the shop? She'd looked so much like my mum in the photo.

And what about the book in the cell: had it been my father's?

Really, there was only one way to find out the answers to all these questions: I had to go to San Luca for a third time.

I knew how dangerous that would be, but I had to put an end to this uncertainty, because if I didn't it would drive me mad.

I went to the same station, the same ticket office, asked for a ticket for the first fast train to Siderno.

"Il treno è pieno," said the ticket seller. The train is full.

"The next train?"

"Pieno."

Then I had a thought. "What about first class?"

"Ci sono biglietti," he said, smiling.

The ticket cost my dad about as much as a round-trip ticket from Sydney to Singapore, but what did I care? It wasn't my money and now, at least, I was on my way to San Luca.

As I boarded the first-class carriage, all shiny wood and old leather, I felt like I was in one of those old, old movies, the ones set on the Orient Express. Where there's a murder and a detective with a serious moustache.

It seemed that I was the only passenger in the carriage.

The train gave a *whoo-hoo* – we were about to choof off – and I went for my phone.

It wasn't there!

Now I remembered that I'd put it on the charger for one final boost and I hadn't taken it off.

I couldn't possibly go to San Luca, to anywhere, without a phone.

I was making my way down the aisle to get off the train when somebody entered my carriage.

Somebody I knew.

Dr. Chakrabarty.

You could've knocked me over with a piece of wet fettuccine.

But if I was surprised to see him, the look on his face told me that he was equally surprised to see me.

The train gave a final *whoo-hoo* and started rolling.

I couldn't get off now.

And I suddenly felt very naked and very vulnerable – I couldn't remember the last time I'd been anywhere without my iPhone.

"Are you unwell?" Dr. Chakrabarty asked.

I didn't think somebody of his advanced age was going to understand just how serious my iPhonelessness was, so I didn't bother trying to explain.

"No, I'm fine," I said. "So where are you off to?"

"San Luca," he said.

Jaw. Drop. I thought I was the only person in the world stupid enough to go to San Luca. "But what for?"

"The Festival of Our Lady of Polsi," he said. "It's supposedly the best festival in Calabria."

I remembered that Father Luciano had mentioned this festival.

"Oh," I said, even though I couldn't get my head around the idea that it might just be a coincidence that we were headed to the same godforsaken place.

"And you?" he said. "May I ask what brings you on this train?"

"The same," I said, but then I thought some further explanation would be advisable. "San Luca is where one of my ancestors is from."

"You don't say?" said Dr. Chakrabarty as he made himself comfortable in the seat opposite me.

I thought he'd be off then, one of his trademark discourses taking in the history of Calabria and various associated and not-so-associated topics.

But instead he took an iPad out of his bag and said, "I hope you don't mind, but I have some correspondence to catch up with."

"Not at all," I said, reaching for my iPhone, the iPhone that wasn't there!

For the rest of the trip Dr. Chakrabarty was engrossed in his iPad and I basically looked out of the window at the changing scenery.

By the time we pulled into Siderno I was feeling nervous again; San Luca had never been the most relaxing destination.

The bus wasn't an option on my own. I couldn't risk having the same driver who would, no doubt, inform the Strangio clan that Silvagni was on his way.

I'd thought that as we were both heading to the same place, we could share a taxi. I didn't even care if Dr. Chakrabarty couldn't overcome his innate stinginess enough to pay half the fare. I would just feel safer with somebody else.

But Dr. Chakrabarty rushed off the train before I could suggest this and I lost him in the crowd.

Out on the street, I put out my hand. A taxi stopped.

"San Luca," I said to the driver.

"San Luca?" he said. "Long way."

"I will pay with a card, is that okay?" I said.

"*Si*," he said. "Card is okay."

I got in, and for the third time in a few days I was heading high into the Aspromonte Mountains.

As I did, I wondered how I would return this time.

In a car, careering around each bend?

On a skateboard?

There was another option, of course.

That I wouldn't return, that I would be third time unlucky.

For a second I considered telling the driver to turn around.

But I knew I couldn't.

I knew I had to find the answers to at least some of my questions.

The San Luca we pulled into was a very different place to the miserable one I had previously visited. The sun was shining, for a start. Colorful bunting was strung across the streets. There was a real air of festivity.

After paying the driver I walked over to the piazza where there was some sort of fair – food stalls and rides for kids and face-painting. There were also a lot more people around, not just the scuttling cockroaches. Whole families with mums and dads and kids demanding stuff. It was just like at home.

It felt good, like a normal place, and I wondered whether I'd imagined half the things from last time, all that godforsaken business.

I bought a slice of pizza and sat down next to a fountain and thought about what I was going to do next.

Just rock up at the supermarket and hope the girl was working there?

Or maybe back to the church and check their records, especially the births on the day my mum was born?

If she was even born that day.

Doubt was breeding more doubt – what was real about my family? Obviously we were real: Gus, Dad, Mom, Miranda, Toby and me, but what of our history could I believe, could I trust?

Back to the supermarket?

Or the church?

I promised myself that by the time I finished the slice of pizza I was going to make a decision.

But I still had a piece of the crust to go and the decision was made for me.

Because she, the girl from the supermarket, was coming towards me.

And she looked even more like my mother in that photo than I remembered.

With her were two other girls, around the same age. One short and blond, the other tall and dark.

Each of them was holding a gelati cone, and they were licking and laughing.

As they came closer I thought about what to do. And then they sat down on the same little stone wall that I was sitting on.

The girl from the supermarket looked at me and smiled.

"Kangaroo?" she said.

She remembered me!

"Kangaroo," I said.

The girl said something to her blond friend in Italian.

"So you are from Australia?" said the friend.

"That's right," I said.

"My friend says she is ashamed because her English is not very good. But she remembers you because you came into the shop where she works."

"I did," I said. "What is your friend's name?"

"Elisa, but we all call her El."

"My name's Dominic," I said. "What are your names?"

"I am Donna and this is Isabella."

At any other time this would have been about as good as it gets: in Italy, eating pizza, flirting with three beautiful Italian girls.

But that wasn't why I was here.

"Elisa seems to be interested in Australia," I said.

Donna translated this for Elisa.

Elisa said something back.

Donna said, "Her relatives went to live in Australia."

"That's fascinating," I said. "Which relatives and where did they settle?"

"Settle?" said Donna.

"Where did they live?"

Again, she translated this for Elisa.

Again she answered in Italian.

"It was the sister and the brother of her mother," she said. "She is not sure where they live, but maybe it is something like the Golden Coast."

It took me a while to process this, but when I did, the final product of this processing was almost too incredible for me to comprehend.

Was Elisa's mother's sister my mother?

Was this girl my first cousin?

And if she was, who was her brother?

A phone rang, Elisa's phone.

She answered it.

I couldn't understand what she was saying, but I could detect a change in her tone.

As she talked she shot me a couple of looks.

She ended the call, said something to her friends, and they got up.

Donna gave me a not-sure-what's-wrong-with-her look and said, "Nice to talk to you."

The three girls hurried off.

The feeling I'd had the last time I was here, that it was a godforsaken place, had suddenly returned.

Despite the other unanswered questions, I had the feeling that I needed to leave.

So for the third time in a few days I had to find a way to get off this mountain.

A taxi was the most obvious way.

But there were none around.

A skateboard?

I'd done it before, I could do it again.

But there were no skaters in the park.

A bicycle?

All the bicycles I saw were securely padlocked. They weren't a very trusting bunch, the people of San Luca.

Steal a car?

I'd hot-wired a bulldozer, hadn't I? But that had been pretty straightforward. And I'd had my iPhone to help me.

And even though the Zolt had made hot-wiring a car look easy, that was because he'd been doing it his whole life.

No, stealing a car wasn't an option either.

And then it came to me: of course, Father Luciano!

He'd helped me before, he'd help me again.

Back across the piazza to the church.

The door was open and there were a few people inside, kneeling, praying.

I hurried through and into the next room, the one where all the stuff was kept and – thank God and all those who work for him – there was Father Luciano, his back to me.

"Father," I said. "I need your help."

"Of course, my son," said Father Luciano, turning around.

Except it wasn't Father Luciano, it was sexy-things-to-the-passing-girls Carlo.

"You're not a priest!" I said.

"Indeed I am," he said.

"But ... but ... but where is Father Luciano?"

"He has taken up, how shall I say, a more permanent position."

It was time to run.

I turned around, and there blocking my way was Droopy Eye and his fellow members of the Strangio clan.

I turned back to Carlo, Father Carlo.

"The feud between the Strangio clan and the Silvagni clan has been going since 1852. I helped you once, but I'm afraid I'm unable to help you again."

Hands grabbed me and I felt the sharp point of a knife in the small of my back.

I was pushed forward, into the room with all the books, and then through a series of other rooms.

Until there were no more rooms.

Were they going to kill me here?

Was this where I was going to take my last breath?

One of the kids took hold of a large steel ring on the floor and pulled it upwards.

It was a trapdoor, and steps inside led downwards.

"Go down there," said Droopy Eye. "And don't bother trying to escape, because there is nowhere you can go."

I knew he was telling the truth.

I took the steps and I was in a tunnel again.

Again the point in the small of my back.

Tunnel after tunnel until we were there again, the cell with the graffiti on its walls, the hiding place.

I wouldn't say it felt like home, but it was deeply familiar, a familiarity my previous brief visits should not have given it.

And I wondered whether this was a memory I'd inherited somehow. That it was in my DNA somehow.

When I saw the empty can I'd used as a pee bomb I couldn't help smiling.

"You think this is funny," said Droopy Eye.

And fear inside me was spreading, its icy tentacles creeping through my guts.

Eventually Droopy Eye said, "Your father killed my father."

"So you keep saying," I said.

There was far-off sound, a sort of clatter, but my captors ignored it so I guessed sounds like that weren't unusual down here.

"What do you want from me?" I said.

"*Il tuo sangue,*" said Droopy Eye.

That I understood – *your blood.*

"You want to kill me?" I said.

"Of course we want to kill you," said Droopy Eye. "Like your father killed my father."

I could see what he was getting at.

In fact, it almost seemed reasonable that I should pay with "*il tuo sangue.*"

I looked around, my eyes flicking from one wall to the other.

How to escape? There was no escape.

Not by running, there wasn't. Or by fighting. I was just a fifteen-year-old kid, not Arnie, Bruce or Tom – not even Hercules, the original action hero.

This was the real world, not ninety minutes of Hollywood.

"Maybe there is another way," I said.

Droopy Eye said nothing.

I rubbed my finger and thumb together, the universal sign of money.

Droopy Eye said something.

Hands grabbed my hands from behind, bending my arms back.

And Droopy Eye was next to me, and his knife was at my neck, and the tip was pushing against my Adam's apple.

"Please don't," I cried.

The knife pushed deeper and I could feel it puncture the skin.

Il tuo sangue.

I was going to die here.

In this godforsaken place.

There was the sound of footsteps.

People running.

People yelling in Italian.

My arms were released.

The knife went away.

There were now two other people in the cell.

Seb was one of them. And the other was Nike, the kid who had swiped my iPhone in the Colosseum.

And Nike was holding a gun.

Seb said something to Droopy Eye in what sounded like Calabrian.

Droopy Eye said something defiant back.

Seb nodded to Nike.

Nike squeezed the trigger and the gun went off, the retort amplified to a crazy volume in the confined space.

At first I thought he'd shot one of the kids, because they all dropped to the ground.

But then I understood what had happened: Seb had told them to get on the ground.

Droopy Eye had refused.

So Seb had given him a ballistic hurry up.

Seb said something else in Italian and, as Nike went around, each of the kids handed over his mobile phone.

Seb still wasn't satisfied, however.

He took one of the phones, scrolled through the contacts.

He called a number.

One of the phones Nike had collected rang.

He called another number.

From Droopy Eye came the sound of a ringing phone.

He had two phones!

I would never have thought to do something like that.

Nike went back to Droopy Eye and casually kicked him in the ribs. Droopy Eye screamed and rolled.

Nike jammed the barrel of the gun into Droopy Eye's guts and used the other hand to remove his second phone. Once he'd done this he stood up again.

Nike was one scary customer and I wondered about the fight I'd had with him in the hypogeum, whether I'd beaten him just a bit too easily.

Now that he had all their phones Seb set about disabling them, removing the backs, taking out the batteries and the sim cards, putting them in his pocket.

"Okay, Dom, we're going to get you out of here now. Just follow us, that's all you need to do," Seb said to me.

Okay, there were a whole lot of questions that wanted answers: How did Seb find me? How did he know Nike?

But now wasn't the time or the place for them.

I concentrated on following Seb and Nike as they scooted from one tunnel to the other.

There were sounds all around us now: footsteps, voices.

"Are they following us?" I asked Seb.

"We're almost there," he said.

We'd reached a sort of cul-de-sac.

An iron ladder ran up the wall.

Seb took out his phone, called a number, said something in Calabrian.

"We're clear," he said.

Nike scurried up the ladder first, pushing a cover aside when he reached the top.

Then it was my turn, Seb right behind me.

I sort of recognized where we were, right near the cemetery, the one I'd run through that day I'd left the church.

"Quick, over there," said Seb, pointing.

Two generic-looking black cars had pulled up.

Seb opened the back door to the first one and said, "Get in."

"What about you?" I said.

"Just get in and get down," he said. "I'll explain later."

I didn't argue: I got in and I got down.

The car took off and I stayed down.

As we rolled down the mountain for the third, and I hoped final, time, I thought about what I'd just been through.

Already it had the feeling of unreality, as if it was a dream, or a video I'd just watched.

After an hour or so the driver, in a voice I sort of recognized, said, "Okay, now."

I sat up.

Slim was behind the wheel.

Now there really was too much to compute: my hard disk was whirring, my CPU was running hot, my brain was about to combust.

Enough!

I closed my eyes and emptied my mind of everything except for one thought: I was alive.

When I opened my eyes again, Slim was smiling at me.

"We going to Roma?" I said.

"*Si, Roma*."

"Apparently that's where all the roads go anyway."

The joke, if you could call it that, was lost on Slim.

THE LEANING TOWERS OF PISA

As I stood in the boarding line, willing it to move quicker, I was sweating like a drug smuggler with a gutful of ganja.

I couldn't help sneaking looks behind me, expecting them to appear. Them being the Swiss gendarmes, Droopy Eye, Carlos, any of those people who were after me.

I wasn't sure if technically I was in Italy anymore – I'd had my passport stamped – but I desperately wanted to be on the plane and the plane be in the air and Italy to be a long, long way away.

Basically, I was a mess.

Something that didn't go unnoticed.

"Are you okay?" said the person behind me in the line.

I turned around – it was the girl-whose-name-I-didn't-remember, dressed in her customary green and gold.

"Sorry, what's your name?" I said.

"Julie, but everybody calls me Jules," she said.

"I'm Dom," I said.

"I know," she said. "Bad luck about the race."

"I ran a really dumb race," I said.

The line moved and Jules shuffled the enormous bag at her feet forward.

"Wow, what's in there?" I said.

"Souvenirs," she said. "I've got, like, this ginormous family."

Souvenirs?

My mind traveled back.

To PJ dropping me at the airport, to her saying "Can you bring me back one?"

To me saying, "Sure."

Her: *You promise?*

Me: *I promise.*

So what, I'd made a promise to a street kid. Even if I did ever see her again, which was unlikely, she probably wouldn't even remember.

The line moved forward.

"My mum, she used to have this little model on her dressing table," PJ had said.

Crap!

"Are you sure you're okay?" said Jules.

"I forgot to get somebody something," I said. "Can you make sure the plane doesn't leave without me?"

Last time I'd been here, I'd deplaned. Now I de-lined. I hurried out of the departure lounge and towards the area where all the shops were.

"Do you have any leaning towers of Pisa?" I asked the woman in the first shop I came to.

She raised a very thin eyebrow, and said "Probably not."

A quick scan of the shop's merchandise and I understood why – very expensive-looking jewelry sparkled under glass cabinets.

I kept going.

But every shop seemed determined to uphold Italy's reputation as an eye-wateringly expensive fashion mecca.

Where was the crap when you needed it?

An announcement came over the loudspeaker.

"Calling passenger Dominic Silvagni, your plane is now ready for departure."

Just as I was ready to give up, I saw it.

A shop full of absolute garbage: plastic Pantheons, gondola ashtrays, the Bridge of Sighs in a snow globe and – oh joy! – leaning towers of Pisa.

I chose the six-inch model (with free postcard and keychain) shoved the rest of my euros at the woman behind the counter, and ran back to the departure gate.

"Mr. Silvagni?" said the lone flight attendant, right emphasis on the right syllables, as I approached.

"*Si,*" I said.

I hurried on board, the other passengers giving me filthy looks as I made my way to my seat.

"You get it?" said Jules as I passed her.

"Sure," I said, smiling.

But that smile dropped right off my face when I saw my seat: I was sitting next to Marge Jenkins.

Boss of everybody. And everything.

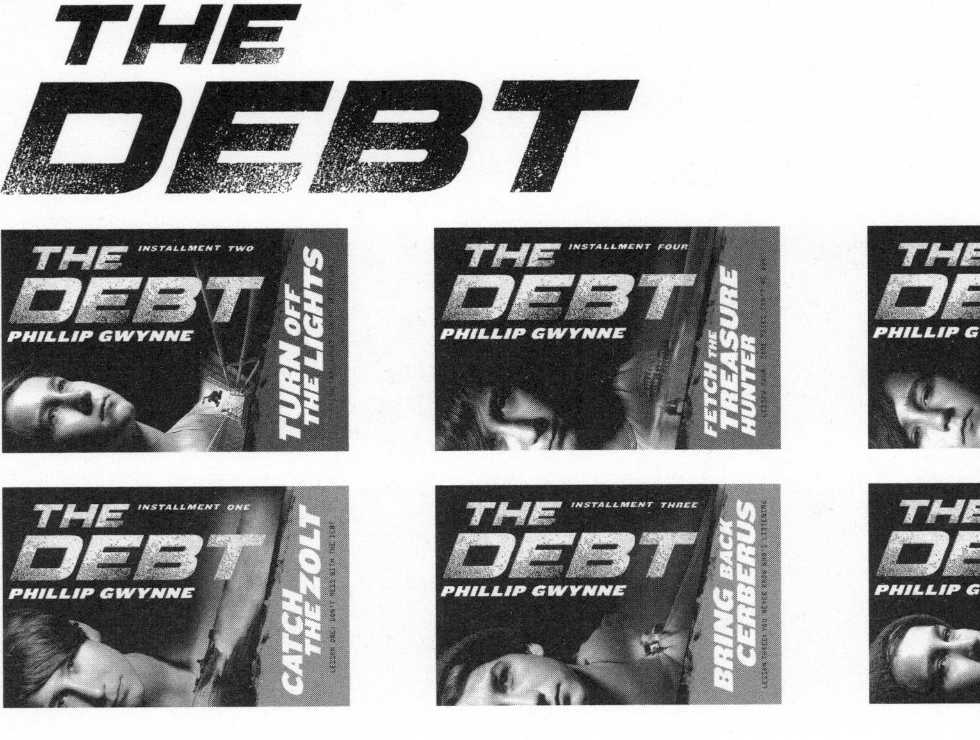
THE DEBT
THE DEBT
INSTALLMENT TWO
PHILLIP GWYNNE
TURN OFF THE LIGHTS
THE DEBT
INSTALLMENT FOUR
PHILLIP GWYNNE
FETCH THE TREASURE HUNTER
THE DEBT
INSTALLMENT ONE
PHILLIP GWYNNE
CATCH THE ZOLT
LESSON ONE: DON'T MESS WITH THE DEBT
THE DEBT
INSTALLMENT THREE
PHILLIP GWYNNE
BRING BACK CERBERUS
LESSON THREE: YOU NEVER KNOW WHO'S LISTENING

THE DEBT
INSTALLMENT SIX
PHILLIP GWYNNE
TAKE A LIFE
LESSON SIX: HE THAT DIES, PAYS ALL DEBTS

THE DEBT
INSTALLMENT FIVE
PHILLIP GWYNNE
YAMASHITA'S GOLD
LESSON FIVE: ALL THAT GLITTERS ISN'T GOLD